Angel of Music

Angel of Music

Tales of the Phantom of the Opera

Carrie Hernandez

Based on Phantom of the Opera Characters
Created by Gaston Leroux

Based on Characters Created By Gaston Leroux

Library of Congress Number:		2004099173
ISBN:	Hardcover	1-4134-7280-X
	Softcover	1-4134-7279-6

This book was printed in the United States of America.

To order additional copies of this book, contact:
Xlibris Corporation
1-888-795-4274
www.Xlibris.com
Orders@Xlibris.com

26505

Contents

Little Lotte

Prologue

The year was 1869. Monsieur Daaé and his eight-year-old daughter Christine had traveled to Perros in Brittany along with their patrons Professor and Madame Valerius, to spend the summer by the sea. Once there, Daaé spent most of his days either on the beach or locked in his room playing sad tunes on his violin. Despite the beauty and tranquillity of the French coast, he sorely missed Sweden, his homeland. Christine, who sang with a clear sweet voice, was his constant companion.

At the time of Pardons, there was a festival in a nearby village and Daaé decided to take his daughter there. He went, as always, with his violin and soon found himself playing at the festival as he had of old with Christine dancing and singing at his side. Some of the people who were drawn by the music into a circle around the two tried to donate some *sous pour la musique* but the Daaés, dressed more like gentry than traveling musicians, wouldn't accept money. The public, charmed as they were, didn't know what to make of them.

The scenario might have made more sense had it been known there was a time – before the professor had taken the Daaés under his wing – that father and daughter performed as a means of survival. A few extra coins in the hat back in those days made the difference between a night spent in a warm bed or shivering in each others' arms in a ditch by the roadside. Even so, Daaé felt nostalgia for that old life when all he and his daughter had was their music and each other. He often dreamed of escaping to the open road once more.

Only his great love for Christine stopped him. In their wandering life, she'd suffered excessively from the cold and lack of food. Daaé had often feared when he looked at her matchstick arms and legs, her hollow-cheeked little face and those blue eyes, so big, so yearning, so hauntingly beautiful in their aspect of privation, that his daughter wasn't long for this world. Seeing her now, so plump and full of life, he knew he could never risk losing her again. And so he bore his disappointment with dignity, stayed on with the professor and played at the fairs whenever he could.

That particular afternoon, a certain young boy caught sight of the two at the fair and was taken by the lovely golden-haired Christine. The boy was Raoul, Viscount de Chagny, who'd gone with his governess to spend the summer with his aunt in Lannion. The beautiful little girl so enchanted Raoul with her sweet child's voice and the plaintive melodies she sang that he kept within sight of her for as long as she stayed at the fair. Towards late afternoon, Christine was getting tired and so her father decided to take her home. As they made their way through the booths of the vendors, Christine spotted something that made her drooping eyes brighten. Her fatigue momentarily forgotten, she ran to a booth where multicolored scarves of silk were fastened to a line and fluttered in the wind like so many butterflies.

"Oh, buy me one, Papa," she cried.

He smiled indulgently and asked her which she would like. She spent some minutes examining each of them until she came upon one that was gossamer white. Even before he had a chance to ask the price, Christine was unknotting it from the cord. She glanced over her shoulder and dimpled at him sweetly. "I want this one, Papa," she said.

"Why that one, child?" he asked, comparing its plainness to the more eye-catching hues of the others.

"It reminds me of the angel," she said.

Daaé knew then there would never be another scarf for Christine and so he handed the vendor some of the coins Valerius had given him.

The two set off down the beach toward the cottage the professor had rented. It was isolated but cozy and boasted a small garden surrounded by a short white fence. It stood at the top of a small hill and had an excellent view of the sea. Neither Daaé nor his daughter noticed that a handsome blond boy and his governess were following them.

Christine skipped in rings around her father. She ran up ahead and sprinted back. She experimented all the while with the scarf by tying it around her neck, over her head and in any way that occurred to her. At last they came to Trestraou, a small inlet where a chill wind had started to blow. Christine held the scarf by two corners over her head and let the wind blow it out behind her as if it were a kite. She ran back and forth in this manner until a particularly strong gust tore it from her hands and blew it into the air. Christine cried out but even as she and her father watched its progress the wind drew it first up and then out over the water. Far from shore, it came back down, snagging on some driftwood wedged amongst rocks.

It was then Raoul reached them and saw Christine weeping. "Don't worry Mademoiselle," he said in his most gallant tone. "I'll bring back your scarf from the sea." He plunged into the waves without so much as removing his shoes. His governess shouted for him to return but Raoul paid her no heed.

The three watched anxiously as the golden head appeared and disappeared, then reappeared at a distance that seemed impossibly far away. Christine, blue eyes dancing even though her cheeks were still wet with tears, started jumping up and down when Raoul reached the scarf and tore it away from the driftwood. Slowly, fighting both tide and undertow, he swam back to shore. When at last, he dragged himself out of the surf, Christine threw her arms around him and kissed him on the cheek.

His governess ran towards him as well. "Monsieur le Vicompte," she shouted, "What will your aunt say when she sees you like this? Your clothing is ruined. I only hope you don't catch your death, walking all the way home in this freezing weather."

Raoul shrugged.

"Oh, Papa," Christine cried, "Can't we take him home with us?"

"Why of course, my dear," Daaé said. "I should have suggested it myself." He turned to the angry governess, so funereal in the dull black of her uniform. "Madame," he said, "we're staying in that house over yonder. The young gentleman could warm himself by our fire and dry his clothing before returning home."

"We would be much obliged," the woman said, looking sternly at the shivering Raoul. "Monsieur le Vicompte has already become famous for his willful conduct and quite frankly, if news of this last reaches his aunt, it might be more than her poor heart can bear."

Introductions were made all around and then the four walked the rest of the distance to the cottage. Raoul, who'd been presented formally as the Viscount de Chagny, sidled up to Christine and told her with all the munificence of his class, "You may call me Raoul."

"You may call me Christine," she said, innocent of any irony.

Raoul was subjected to much fussing on the part of Mama Valerius when he first made his bedraggled appearance on her doorstep. She packed him off to her bedroom, supplied him with towels and a blanket and demanded that he strip and pass her his wet clothing so it might be dried. He went into the bedroom and emerged a minute later wrapped in the blanket. Mama Valerius retrieved the dripping bundle he'd left on the floor and led him back out to the parlor where Christine, her father, the governess and Professor Valerius were all seated. Christine was sitting at her father's feet, her right hand resting on his thigh. Daaé himself seemed unaware of his surroundings. His eyes were half closed and he was quietly scratching out some melody on his violin. Raoul took a seat beside Christine. Mama Valerius, after arranging his clothing to dry on the hearth, brought him a cup of tea.

Christine called her father back to the world by demanding in her piping voice that he tell them a story. Absently, he set down his violin, his eyes slowly focusing on the assembled group.

"Oh yes, Papa Daaé," Mama Valerius said, sitting in a rocking chair near the professor, "There's nothing nicer on a cold, windy evening that a hot cup of tea, a warm fire and a cozy story."

"Very well, my dears," Daaé began, looking benevolently around at his assembled audience. "There once was a king who sat in his little boat upon one of those deep tranquil lakes that open like a brilliant eye in the middle of the Norwegian mountains . . ."*

"No, Papa," Christine said with a charming little moue of distaste. "I want the one about the Angel of Music."

"Ah," Daaé said with a knowing smile. "The story of Little Lotte. I should have guessed it would be that one tonight."

Christine nodded and her father sat back once again in his chair.

The Story of Little Lotte

There once was a young girl whose name was Charlotte but everyone called her Lotte. Little Lotte thought of everything and nothing. A bird of summer was she, who soared through the rays of the sun as golden as her own blond curls, crowned in springtime. Her soul was as clear and as blue as her eyes. She loved her mother dearly, was faithful to her doll and took good care of her frock, her red shoes and her violin. But above all else, she loved to go to bed at night because in her dreams she heard the voice of the Angel of Music.*

At first, all she heard was the loveliest of music, not unlike the rustling of leaves in an autumn breeze, or the lonely cry of a marsh bird at twilight. The closer she listened, the further away and more indistinct it seemed until she learned not to pursue it but rather to open her mind and allow it to fill her. And when at last she'd mastered the art of hearing without listening, the angel was able to speak to her in a voice of such sweetness that her heart was filled with longing.

"I can feel the change within you now," the voice said. "I know you can understand me and I rejoice. For I am the Angel of Music and have come because yours is a pure heart and good. I know that if I were to bestow the gift of music upon you, it would be used only for the benefit of others. With it, you could tame the fiercest heart. With it, you could bring back the lost to the light. But know also that the road to great music is hard and that I as your master would be strict and demanding. You need not respond now but think on it carefully. If, when next I come, you open your heart to me as you did this time, I'll know you have accepted my gift."

Lotte didn't respond for fear of upsetting that fragile state of mind that allowed her to hear the angel. As his presence drew distant, she struggled to retain the tenuous link. Instead, her very struggles brought her wide awake. She sat up in bed, overwhelmed by what had just happened. An *angel* had come and offered her a gift!

Now Lotte was a good girl and always said her prayers but she was also very humble and couldn't imagine why an angel would choose a little peasant girl like her. She thought about it very hard and came at last to the conclusion that the angel must have confused her with some other more deserving child. She imagined he'd soon realize his error and find the person for whom his gift was truly intended. It made her a little sad because she already loved the angel with all her heart. But she told herself she'd probably never hear his voice again and that this was as it should be.

The following night, when Lotte once again hovered in that nowhere place between sleeping and waking, she was surprised to hear the voice of the angel once more.

"Hello again, Lotte," he said and this time she heard sadness in his voice. "Why have you given no thought to my gift?"

She gasped, realizing too late that she'd been worrying so much about the angel making a mistake that she'd never considered any other possibility. "I'm sorry," she whispered.

"I too am sorry, child," he said, "for I believed you to be worthy."

"Oh, Angel, please forgive me," Lotte said.

But the angel only replied, "Now I fear it will be necessary for you to prove yourself."

Lotte felt her heart sinking.

"I shall set for you, three tasks," the angel continued. "It will be necessary for you to use all your cunning to accomplish them. But you must also follow your heart. If you choose to undertake them and successfully complete all three, you will be worthy."

His words chilled her, for she imagined she wasn't clever enough to complete the angel's task and that then, when she failed, he would leave her forever. But she was so upset with herself for not accepting the gift in the first place and so glad the angel was willing to give her a second chance that she said, "Very well, Angel. Please tell me what to do."

His voice seemed to strengthen then. "Bring me the song of the wind in the willow trees out in the marsh by the clear flowing stream."

Lotte didn't dare comment upon the nature of this task, so afraid was she of saying anything that might drive the angel away. And so, all she said was, "I shall try to do as you ask."

A feeling of warmth and well-being enveloped her. It faded slowly and she faded with it into peaceful slumber.

* * *

In the morning, Lotte awoke rested and determined. She had no idea what she needed to do to bring back the song of the wind but was angry with herself for having disappointed the angel. She got up and dressed with a firm set to her jaw that had not been there before. After breakfast, she took the road that led toward the forest and came to a crossroads. Crossroads could be dangerous places. Lotte's parents had warned her that the spirits of the dead often lingered there but she herself saw nothing of the sort as she walked past. Just beyond was the forest and the path that led through it to the marsh.

Once she entered the forest, Lotte walked for an hour before reaching a break in the trees. There, stretching out before her was the marsh, covered with a thin layer of fog. Lotte hesitated. She was uncertain how to proceed and decided to stand still for a time in case she could hear the music of which the angel had spoken. Without the sounds of her own footsteps, the quiet of the marshland closed in. Lotte was struck first by the loneliness of the place. She became aware next of the wind blowing around her.

She focused upon the sound of it and tried to find the music. The wind did rise and fall in volume as music often did but the pitch seemed to vary only slightly. She closed her eyes and allowed her senses to extend outward like invisible fingers until she touched the more distant sound of a clear flowing stream. Her heart gave a bound but she forced her breathing to remain slow and her muscles to relax. She let her mind continue its questing journey until at last she heard it, the rustling of the wind in the leaves of the willow trees.

Lotte headed toward the sound, impatient with the bogs and patches of quicksand that dotted her path, obliging her to take a circuitous and time-consuming route. She navigated with such single mindedness that it didn't occur to her that many people had been lost forever in that very swamp as the result of a single incautious step. Only much later did she realize that even then the angel must have been guiding her, making the camouflaged traps as obvious as if they'd been brightly illuminated.

She arrived safely at the bank of the stream. Unlike the brackish pools through which she'd just come, this water ran swift and pure. She looked further downstream to see that it divided into two smaller rivulets, forming an island at the center. The island, unlike the surrounding swampland, was solid and supported a small grove of willows. Lotte crossed to the island, making use of stones that cleared the surface of the water in order to keep herself from getting wet.

Even as she crossed, she was aware of the soughing of the wind in the trees and found herself anxious to get to dry land where she could stand still and absorb this sound. At last, she was able to close her eyes and slow her breathing. She focused her attention on the music. At first, it was as monotone as the wind in her ears. But as she opened herself to it and relaxed all thought and all judgment, she became aware of infinite variations in the apparent sameness. Each gust brought forth a slightly different timbre as different numbers of different leaves of different size and thickness were stirred at varying intensities. It was indeed a symphony of sound in infinite variation, each time newly created.

Eventually, her body could no longer stand the intensity of deep concentration and began to return to a more normal state of awareness. Reluctantly, Lotte shook her head to dispel the remnants of her trance only to discover that she could still hear the music as clearly as before. All the time it had been only a matter of knowing what to listen for.

Lotte wondered how many people lived their entire lives without ever noticing the music that surrounded them.

She knew without any doubt that this was the music to which the angel had referred. The question then was how to transport it. How could she bring the music to him? She decided to concentrate on the way the sound was produced, the notion forming in the back of her mind that if she could learn what created it, she could reproduce it.

After all, wasn't music usually played on some kind of instrument?

Lotte watched the swaying of the branches and the rippling, almost wavelike motion of the leaves. She stepped closer to observe a low growing clump, noting the way the wind made each leaf flutter. It was the fluttering that created the sound, magnified thousands of times as all the leaves fluttered simultaneously. Added to this was the creaking of the branches and the click of smaller twigs coming into contact. In that moment of clarity, Lotte understood. All she needed was a good-sized branch to hold behind her as she ran. A branch she could raise and lower and perhaps even drag along the ground at times to create a special accent. It might be a little different from the music of the grove but then again what was the music of the grove if not forever changing? She clapped her hands with excitement.

"I'm going to bring it to you, Angel," she shouted. She'd never before heard anything as wonderful as this music. And to be able to present it to him as a gift was the greatest of privileges. She thought of the happiness he'd feel when she played it for him and felt butterflies of excitement dancing inside her.

She went to the trunk of a tree that had a thick, healthy shoot growing from its base. It was the perfect branch for what she had in mind and so she stooped to break it off. But with her hand firmly around it, she hesitated. There was life within that branch just as surely as there was life within her. She could feel it, somehow, radiating outward from the body of the shoot. It would doubtless make an admirable instrument but what then? What would happen after the performance was over and she no longer had any use for it? She pictured it drying up, the leaves curling and the color fading as it lay forgotten on some garbage heap. She was ashamed of herself and released the young branch as if stung.

Still, her mind continued to work and a gnarled-looking tree at the very edge of the grove drew her attention. It was a poor, twisted thing that had been struck by lightning. Part of it was still alive and had survived the angry burn that split it down the middle. The other half was charred and dead, and upon this half were still some branches that bore the remnants of leaves. Lotte went to it. She stood before it and reached out to touch the ugly burn. She noticed that the left-hand side of the tree looked almost as though it were beginning to flow right over the scar whereas the right looked more like it was eroding away. When she touched the two sides, one with each hand, she could even feel the difference. The left side seemed somehow harder and fuller, the right, lighter and more brittle. As her hands explored, her vision became unfocused and without realizing it, her mind slipped into that agreeable state of awareness that allowed her to hear the angel's voice. Words began forming in her mind. "Take from the dead side. Removing those branches will do no harm."

She nodded and her glazed eyes took on their accustomed brilliance. She turned her attention to the disfigured side. There was a wealth of dead branches to choose from. She made her selection without further compunction and snapped it off with ease. Then she faced the tree and said, "Thank you." She lingered, even then, wondering if there were anything more she should do. But the wind had died down and the grove was still. No answers came either from within or without and so she turned away, traveled back through the grove, across the stream and over the swampland to her home.

For the remainder of that day, Lotte spent her time near and around her house, running about with the switch trailing behind her. Her mother was surprised for this was not Lotte's usual way. But since she was doing no harm her mother left her to experiment with her newfound music. In the evening, the angel came to Lotte as she'd known he would. His voice was even warmer than before and she noted within it, traces of the very windsong that had become so familiar.

She responded with excitement. "Oh, Angel, I've brought you the music you wanted. Shall I play it for you now?"

His laughter was rich and heartening. "Yes, child," he said. "Play it for me."

So she felt under her bed where the branch was concealed and brought it out. Her window was easy to open and was close enough to the ground that she didn't hurt herself at all when she slipped out. Slowly she began the motions she'd practiced in the afternoon but awareness of the angel's presence inspired her to new heights. She began to improvise upon her own theme, creating something new and never before experienced, something that was unique and belonged only to Lotte. It was this she gave to the angel and she was able to sense how deeply he was pleased. Her own heart swelled with the knowledge.

"Have I made you happy, my angel?" she whispered.

His response would best be likened to a spiritual embrace, enveloping her with the essence of joy and the certainty of being loved. "You are my happiness," he said. "And you have pleased me beyond measure. But tell me, child, what have you learned?"

Still basking in the warmth of his approval, Lotte said, "Music is everywhere and in all things but you must always be listening for it."

"Yes," he said. "Perhaps knowing this, your next task will not be as difficult as the first."

"I'm ready," she said, without having to feign the confidence she felt. "Tell me what I must do."

"Bring me the song of the swans on the lake," he said.

"I will," she answered, bounding toward the house in great exuberant leaps, scrambling back up to her room and diving into bed, happier than she'd ever been before in her life.

* * *

The next morning, after helping her mother with the breakfast dishes, Lotte set out to follow the stream that led to the lake. It was nestled amongst low rolling hills that were dotted with sheep. Lotte had been there one summer when her family brought a picnic lunch and she remembered the way the swans floated on the water like regal white boats. She didn't remember hearing them sing. But confident in her ability to sense the music everywhere, she felt certain her new task would be interesting and fun.

She arrived at the edge of the lake and found a nice, flat stone, warmed by the sun. She sat on it and observed the swans without disturbing them. It was soothing to watching them drift from one part of the lake to the other and with simple pleasure Lotte allowed her senses to extend beyond her once more. To the lapping of the waves. To the ringing of a goat's bell. To the bleating of a lamb. To a folktune played on a flute.

For some time, Lotte enjoyed the music of the valley.

But slowly, a creeping doubt cast its shadow over her tranquillity. The angel had said he wanted the song of the *swans.* She redoubled her concentration but the swans remained mute. With rising uneasiness, she cast about for some clue as to what she was missing. The swans made a splashing sound when they dove. Could that have been what he'd meant? Perhaps the patterns in which they swam were like the steps to a dance. But no. She'd immediately recognized the music of the wind in the willows and knew in her heart she'd recognize the swansong as well.

If only she were to hear it.

She stayed until the sun dipped below the hills and then walked back to her house.

When she went to bed that night, the angel didn't come.

The next day, a much subdued Lotte returned to the lake. The swans were there as always. Silent as death. Lotte sat back on her stone but then she stood up again. She hadn't found the answer there yesterday. Wondering if perhaps there was some other place she should be looking, she wandered in the direction of the hill where she'd heard the flute. There, a shepherd was tending his flock. Lotte waved to him.

He smiled a little and raised a hand in greeting.

"Was that you playing the flute yesterday?" she asked.

He nodded.

"Could you play something now?"

His smile broadened and he produced a hollow reed from his pocket. It was clearly a flute he'd made for himself. He raised it to his lips and played a merry tune. Lotte listened attentively and applauded when he was through. Encouraged, he played two more melodies but his flock had started to wander and he had to go gather them in. Lotte waited for him to return because she was a polite girl and wouldn't leave without saying goodbye. But she knew she had to go because the flute music, though lovely, was not the music the angel had sent her to look for.

The shepherd returned, smiling when he saw Lotte was still there and started to reach into his pocket.

"I liked your music very much," Lotte said. "But I can't stay. I made someone a promise and I must go if I'm to keep it."

Instead of saying goodbye, though, the shepherd gestured for her to sit on the ground. He sat down next to her and produced from his satchel a checkered cloth, some crusty bread and a lump of goat cheese. He set it all out as if for a picnic. Lotte unwrapped the bundle her mother had given her that morning and added an apple, some grapes and several dainty sandwiches. They shared their meal without speaking though sometimes they looked at each other and smiled.

When their meal was over, Lotte helped the shepherd gather everything up and put it back in his satchel. She thanked him. She complimented him again on his music. She even said goodbye. But as she was turning to walk away, she had a thought.

"Shepherd?" she said, turning back around. "May I ask you a question?"

He nodded.

"I was here yesterday and sat by the lake watching the swans. Someone told me they could sing but they seem not to have any voice at all. Is there some other lake nearby? Could it be the swans *there* that he meant?" Thoughts of the night before when the angel didn't come flooded her memory. The fear of disappointing him again choked off her words.

The shepherd watched her with concern but said nothing.

"I'm sorry," she said. "I have to go now."

She hurried away, realizing that in another moment she was going to cry and fearing the boy would laugh if he saw her. Instead, he ran after her. "Wait," he said.

She looked back at him in surprise for she'd come to think he couldn't speak.

"Uh," he said and the sound of his voice was distorted and forced. He turned his face away from her and began making other sounds accompanied by a great deal of spitting. At first Lotte was disgusted. But then, all at once, she realized he couldn't help it. He was answering her question. And that was the only way he could speak.

Lotte concentrated as hard as she could. Her mind slipped again into that place where she met the angel and the shepherd's words came to her clearly.

They can sing.

But only when they're dying.

A soft breeze tickled her ears. The shepherd had stopped speaking. Lotte looked up and saw him watching her. It was the first time he'd done so without smiling.

"They can sing when they die," she said.

"Yes."

"Thank you."

They both became aware of the rumble of hooves. A moment later the sheep began running in all directions as the prince and his followers crested the hill on their horses. With a cry, the boy ran after his scattering flock. Lotte barely had time to cower beside the trunk of a stunted tree before the riders thundered past. She watched as they galloped down the hillside and into the shallows. The swans took flight. The huntsmen fit arrows to bows and shot them down. The heavy white bodies fell from the sky and landed on the ground and in the water. Lotte watched in horror.

But in the midst of the slaughter came a music she'd never known. A chorus of swansongs rose up all around her even as their blood turned the water crimson. Lotte was blinded by her own tears. She sobbed and she gasped but couldn't avoid hearing that terrible music. Not once did she pause to question whether or not this was the music she was meant to hear. She only hoped that at least some of the birds would survive it – that she would survive it.

A few of the swans had escaped. Lotte could see them aloft in the distant sky. The noblemen jerked the reins of their foaming horses, dug in their spurs and turned with mighty scarlet splashing to gallop back the way they'd come. They trampled the dead and dying swans as they pounded up the hill and away. When the last of the hunters had gone, Lotte ventured from her hiding place. The swans, so graceful in life, now lay twisted and broken in the mud. Lotte flinched from the sight, looking instead toward the hill where she'd seen the shepherd running.

He was there, a small figure in the distance, a group of sheep gathered closely around him. She thought to go up and help him with the strays but at that moment her attention was caught by a splashing amongst the reeds along the bank. Moving closer, Lotte saw what the hunters had missed. Tangled in the vegetation with an arrow through its wing was one lone swan that had survived. It redoubled its efforts to escape when she approached but it was so weak that she caught it easily. When she held it in her arms, one wing folded normally but the other remained extended. The wound dripped blood on her hand.

Lotte carried the swan home. Her mother helped her bandage the broken wing. Lotte trembled as she worked. She couldn't get the memory of the hunt out of her mind. Only later, when she saw the swan waddling around the yard by itself was she sure it was going to live. Only then did she wonder how she was going to play the swansong for the angel. Without consciously willing it, Lotte found herself considering the unspeakable. Would she have to hurt the swan she'd just saved in order to get it to sing?

Ashamed, she pushed away the thought. The angel would never approve such an action. And that meant there had to be another way. Remembering the windsong she'd played on the branch, she realized it had been similar to the music in the willow grove but not exactly the same. What she'd played had been an interpretation.

And she could interpret the swansong as well.

Unlike the first music she'd learned, Lotte couldn't practice the swan's music out in the open. Someone might hear and this music was too private for anyone but the Angel of Music himself. The best she could do was replay it in her mind, tears rolling down her face each time she remembered.

When at last she went to bed that night, Lotte had no doubt that the angel would come. She'd become so adept at quieting her mind that she made out his voice just moments after her mother kissed her good night and blew out the candle.

"I missed you last night," the angel said. His voice was perfectly clear in her mind and she had no trouble making out every word. The timbre too seemed clearer and the melancholy tone seemed reminiscent of the music she'd so recently discovered.

"I missed you too, Angel," Lotte said.

"Are you ready now, child?"

Lotte climbed out of bed. Once again she slipped out the window and walked far enough away from the house so no one would be disturbed by the music she'd make. She began a little self-consciously, for the instrument now was her own voice. As faithfully as memory allowed, she reproduced the song she'd heard. She could sense the angel's presence all around her and knew he listened. Encouraged, she dared to sing louder, filling her lungs, opening her throat and giving voice to music so compelling that tears began forming in her eyes once again at the memory it evoked. She tried yet again for she felt something lacking. Hers was a song of loss while that of the swans had embodied a different quality.

All at once she understood. Her last attempt, though different from the melody produced in the throat of a swan was, if anything, even sweeter as it gave voice to a yearning that came straight from Lotte's soul – a yearning that could never hope to find relief while on this Earth. Lotte stopped abruptly, unable to sing more. She was exhausted for she'd used all her strength to bring forth secrets she hadn't even guessed were inside her. She sat down, right where she was in the grass. "I'll never be able to do that again," she said.

"No," the angel responded. His voice sounded wistful. "There is some music so glorious that the human soul has only the strength to create it once in a lifetime. Thank you Lotte, for bestowing such a gift upon me."

She sensed the angel's gratitude and was humbled.

But then he spoke again. "I know you've learned a great deal about the swans and about yourself. But tell me, child, what have you learned about music?"

"It's everywhere," Lotte said. "Even in death."

"Yes."

"But Angel," she said, "how can there be beauty in something so horrible?"

"Was it the horror that created the music?"

"The swans were in pain. They were dying. And so they sang."

"Everything you say is true, and yet you've missed the point," he said. "The good, as they die sometimes catch a glimpse of the paradise to come. The swans who are mute all their lives, find their voice only at that final moment, for the greater glory of God."

Lotte nodded. She did understand and felt the angel's love, starting as a balm of contentment in her troubled heart and radiating outward. She'd thought the killing horrible. But when viewed in terms of eternity and spiritual bliss, what was death, really, except a gateway to a better place? She relaxed and felt her doubts dissipate like morning fog on a warm summer's day.

Only then did the angel speak again. "You have but one task remaining."

"I'm ready, Angel," Lotte said. Her voice was quiet but her heart was certain.

"Your third task will be both harder and easier than the two that came before it," he said. "What you have learned will help you. But never forget to listen to your heart. Do as it tells you even when it contradicts your mind."

"I wish only to please you," Lotte said.

"Then bring me the music of the spring in the forest."

Lotte had no doubt she'd find the answer to this riddle as she had the other two. But her joy was tempered with the knowledge that answers could be painful. The swansong had tired her past any exhaustion she'd ever known. She got to her feet wearily and plodded back toward the house. The only reason she bothered to climb back through the window was to keep from upsetting her mother if she were to check on her in the night and find her missing.

* * *

The next morning, Lotte didn't rise early as was her custom. She stayed in bed, thrashing fitfully until she realized it was already late in the morning. Reluctantly she got up, reassured her mother and had a late breakfast. She knew she must go into the forest but found herself drawn elsewhere. Heeding her intuition, she climbed down into the cellar which wasn't dank and creepy the way many cellars are but dry and comfortable, smelling faintly of apples. There were windows all around the upper walls so that the light was able to find its way in. Lotte walked amongst the shelves neatly stacked with jars of preserves. She remembered her father stored his odds and ends on one of the shelves in the corner, beyond the barrels of apples. So she poked amongst the forgotten items, finally choosing an old water skin, a rope and a length of sail cloth from the neat stacks by the far wall.

With the items she'd taken from the cellar, Lotte took the road to the forest. Again she passed the crossroads without seeing anything unusual. Again she entered the forest. This time, she chose the path that ran parallel to a stream that gurgled cheerfully as it tripped over pebbles in its bed. Lotte, with her newly awakened senses couldn't help smiling at the sound.

At last she arrived at a small waterfall. Just above it was the spring where water bubbled up from under the ground. Lotte sat down and quieted her mind. She listened to the sounds with eyes closed and a smile of contentment on her face. She couldn't help being happy because the music of the little waterfall was the music of laughter. For some moments, Lotte just allowed herself to enjoy it. Without permitting any of her cares or apprehensions to interrupt her serenity, she began to focus on each different aspect of the music. There was the sound of water falling from different heights, landing upon different stones of different sizes all at the same time. This she recognized at once, as it had elements in it of the windsong. But it didn't rise and fall as the windsong did. It created a specific pattern. For a time, Lotte thought it just repeated over and over. She was even able to memorize the sequence so she could replay it whenever she wished in her mind. Just as she was thinking how easy this had been compared to her other tasks, Lotte heard a different splash. Curious, she opened her eyes and watched the progress of the water.

The pattern was not just something she heard. She could see it. Water built up slowly in a crevice from splashes caused elsewhere. When it was full, it overflowed, causing another small pool to overflow and then another, creating at odd intervals that other splashing sound she'd heard. She saw another pool filling with the runoff and knew that it too would eventually spill. When it did, the whole secondary sequence began once again with the filling of the smaller pools. She realized that what she was actually witnessing was a music of patterns within patterns. The more she observed, the more she found until she wondered if there really were any pattern at all or only the semblance of one. Lotte was uncertain she'd grasped the concept but it occurred to her that she might be able to recreate the music even without understanding it.

She spread out the sailcloth on the ground beside the cascade and began piling some of the river rocks on top of it. When she'd made a stack, she filled up the skin with water. This very act, she noticed, slightly altered the pattern of sound she'd observed and she couldn't help wondering what other disturbances such as a fish rising up to catch an insect or a deer coming to drink might cause. The skin full, she poured the water over her stone pile. The sound it made was similar to the stream flowing next to it but Lotte wasn't satisfied. She adjusted some of the stones and tried again. The second time was better but the water in the skin ran out much too soon. There was no possibility of creating the patterns within patterns that were so essential.

Still, Lotte knew she'd made a good start. She decided to take the rocks home and some of the water too, restack the stones and experiment some more. She refilled the skin and wrapped the stones securely in the sailcloth, tying the mouth of her makeshift sack with the rope. Only then did she discover that the stones were much heavier than she'd thought. She was able to drag the sack short distances but then she had to rest. It was clear she wouldn't make it home by nightfall. Still, she tried. She dragged it a little, stopped, rested and dragged it a little bit more. By early evening she'd barely made it to the edge of the woods. Tired, exhausted and dirtier than she'd ever been in her life, Lotte realized that if she were going to get home before dark, she'd have to abandon the stones. She hid the bag under some bushes and walked the rest of the way home.

That night, she could sense the angel hovering. She'd begun to recognize his mere presence even when he didn't speak. She was comforted by the thought that he was near and silently promised him that she'd soon have the music he requested. There was the faintest echo of response in her mind.

Soon.

Lotte was up again before dawn. When her mother came to the kitchen, she was surprised to find that Lotte had already made breakfast. As soon as she was allowed, Lotte raced back to the forest. She gathered some more water from the stream, having saved the water from the night before in a bucket. She had the vague notion that she might, over time, collect sufficient water to complete at least one pattern cycle. Her mind that morning was filled with ideas of ropes and pulleys and pipes and spouts that would have done credit to an engineer. But she was still concerned that she hadn't captured the essence of the music she was to play.

Doubtful, but with a full water skin strapped over one shoulder, Lotte returned to the sack of stones and began struggling with it once more. Oddly, she seemed to sense the angel even then. It was strange. She'd never before sensed him during daylight hours. She decided her mind was playing tricks on her because she was so tired, and continued the process of dragging and resting.

What would happen, she wondered, if she piled the stones beneath the outdoor pump? Perhaps she could bring forth a steady enough stream to produce the desired effect. She remembered the patterns within patterns and wondered if she'd have the strength to pump the water that long.

A whisper in her mind brought her back to the present. That must have been the angel. She couldn't understand why she was sensing him. She sat down, trying to calm herself enough to hear him if he had something to say but instead of becoming clearer the feeling of closeness receded. Her mind returned to the problem of the water. She wondered if she could get other people to take turns pumping when she got tired. She wondered who she could get to do it at night. And it would have to be done at night as well as during the day if she were to capture the greater cycles as well as the lesser. How long would it have to go on? Would there even be enough water in the well?

"There will never be enough." She'd spoken out loud without realizing it. A moment later she felt the presence of the angel.

"I'm trying," she cried.

She was much too agitated to have heard any response. But he was there and his presence was more palpable than it had ever been before.

She began to fear that she'd soon be able to hear him without quieting her mind. And though such a thing would have normally been welcome, she was terrified because she wasn't ready. She'd been on the brink of discovering that to accurately produce the music by way of water and stone would be beyond the means of any mortal. That meant there must be another way. She just needed to find it.

"Oh, please," she cried. "I'll figure it out if you just give me time."

Lotte dragged her bag as far as the crossroads and could feel the angel all around her. She knew that at any moment he'd speak and when he did, she'd be required to perform. But how? Hurriedly she thought of opening the sack with the stones and pouring the water that she had over them, trickling it slowly enough so that she could complete at least one minor cycle.

Suddenly, a voice broke into her thoughts. It was not the voice of the angel but the cracked and broken voice of a very old man.

"Help me."

She turned toward the sound and found that someone was lying in the ditch beside the road. She was annoyed by the distraction for she could sense the angel as strongly as if he were standing beside her. But Lotte was a good girl and she had a kind heart. With a sigh, she dropped the rope and approached the ditch. Peering over the edge, she saw the filthiest person in the world. He'd worn his clothing for so long that it looked like it had grown into his skin. His face had a grayish pallor beneath a thick layer of dirt. His eyes were sunk deep into his skull. His sparse hair reminded Lotte of a partially plucked chicken and she remembered what her mother had once told her about dirty hair breeding lice. Worst of all, she was downwind of him so when a sudden gust blew her way she caught the sickening odor of filth and disease. With an effort she controlled the urge to gag and squatted down by the side of the ditch.

"What should I do?" she asked.

"Water," he moaned.

Lotte couldn't answer because of the lump in her throat. If she gave the man water, she'd never complete her third task. Somehow she knew the angel would speak the moment the water was gone. How could she possibly play the music for him then? She looked back down at the man in the ditch and knew that without water he'd die. Someone must have treated him very badly for him to end up where he was. What he needed was a nice long drink. What he needed was for Lotte to bathe his poor face with cool water, to revive him and to support him as he walked the rest of the way to her house. Her eyes filled with tears as she unslung the skin from her shoulder.

"I love you, Angel," she whispered. "Please forgive me."

She uncorked the skin and reached down with it into the ditch.

The man's eyes were closed and he didn't take it.

"I have some water for you," Lotte said.

Still he didn't respond.

She poured a few drops to wet his lips but the water only dribbled down his cheek. With some misgivings, Lotte climbed into the ditch with the man and put her hand beneath his head, carefully lifting it so that he'd be in the proper position to drink. Her hand had only been there a moment when she felt a tingling sensation that started in her fingers and moved up her arm. She had to control the urge to snatch her hand away, forcing herself to stay as she was and to offer him water again. He reached up and took the pouch from her. She stood and took a fearful step backward as he moved to sit up but she was kept from fleeing by the curious look of tenderness in his eyes.

"Don't you know me, Lotte?" he asked.

As she watched he parted his garments, revealing a blinding white light that burst from his core. With a cry, she turned away and covered her eyes but the sweet, musical voice soothed and consoled her.

"Have no fear, my beloved. Don't you know your Angel of Music?"

"Is it really you?" she asked, though she dared not uncover her eyes.

Musical laughter like that from the forest stream, rose up and enveloped her.

"I can't look at you," she said.

"No, child. An angel can't be seen by mortal eyes. Even so, I am with you. And I will always be with you."

"But how can that be?" Lotte asked, uncovering her eyes but keeping her back to the radiance. "I didn't bring you the music you wanted."

"You carry it within you, Lotte," the angel said. "The music of the stream is the music of eternity. The patterns within patterns that go on forever. Don't you remember? A whole mortal lifetime wouldn't be enough to recreate it but recreation is unnecessary. Your soul is the music and it is eternal. Search within yourself and you will find what you seek."

Lotte turned her focus inward, becoming aware of a brilliant spark inside her – a small thing, really, compared to the angel but every bit as bright.

His voice returned as a whisper in her mind. "One day you will see me, Lotte, but not until that spark has grown, long after it has left its earthly home. For now, rejoice in the music you can reach and have faith in me. I will show you the way."

"You will teach me then?" she asked, new hope dawning in her heart.

"Of course, child," he responded. "Have I not been teaching you all along?"

Lotte stopped to consider and realized it was true. "How can that be?" she asked. "I thought I had to prove myself worthy."

"Did you complete the tasks?"

"Yes."

"Are you worthy, then?"

She considered. "You knew even before I began that I'd succeed."

"The windsong. The swansong. The dance of the waters. All of that and more lies within you. You succeeded before you started simply by coming to me."

"Then why did you make me think I was being tested?"

"Make no mistake," he said. "You were being tested. Your thoughts and actions were being judged by a very critical and unforgiving observer."

Lotte felt herself pale. "Who was judging me?"

"You," he replied. "Right from the beginning you lacked faith in yourself. You needed proof of your own worth before you could accept me. Do you understand why?"

"I thought you'd made a mistake in coming to me," she said.

"What do you think now?"

Lotte reflected upon all she'd learned since the angel first revealed himself and upon all the things she had, in truth, taught herself. She remembered too, the spark that was inside of her, itself like a tiny angel. And knew it to be beautiful.

"There was no mistake," she said, realizing the truth of it as she spoke.

And then with a sudden burst of joy and gratitude, she clasped her hands together.

"Oh, Angel," she cried. "I do understand. Thank you so much for all you've shown me."

Epilogue

Christine's eyes were radiant at the familiar close of the story. Mama Valerius rocked contentedly in her chair. The professor wore a secret, knowing smile.

"Papa, how old was Little Lotte?" Christine asked. "Was she older than me?"

"I don't know," Daaé said. "Why do you ask?"

Christine looked away shyly. "I was just wondering if he might come to me one day."

"You can never tell for sure when, or even if, the angel will come," Daaé said. "All the great musicians, all the great artists have been visited by the Angel of Music at least once in their lives. Sometimes, the angel will come during childhood, as he did with Little Lotte. That is the reason there are child prodigies who play the violin better at the age of six than many men can at the age of fifty . . . Sometimes, the Angel comes later in life because some children are not wise and refuse to study their theory or practice their scales. But in most cases, the angel never comes at all since most people don't have a pure heart or an easy conscience. Only those whose souls are predestined can ever hear him. And even they can never see him. He often comes at the least expected times, when you are sad or discouraged. It is then that you suddenly perceive the sound of celestial harmonies and a divine voice that haunts you for the rest of your life. Those who have been visited by the angel become impassioned. They experience a rapture unknown to other mortals. They are privileged in that they are unable to play a musical instrument or raise their voice in song without bringing forth sounds so sublime as to shame all other human sounds. Those who don't understand about the angel believe that such people are geniuses."*

"Have *you* ever heard the Angel of Music?" Christine asked.

Daaé shook his head sadly but then his eyes brightened. "You will hear him one day, child! When I am in heaven, I shall send him to you. I promise!"*

Daaé's unexpected vehemence brought on a fit of coughing that Christine barely noticed, for upon turning to Raoul she discovered that he'd curled up in his blanket and fallen asleep.

"Look, Papa," she cried, her voice rich with laughter. "Raoul's sleeping."

"So he is, dear," Daaé said, discreetly folding the blood-specked handkerchief he'd been using.

The governess stood, felt the clothing spread upon the hearth and declared it dry enough for the viscount to get dressed. She roused Raoul and sent him off to change.

"I wish to thank you again for your hospitality," the governess said.

"It was nothing," Mama Valerius said. "We were glad to be of some small service to the viscount."

"Can he come again?" Christine asked.

"Come now, Christine," said the professor from his chair in the corner. "I'm sure a viscount has more important things to do than visit little girls in their marshland cottages."

"I'll bet he'd like to hear more of Papa's stories," she said. "And Papa could teach him to play the violin. Couldn't you Papa?"

Daaé had placed the violin back under his chin and recommenced his scratching. "Of course, dear," he murmured absently.

Just then Raoul returned. His clothing may have been rumpled but his expression revealed just how pleased he was with himself.

"You'll come again, won't you Raoul?" Christine asked, throwing an impudent glance in the direction of the professor.

"I would like very much to come again," he said in his most gallant tone.

And he did return. Every day. The viscount and the itinerant musician's daughter spent the whole summer together, playing on the beach, listening to stories and having their own little adventures. Raoul even found himself learning to play the violin.

*Any passage ending in an asterisk is from Gaston Leroux's, *The Phantom of the Opera.*

Phantoms of the Mind

Prologue

My earliest memories are of growing up, during the late 1840s, in a farmhouse outside the French town of Écouen. From a very young age I was able to recognize within my parents a defined polar opposition that became my criteria for judging "rightness" and "wrongness" throughout my life.

My mother always said, "And so they lived happily ever after."

My father always said, "Good works draw the devil's attention."

Preceded by a situation rather than a story, he would say this when he caught me giving milk to a stray cat or trying to straighten the wing of a wounded bird. In the early days when I was still his flaxen-haired princess, he spoke those words as if imparting advice. Later, after my mother passed away and my continued existence became a burden rather than a joy, he spoke them with bitterness. By then I'd already come to suspect he was a liar. He claimed for instance, that I'd been the death of my mother, that the beatings he gave me were "for my own good," that my poor doll Anabelle had to be burned because she was filthy.

So even when the cat gave me a nasty scratch or the bird flew away, I clung to the essence of the tales my mother had told me, still believing that if only I were kind and good, God would protect me from all evil in the world. Perhaps I was able to do this, despite all the evidence to the contrary, because of a beautiful secret locked safely away in the depths of my soul, a secret made mine as the direct result of an act that for many years I viewed as the best and most noble of my life. It was only later I understood that "goodness" and "kindness" can be judged only relatively and that reality, though seemingly solid and constant, is as capricious and amorphous as any god of mythology.

It was only later I understood that the little girl I thought I once was turned out, in the end, to be somebody else.

Chapter One

Even now I remember the beginning of the end. I was in my ninth year and two summers had come and gone since Maman died. By then, I'd learned that keeping from under foot at home was an excellent strategy for preserving both my health and good looks. Because of this, the arrival of the circus one June morning was especially fortuitous. I'd been sawing away on my violin at a safe distance from the house when a brief pause allowed me to hear the sounds of distant activity. I walked to the top of a moderate incline and gazed down the other side at a busy scene of countless people, animals, and wagons, all moving about with industry. From my vantage point I was able to observe a number of barrel-chested, thick-armed men unrolling yard after yard of brightly colored material and staking it to the ground with big wooden mallets. Next, a duo of harnessed elephants came forward. I decided it would be fun to have a closer look. The sudden rush of anticipation at the idea tempted me to leave my instrument in the grass by the tree. Without a doubt, it would have been safe there. But my violin was my treasure and I couldn't bring myself to abandon it. So I took the time, despite my impatience, to wipe away the white flakes of rosin spotting the wooden body and return it to its padded case.

Not until I'd brought it inside the house and slid it back under the bed did I feel I could depart. I ran all the way up the hill and down the other side, arriving at last and attempting to mingle with the circus folk. By then the elephants, hauling on a rope, had managed to raise the peak of the tent to the top of a central pole. This accomplished, a few of the workmen went inside with additional supports to finish the job. The rest drifted away to involve themselves in other chores such as pitching smaller tents or driving the numerous wagons – some of which were actually cages – into symmetrical lines on either side of the main tent. Keeping within sight of the elephants, I watched as a slender, olive-skinned man drove them around toward the back of the Big Top by means of a nasty-looking hook. Oddly, they didn't seem to mind its bite, lumbering without complaint in the direction he indicated. They even remained complacent when he chained the left foreleg of each to a stake. As he worked, he spoke to them, roughly affectionate, his easy manner serving to increase my confidence until at last, itching to be involved, I approached him.

"Hi, I'm Lotte. Can I help?"

He stopped what he was doing and turned a critical eye on me. "This is no work for a girl," he said.

Despite his attitude – or perhaps because of it – I followed him after he'd finished with the elephants. Quiet yet conspicuous, I loitered nearby, watching as he pounded stakes into the ground. It took several long minutes of this uncomfortable stalemate before he weakened and commanded me to bring him more stakes, pointing in the direction of a nearby wagon. I jumped to comply. But when I returned and dropped my burden on the ground beside him, I could tell by the stubborn set to his jaw that he still didn't want to accept me. I persevered and as the day wore on he found it necessary to call upon my assistance several more times. Each additional task afforded me the opportunity to prove to him I was capable and reliable. It wasn't until early afternoon – when he gave me the job of shoveling manure – that he decided to trust me. Up until then, he'd scrutinized my every move but all at once he nodded to himself and wandered away.

Determined to finish before he returned and show him that his trust was not misplaced, I shoveled with enthusiasm. By the time the area around the elephants had been cleared, though, I discovered that the area by the tethered horses needed cleaning as well. I was unsure as to whether or not he'd meant for me to move on but I must have decided it wouldn't hurt to show initiative. I continued my work around the tethered horses and cleaned up anything that might have been manure and probably a lot that wasn't.

It's hard for me to explain or even to understand the voracious need I had back then to be accepted and praised. Perhaps it had something to do with the knowledge that I was nothing but a burden to my father. Perhaps it was in reaction to the festering guilt I harbored over the death of my mother. The only certainty was that I was driven to excel. And so, despite the filthy job he'd given me, the sweat burning my eyes and the stiffening of my muscles, the only thought in my mind was to finish before he came back. Had I taken an objective look at the area around me, I'd have realized no sane adult would expect a child my age to complete even half the task. But no such thought occurred to me and I kept myself going by playing and replaying an insipid little scenario in my mind.

The man returns and Lotte hasn't only finished with the manure but has further made herself useful by carrying water. The man stands and watches her for a minute. His surly expression is replaced by a dazzling smile.

"What a good little helper you are," he says, patting me affectionately on the head.

It seems, though, that such a destiny was not to be mine. Quite suddenly my silly daydream was interrupted by the sound of irregular footsteps. Turning, I found myself face to face with what must once have been the circus strongman. He wore his bushy black eyebrows and mustache waxed in the most flamboyant configuration of twirls and whorls I'd ever seen. Our eyes met.

"Are you el Moco's little helper?" he asked.

"El Moco?" I repeated.

"The elephant man."

"I guess so."

"You *are* a little cream puff, aren't you?"

I didn't know how to respond. I could think of nothing better than to return to my work, hoping that if I ignored him he'd go away. Undaunted, he continued to regale me with similar remarks in a voice that became increasingly husky and intimate. At last, despite my resolution to ignore him, I glanced up and caught him rubbing his pants in a way I found utterly disgusting. Never before had I witnessed such a thing and although his words were nothing but endearments, I felt somehow as if I were being assaulted. He watched me avidly, unconcerned that I saw what he was doing. And although I was repulsed, I was incapable of tearing my eyes from the spectacle.

His gaze flickered past me and he stopped what he was doing with guilty abruptness. The hand however, wasn't long idle. During a moment when I must have blinked, he produced a chewed-up strip of colored pasteboard that looked for all the world as if it had appeared from thin air. "You're such a hard worker," he said with exaggerated solicitude. "I think you deserve something for your efforts." He extended me the pasteboard strip. "Take this. It's a ticket for the show."

Before I could take it, el Moco arrived, winded as if from running. "Leave her alone, Piojo," he said.

Piojo raised his hands in a gesture of innocence. "I've done nothing, Moco. Ask her yourself." And then to me, "Tell him, precious. Have I hurt you?"

"No."

"You see," he said with an ingratiating smile. "All I did was offer the child a ticket for the show. Unlike you, I'm willing to pay for my help. You know how badly those cages need cleaning." He gestured toward a nearby tent with a careless toss of the head.

"No," el Moco said. "I have more than enough work to keep her busy and I've already promised her a ticket."

He hadn't.

"That's a lie," Piojo said to me in a stage whisper. "El Moco never gives away tickets. But *I* do. I'll even let you have it right now, if you want. Just come with me to my tent so I can show you what you need to do."

I shrank from the nastiness of his chuckle.

"Get out of here," el Moco said without hiding his disgust. "Lotte is a good girl and she's working for me."

Piojo's muttered response could have been nothing nice but he turned and hobbled angrily away, leaning heavily upon a black wooden cane. His right knee, whenever he put his considerable weight on it, bent inward at an impossible angle while his left leg swung wide. The sight of his affliction filled me unexpectedly with guilt at the uncharitable thoughts I'd had at his expense. But guilty feelings or no, nothing could have induced me to follow him into that tent.

"You stay away from el Piojo," hissed el Moco, suddenly at my elbow. "He's an evil man who eats little girls like you for lunch."

I was so grateful for his intervention that I might have hugged him. His warning glance was enough to stop me however. Instead of thanking him as I'd originally intended, I asked, "Are you really going to give me a ticket to see the show?"

He grunted, gave me a stern look and walked away. Still, before he'd passed out of earshot, he turned back to shout one last time, "You stay away from him, you hear?"

Chapter Two

It was late by the time I cleared away all the manure and el Moco was nowhere to be seen. Tired and dirty but still hoping he'd appreciate the amount of work I'd done, I began to roam the grounds, looking for him. At one point in my wanderings, I found myself dangerously near the tent to which el Piojo had gestured earlier. I quickened my pace and fully intended to dash right by. But before I was able to make good my escape, I heard a sound that halted me mid-stride. I listened. Someone inside the tent was sobbing and I, with my overactive conscience, found it impossible to continue without at least attempting to help.

"Are you all right in there?" I called.

The sobbing continued. For a time I hesitated, torn between the fear of remaining and the inability to abandon a creature in need. But as the minutes dragged by and neither el Piojo nor anyone else appeared, I decided to make a very quick investigation, ducking under the tent flap into a humid, twilit world. My first reaction was to gag, for the stench was overwhelming. El Piojo hadn't been lying when he said the cages needed cleaning. The ones in the tent just like those outside were actually wagons, the floors on a level with my face so that the stinking piles of fly-ridden excrement were impossible to miss. Many of the cages were occupied by the mangiest collection of animals I'd ever seen. For an instant, I imagined it must have been one of them crying, for the sound, suddenly close to me, was coming from one of the platforms. Turning toward it, my attention was caught by a sight so incongruous as to be absurd: a golden harp, its lowest string conspicuously missing, locked like a prisoner in a cage full of filth. Approaching it with something like religious awe, I was struck by a profound sadness. How could such a treasure be kept in such a way?

Yet the magnitude of the travesty was even greater than I first realized. The treatment of the harp was indeed an outrage. But the condition of the man I found crouched beside it was nothing short of a crime. His pitiful, rag-covered form was huddled on the floor, facing away from me so that all I could clearly see were the cracked and dirty soles of his bare feet. He seemed unaware of my presence and continued to weep, his malnourished body wracking with sobs. The sight of his suffering was terrible. It awoke in me the realization that someone had done this to him and judging by his state, he'd been captive for some time.

At precisely that moment, I saw a shadow on the canvas of the tent that could only have been el Piojo's, lumbering toward the entrance from the outside. In that moment of sheer terror, I didn't think, only reacted, dashing toward the back wall, rolling beneath the canvas and barreling straight into el Moco.

"Hey," he shouted. "What were you doing in there?"

"There's a man inside, locked in a cage." I cried.

Before I was able to do anything more, he gripped my upper arm and steered me away. "There's no man in there," he said.

"But I saw him."

"I know what you saw but it wasn't a man."

At a loss, I thought back upon the scene I'd just witnessed, stumbled over a rock, was jerked back onto my feet, and came to the conclusion that el Moco was either lying or ignorant. The only certainty was that he was in a hurry to put some distance between me and that tent.

He released me when we got back to where the animals were tethered.

I rubbed my arm where his grip had cut off my circulation. "So if it wasn't a man, what was it?" I asked.

He picked at a yellow callous on his palm and glanced back toward the tent. He still wasn't looking at me when he finally responded. "It was a demon you saw."

"There are no such things as demons," I said. Even now I remember how insulted I was at his attempt to scare me with nursery stories.

"You can't have seen his face, then."

"How would you know?"

"Because if you'd seen his face, you'd never have mistaken him for a man."

It was then I realized el Moco believed what he was telling me. The man in the cage had something wrong with his face. And for that, they'd locked him up. The idea terrified me. I took hold of el Moco's hand with both of mine. "We have to do something, Moco," I said. "He was crying."

He jerked his hand away from mine. "You'd cry too if you had to spend your life in a cage."

"He can't be a demon."

"Get out of here before el Piojo finds out what you've been up to."

I hesitated.

"Go," he shouted, making a move as if to strike me.

Long experience had honed my instincts and I bolted. I didn't stop running until the curve of the hill finally hid the circus from my sight.

Chapter Three

When I got home I found that Papa had taken himself off somewhere, a fortunate development as I was famished. In his absence I was able to go into the kitchen without any fear of being cornered. But despite this initial stroke of luck, the larder was empty and I had to resort to the tin of rapidly diminishing coins Papa hid on the top shelf of the cupboard. I took what I needed and left the house, walking the mile to town where I could buy myself a few rolls at the *boulangerie.* I was careful to guard my change in my apron pocket before wolfing down my prize. My own piggishness embarrassed me but I couldn't control myself. I thought again about the poor creature I'd seen, weeping and alone in that horrible place, and wondered what *he* might have eaten that day. He occupied my thoughts for the rest of the evening. My dreams, too, were full of him. I awoke the next morning more tired than when I'd gone to bed. I knew I had to go back.

It was late afternoon when I returned, having decided to stay away in the morning when I expected el Moco to be around. When I arrived, it seemed a performance had just concluded. The grounds had undergone an amazing transformation. Game and concession booths were set up all over. Hucksters conducted their business to the merry tunes of a calliope while hawkers outside the smaller tents tried to convince passers-by to pay a few *sous* for a glimpse of whatever curiosity was inside. I did what I could to blend into the crowd and follow the flow around the many stands and tents until I came within sight of the one that was my goal. As I approached, my heart pounding with apprehension, an explosion of white doves burst from the entrance like a vision from paradise. I paused to watch them as they winged their way toward the hills. Only once they'd disappeared beyond the horizon did I turn back toward the tent. El Piojo stood in front of it, his back to a gaudy poster depicting a dead body rising from the grave and captioned, "The Living Corpse." Caught up in an argument with a beefy man whom I recognized as one of the hands who'd set up the Big Top, el Piojo was oblivious to my presence. I used the opportunity to peek through the partially opened flap of the tent.

A good-sized crowd had gathered within. I detected the faint sound of music though the cacophony that surrounded me drowned out most of what I heard. Certain strains did reach me, however. It was far too little to satisfy but more than enough to tantalize. Unable to resist, I edged closer, closed my eyes and listened with all my might.

I could just identify the crystalline tones of a harp, lovely in and of themselves but serving merely as a backdrop for the voice, which I clearly heard for the first time a moment later. All it took was that first note, that first single voluptuous note, enfolding me in its vibrant warmth, and I knew I was experiencing something completely beyond my comprehension. It awoke within me a fierce desire that I hadn't known was a part of me, filling my soul with the longing to capture and hold that glorious richness, to cherish and keep that painful sweetness, to preserve and maintain that physical resonance so deep within my body, as a part of me forever. I could feel my heart opening, calling the music to me, could feel the very moment when it entered, coursing through and possessing me, imprinting itself indelibly on my mind. In that instant, the two years of emptiness inside me were filled with a healing and radiant light. I understood, then, that love really did exist, that beauty could be found if one were only willing, that the music was magic and the fairy tales all true. There would be a happy ending. Of that I was certain.

A pair of meaty hands caught my shoulders from behind.

"No peeking, angel," said a voice that I recognized with a sinking heart as el Piojo's. "We can't have you watching the show without a ticket."

"I was only listening – "

"Silly girl," he interrupted, massaging the flesh of my upper arms with his thumbs. "You should have taken the ticket I wanted to give you, back when you had the chance."

I tried to pull away but his grip tightened.

"Now, unfortunately, we have a little problem: You see, I happen to know that you've stolen something of mine."

"I haven't," I cried.

"Don't you know that watching a show without a ticket is the same as stealing?"

I gasped, beginning to know real fear.

"I see you don't," he said, restraining me with ease. "And for that reason, I'll forgive you. See? El Piojo isn't angry. But even so, you must find a way to pay him for what you've taken."

"Pay you?"

"Why yes," he said, deftly spinning me so that I faced him. "You heard the music from my show and you remember it even now, don't you?"

I nodded miserably.

"So then you *did* take it," he crowed, "without permission and without payment. The question is, can you give it back?"

I shrugged and looked at my feet. My lower lip began to tremble.

"There, there," he said, patting my cheek with one hand though the other remained clamped to my arm in a numbing grip. "It's not your fault, precious. You didn't know. And since el Piojo is your friend, he'll make it easy for you. He won't ask for money. Oh no. What use has el Piojo for money? Just a kiss. That's all he asks. A nice, sweet kiss from his little friend."

The bile rose to my throat at the very thought of bringing my face as close to his as would be required to deliver a kiss. Then I remembered the change from the *boulangerie.* Infused with sudden hope, I had the courage to look him in the eye for the first time. "How much is a ticket?" I asked.

He gestured impatiently at the poster with the prices and I realized the required amount was in the pocket of my apron.

"I have the money," I said in a rush. "I'll pay you, instead."

Reaching into the pocket with my free hand, I withdrew my coins and held them out to him. It was a relief to be able to do so. He looked around him quickly, noticing the number of people in the vicinity and deciding, I suppose, that it wasn't the right time to make a scene. Still, he seemed almost resentful as he pocketed the cash and released my arm. I entered the tent with every hope of recapturing the ephemeral thread of that music, only to arrive as it ended.

I hung my head.

"Go now," the mesmerizing voice said, beautiful even in speech. The crowd turned and shuffled out, obedient sheep, every face reflecting a dazed, ethereal wonder. I wanted to recapture the world within that music. I wanted to feel what they were so obviously feeling. But I'd been awakened from the enchantment while still outside. Never had I felt so cheated. I walked against the crowd, penetrating deeper into the tent as everyone else headed out. With the tall lines of the harp and the framework of bars clearly visible even above the heads of the retreating masses, the single remaining cage inside the tent was easy to spot. The first thing I noticed when I emerged from the throng was that someone had even taken the trouble to clean it. Looking up then, from the floor to the harp, my attention was quite suddenly drawn to the figure beside it. Our eyes met and I drew in a breath that nearly choked me.

The sign had called it "The Living Corpse," though it seemed impossible that such a thing could be alive. Upon its head, tight flesh, the color of Dijon mustard, had been eaten away in places so the teeth were partly visible even though the mouth was closed. The nose, too, was gone and the scars of ancient sores – as well as some that still seemed to be oozing – covered face and scalp

Then, unbelievably, it spoke.

"Why are you still here?"

The sweetness of the voice gripped me at once and with eyes closed, I found myself savoring the sound of it.

There was a sigh when I didn't respond. "Just have a good look and then go, won't you? I've just finished a show and I'm tired."

Indeed, it was the very "tiredness," that finally made it possible for me to bridge the gap. Voice, face, music and weeping figure. I suddenly understood that all of those were nothing more than aspects of the *man* I saw before me. I couldn't begin to fathom the enormity of his misfortune but I felt as though there were a kinship between us. Struggling to keep from gagging, I forced myself to face him and to answer him as frankly as I could.

"I didn't come to look at you. I just came to make sure you were all right."

With a startled motion, he came forward, grasping the bars of the cage and looking into my eyes with disconcerting intensity. "What a strange thing for someone to say. Do I look all right to you?"

"At least you're not crying anymore."

"Ah," he said. "You're the little one who came sneaking in here yesterday."

"I wasn't sneaking," I said. "I heard you crying and I thought someone was hurt. I just came to see if you needed any help."

A loud bark escaped him. It made me jump. Only a moment later did I realize he was laughing.

"Forgive me," he said, still stretching back his mottled lips in a parody of mirth. "It's just that I've never heard such an understatement in the span of my whole miserable life and you said it with such a straight face."

"I don't understand."

"No, of course you don't." His voice became gentle. "Sarcasm has no meaning for an innocent such as yourself. I only meant to say that you were right. I wish there really were someone who could help me."

"I could help you," I said, looking up at him with conviction. "Just tell me what to do."

"You, child? There's nothing *you* can do." His tone was wistful. "Thank you for concerning yourself, though. I believe you're the first who ever has." He paused for a moment and looked me over. Then he beckoned saying, "Come here. I think maybe old Erik has enough magic left to do one last trick for you."

I came nearer. He sat cross-legged on the floor of the cage so that he was more on a level with me. His hands flew into motion. Their long-fingered spidery motion held me rapt until there appeared in one of them a piece of paper where nothing had been before. It was to this I turned my attention. With deft, theatrical flourishes, he tore away at it, his mesmerizing voice keeping up a patter that I heard only as indefinite music in the background. I watched with fascination as the paper took on familiar form.

"There," he said, balancing the finished creation on his open palm. "What does it look like?"

"A butterfly," I cried in delight. He really had done a masterful job.

"Yes," he continued, giving it a few finishing touches. "It does indeed *resemble* a butterfly. But it's only paper after all."

He closed his hand, crushing it. I couldn't restrain a small cry of disappointment and he smiled a little at my distress. But before I had a chance to do anything else, he turned his predatory gaze upon me and for one suspended moment I lost myself in the depths of his eyes. I cannot say how long our gazes remained locked. I heard a soothing voice speaking to me, as if from far away. I couldn't comprehend the words but they became the center of my universe. Strange, ephemeral visions flashed across my consciousness and were forgotten. A barely recalled jerking of the eyelids was answered by twitches in different nerve centers throughout my body as even my brain began to alter subtly. Slightly frightening, the sensation was somehow pleasurable as well and although somewhere I knew I had the power to stop it, I didn't choose to do so.

"But wait," he cried, startling me out of my reverie. He opened his hand and the crumpled piece of paper burst into flames. "The monarch," he said, "like the phoenix, rises from the flames of its cremation, to live again."

Even as I watched, the flames altered, taking on solid shape, combining with the black of the ashes to stand at last as an orange and black-striped butterfly, opening and closing its wings as if it were alive.

"Oh," I cried.

"Give me your hand," he whispered.

I slipped it in between the bars and he took it firmly in his oddly frigid grasp, turning it palm upward and coaxing the butterfly to walk onto it with its spindly black legs. A moment later I'd withdrawn my hand and was examining the beautiful creature.

"It's real," I whispered.

"Oh yes," he said. "For you, it's quite real."

"Thank you, Erik." I looked up at him reverently. His eyes as he looked down at me seemed to hold within them an expression of deepest tenderness. I met his gaze easily and though I sensed he was doing nothing to hold me this time, I chose to prolong the contact myself. So focused did I become on his eyes that I found I was unaware of the rest of his face and for one, brief instant, I saw him to be beautiful. Moments later my awareness flickered back to the reality of twisted flesh and jumbled brown teeth. But he no longer disgusted me. I knew what I'd seen.

And somehow I could tell he knew it too.

"Keep it," he said, when I tried to hand the butterfly back to him. "Take it out into the sunshine and let it go free. No creature should have to spend its life in darkness and imprisonment."

I walked with it toward the tent flap, nearly running into the group of big, preadolescent boys who were just pushing their way in. One of them gave me a shove that almost knocked me down but then they were past and I made it outside without mishap. I noticed that el Piojo was occupied, trying to convince a group of people who'd gathered around him to go inside and have a look at the living corpse, "Hear it sing. Ask it questions. See its eyes moving behind its rotting skull." I found myself experiencing growing resentment at the way he talked about Erik. But I forgot about that when I heard the sounds that were issuing from inside the tent: laughter and taunts. A sick, desperate feeling invading my stomach. I forced the butterfly, so strangely disinclined to fly, to transfer itself to the canvas of the tent as high up as I could reach, and ran back into the tent. The boys were pelting Erik with rotten tomatoes that they'd brought in a burlap bag. Helpless and pathetic in the protective stance he'd assumed, Erik huddled against the one solid wall of the cage with his arms around his head. As if that weren't enough, the boys were shouting the sort of childish insults I'd so often experienced firsthand before Papa pulled me out of school. They seemed to think themselves uproariously funny.

"You're so ugly your maman probably fainted the first time she saw you . . ."

"You're so ugly all the girls probably faint when they see you . . ."

"You're so ugly that if you kissed a girl she'd probably turn into a frog . . ."

"You're so ugly that . . ."

One of them had acquired a stick and was reaching in with it through the bars. I knew I was too small to stop them. I knew that if I called attention to myself they'd turn on me. I ran out of the tent, through the crowd gathered around el Piojo and started tugging on his sleeve.

"Quick," I cried. "Make them stop. They're hurting him."

Somehow he managed to twist my flesh in a cruel pinch even as he was shaking me off. But he did pick up his cane right away and hobbled laboriously through the crowd toward the entrance. I followed in his wake, still fearful of him but reluctant to leave until I was sure Erik would be all right. When I got back inside however it was a different tableau that met my eyes. My "helpless" friend had somehow managed to grab one of the boys by the neck and to pull his struggling form against the bars while the others, completely forgetting their tomatoes, were trying with all their might to release their companion. Erik's bruised and livid face was truly horrible to behold, twisted with murderous rage, his ruined lips drawn away from the decaying, broken teeth, his eyes, nearly popping out of their sockets and covered with straining red blood vessels that seemed ready to burst. El Piojo took in the whole scene and didn't hesitate in his action. Raising his cane, he slammed it down on Erik's head. He did this three times before the claw-like hands released their hold and the boys beat a hasty retreat. The punishment, however, was far from over. Forgotten, I cowered in the shadows, watching as the cane came down again and again on the prostrated form. Erik tried at first to crawl away from the beating and then, giving up in exhausted resignation, simply lay there, absorbing the impact of the blows like meat.

I kept my sobs silent until el Piojo had left and then I ran back to the cage and to the bloody figure on the floor. I didn't know what to do but found myself repeating his name over and over. Eventually I thought to remove my apron and moisten it in his water dish. With it, I tried to clean away the blood and rotten tomato that was all over him. Blood leaked from the hole that was his nose. I didn't know what to do about that and was afraid to put my fingers inside, even with the fabric of the apron wrapped around them.

There was also nothing I could do about the ugly purple flesh swelling up around his eyes, cheeks and lips. Useless as I was, I still felt compelled to do something. So I smoothed the pitifully few locks of his limp, dark hair, noticing again the unnatural coldness of his flesh.

By then he'd lain there so long I thought he must be dead. It was hard to believe that just a short while before he'd been singing so beautifully. The music and the magic were still so fresh in my mind. I remembered too, the tender way he'd looked at me right before sending me out. It was this that caused my grief to burst forth in an ugly, guttural wail. Resting my head against the bars of the cage, I stood there crying with uncontained violence, thoughtlessly caressing his wounded head and repeating the word "no" again and again in tones of pain and disbelief.

I don't know how long I actually stood there but at last his hand moved and I pulled back, embarrassed for having touched him, and tried to stifle my tears. He moved his head to regard me from where he lay. He tried to say something but the only sound that came out was an alarming gurgle. Angrily, he hawked up a big gob of blood for which I was totally unprepared. I only had a moment to turn away before my stomach heaved. As it heaved a second time, I was vaguely aware of the hand that reached out from between the bars to clasp my arm, silently supportive. Numerous spasms followed but since I had nothing on my stomach, the entire scenario wasn't nearly as embarrassing as it might have been. When the fit had passed I looked back at him apologetically. And then at the same time, we both said "I'm sorry."

Despite everything, I laughed. He, too weak even for that, gave my arm an extra squeeze. Our eyes met once more and I saw in his, despite everything that had just occurred, a twinkle that could only be interpreted as humor.

"What's your name, child?" he asked.

"Lotte," shouted an angry voice.

I whipped around at the sound of my name to see el Moco standing at the entrance. Erik immediately released my arm.

"I told you to stay away from here," el Moco said.

"Oh, Moco, look at him," I cried. "He needs help."

But without sparing Erik so much as a glance, el Moco strode toward me, caught my upper arm and steered me out of the tent.

"Aren't you going to do anything?" I asked.

"There's nothing to be done."

"But he's hurt."

"There is nothing anyone can do for *his* hurts."

"You could let him out."

We were outside the tent by that time, and my suggestion was enough to make him stop and look at me in dismay.

"Don't even think such a thing," he said in a lowered tone. "Do you have any idea the reign of terror he would cause if he were ever to get loose? He has no conscience. No mercy. And he hates anyone fortunate enough to be born with a normal face."

"He doesn't hate me," I responded with feeling.

"He hates you most of all," el Moco said, a sharp edge of malice to his voice. "He hates you because you're beautiful. If he ever got out, you'd be the one he'd go after first. He might lurk in the shadows so you'd always be afraid. Or maybe he'd bide his time, winning your trust and pretending to be your friend. But make no mistake, in the end he would surely destroy you."

I jerked my arm from his grasp. "You're lying," I said. "You're just trying to scare me away so you won't have to give me a ticket. But I know him now. He's not mean. He's just sad. And he's a lot nicer to me than you are."

El Moco squatted down in front of me, a look of alarm on his face. "What do you mean, he's nice to you?"

I shrugged, uncomfortable at his proximity.

"Tell me," he demanded, shaking me by the shoulders. "What did he do that was so *nice*?"

I looked down at the ground and muttered, "He gave me a butterfly."

"A butterfly," he repeated as if his worst fears had been realized. "It wasn't by any chance a *monarch* butterfly, was it? The kind that rises from its own cremation to live again?"

He almost dragged me back to the tent, seeming to know right where I'd left it and indeed, I could see as we approached that the orange and black form was still there. But the closer we got, the more uneasy I became. I could already tell that something was wrong, though it wasn't until I stood in front of it once more that full realization dawned. It had been crushed.

"Is this it?" he asked.

I covered my mouth as if to stifle a scream. My voice when I spoke was distorted and near tears. "They killed it."

"No," el Moco said quietly. "It was never alive."

"But I saw it. I felt it walking on my hand."

"Look at it closely," he said, lifting me up so my eyes were on a level with it. "Touch it, if you have to. It's just a painting. El Piojo did it himself."

Impossible as it seemed, I could see he was right. The butterfly was nothing but a painting on the canvas and a very crudely rendered one at that.

"You let him look into your eyes, didn't you?"

I nodded as he set me back down. The malicious look was gone and his voice when he spoke expressed only the deepest compassion.

"Then he's inside you now. God have mercy on your soul."

Chapter Four

That night I lay in bed, nursing a bruised backside and an empty stomach. Resentment burned in my heart. Papa had been furious after discovering that some of the coins from the tin had been taken. I too had been furious for he hadn't allowed me to say a single word in my defense, laying into me with an enthusiasm that belied his statement that it was hurting him more than it was hurting me. My thoughts, as I spiraled downward toward sleep, were pure venom, doubtless the cause of my bizarre dreams. At first I found myself bent over the bed, buttocks exposed to the air. Only when I'd become fully aware of my situation did I hear the sound of the riding crop slicing through the air. Only then did I hear the meaty *whap* and the sting of it on my naked flesh. Screaming with each blow, despite my stubborn resolution to remain silent, my attention was nevertheless drawn to the shadows in the room. They were far deeper than I'd ever seen them. And in that moment of realization, they came to life. A horrific apparition detached itself from the darkness. Erik. Advancing on my father in all his monstrous splendor, Erik jerked the riding crop from him and threw it aside. I, temporarily forgotten, pulled my dress back down and turned to watch. My father was backing away, holding his hands defensively before him.

"Leave here," Erik roared.

My father turned and ran.

Only then did Erik look at me, the maniacal fury that had burned in his eyes fading away as I raised my arms to him. He came to me and lifted me up, kissing away my tears. And when I closed my eyes, the lips that touched me and the arms that held me felt warm and whole. He murmured words of comfort. At some point those words took on the aspect of song. I awoke, still in darkness, basking in the afterglow of the sweetest dream I'd ever known. El Moco had been right about one thing. Erik was inside my mind. But rather than a curse to be feared, his presence was a miracle to be cherished.

Still, as consciousness blossomed more fully, the delicious sense of well-being evaporated and left in its place the coldness of reality. I remembered that despite his mental powers and his spiritual gift to me, in physical fact Erik was injured and alone. I wondered if el Piojo even bothered giving him a blanket on cold nights. Somehow, I doubted it. And with that doubt came the excuse I needed to go back and see him one last time. I would bring him a blanket. Taking one from my bed, I folded it neatly, got dressed and slipped out the bedroom window. It wasn't until I found myself outside that I was hit by the full impact of my plan. Though it was still night, the details of the countryside were visible, the full moon casting its eerie bluish glow over the landscape, the branches of the tree in the garden rustling in the breeze. And I realized, as the goose-flesh prickled my skin, that unlike the actions of my dreaming self, anything I did at that point would be real. I really meant to cross the fields at night, alone and without permission. I really meant to trespass on private property and to sneak into a tent that didn't belong to me. Marveling at the enormity of my own gall, I hesitated. But only for a moment. Then I thought of him. I thought of him and a bittersweet longing welled up within me. I thought of him and found myself walking, the excitement and anticipation I experienced as I approached the place where I knew he lived, increasing to such a point that nothing mattered except that I was going to see him.

At last I was standing outside his tent, sweating and shivering simultaneously. No one was around. The circus, except for the animals standing or lying in their compounds, seemed deserted. With the folded blanket still hugged against me, I took a deep breath and entered. Immediately, despite the greater darkness inside, I realized that the other cages I'd seen the first time were back. These were the cages that housed the fiercer of the circus' menagerie: the great apes, the bears, the lions. Unable to identify the shadowed, sleeping forms, I did my best to keep my distance. I wove my careful and silent way amongst them, guided by the black silhouette of the harp, only just distinguishable in the darkness.

It took several minutes for my eyes to adjust enough to identify the shape of Erik's body curled up against the bars. My heart was full to bursting when I saw him and somehow the offering of one threadbare blanket seemed paltry. It dawned on me then, quite suddenly, that it might be within my power to set him free. My heart redoubled its pounding at the thought and I walked around the cage, climbing up the wooden blocks that served as steps to more closely examine the door. Unfortunately, it was padlocked and the key was nowhere in sight. Even so, I gave it an experimental pull, accomplishing nothing except to make a loud, clattering sound that awoke the occupant of the next cage and set it to nervous pacing.

Afraid of making any more noise, I hurriedly climbed back down. My original plan had probably been the best. Without wasting any more time, I slipped the blanket between the bars and left it next to him where I was sure he'd find it if he awoke. Before I was able to withdraw my arm, his motionless figure came to life, catching my wrist in an iron grip and twisting it painfully. Stifling a scream, I tried to pull away. But my struggling did me no good at all even when he switched hands in order to raise himself to a sitting position. With both his feet braced against the bars of the cage, I realized in growing panic that he was stronger, even, than my father. I could feel the hatred and wrath radiating from him and knew in that moment he had the strength to tear my arm off and meant to do it. With an aloof efficiency that was frightening, he twisted it still further. And though I'd meant to stay quiet a cry at last escaped me. Only at the sound of that pathetic little squeak did he hesitate. Still holding tight to my arm but no longer twisting, he leaned forward and attempted to plumb the depths of the darkness with his burning, golden eyes. It was then I understood that he didn't know whose arm he'd caught.

"Erik," I whimpered. "Please let me go."

"Lotte?"

"Yes."

A moment later my arm was free. I withdrew it and shrank beyond his reach. From the other cages were emerging sighs and moans. My noise had awakened the animals. Still, I never took my eyes from Erik and could just make out his change in position as he crouched forward and grasped the bars with both hands. "Did I hurt you?"

"Yes."

"I'm sorry." His tone was stricken. "I had no idea it was you. People come here sometimes, people who mean to do me harm though I've done nothing to them. How could I know it was you when you didn't speak? What was I to think when you started banging around and coming at me through the bars?"

He paused and though I kept my eyes averted, I could tell he was trying to look into them.

"Lotte?" His voice sounded suddenly much colder. "What exactly were you trying to do?"

"I thought . . . you might be cold," I responded, interrupted every few words by the spasming of involuntary sobs. "I just wanted . . . to bring you a blanket."

"Where is it?"

"Inside."

I could make out his searching motions. I could tell when he found my gift, unfolded it and wrapped it tightly around himself. He sighed. "God bless you," he whispered, all traces of anger gone. "You are a kind and giving child, though even now I scarcely comprehend your desire to be good to *me*."

I drew in a big gulp of air, a futile attempt to control my shuddering breath. "It's . . . because of what you said. No one should have to live in the dark or be . . . locked in a cage."

"Is that why you were examining the lock?"

"I was trying . . . to open it." In a wave of self-righteous pity, the tears renewed themselves.

"Lotte, are you all right?" There was a new tone of concern in his voice.

"It hurts."

"Let me see."

I approached, allowing those long-fingered, spidery hands to probe the swollen area. His touch was so light that it was hard to believe those very same hands had been responsible for the ruthless brutality in the first place.

He cursed under his breath. "I'm afraid I've dislocated your shoulder, Lotte. I think I can fix it. Can you keep from crying out?"

Another shuddering sob. "I'll try."

"Give me your hand."

With an apprehensive whimper, I placed my hand in his, though even that small amount of motion caused a nauseating pain. Understanding, he gave me a moment to recover before placing his other hand on my shoulder and beginning to raise my wounded arm. Not crying out proved to be the hardest thing I'd ever done. Uncontrolled but silent tears pumped from my eyes. The animals, as if sensing my agony, became increasingly restless, pacing within the confines of their cages, moaning and roaring at growing volume. Even so, he continued to raise my arm, to pull it taut and to manipulate my shoulder until at last, with a sickening, dull pop, I felt it go back in. The pain was suddenly much less and I rested my head against the bars in an aftermath of exhausted relief. As I recovered, he remained quiet. His hand reached toward me twice, only to pull back at the very last moment. On the third attempt contact was made, a brief, stolen caress, hastily withdrawn.

"Lotte," he whispered, caressing me with his voice instead, "I need you to promise never to sneak up on me again. Just let me know it's you and you'll be safe, for I could never intentionally hurt you. But the same does not apply to the rest of miserable humanity. You have no idea how close you came to losing that arm."

"Yes, I do," I said.

He sighed. "Go home, Lotte. Go back to bed where you belong. Cold compresses on your shoulder for the first two days should help with the swelling. After that, keep it warm."

"What about you?"

"I'll be all right."

"In here?" I shuddered. "How could anyone live in a cage like this?"

"Never underestimate the human capacity for suffering, child. I myself am only twenty-seven and the average human life span is at least fifty-five."

"I think they'll kill you before you're fifty-five."

"That would be a blessing."

"How can you say that?"

"Look at me, Lotte," he commanded. "Really look at me. What kind of a life do you think I could lead even if I weren't locked in this cage?"

I shrugged. "You'll never know until you try."

"How am I to try when there is *no way out?"* he snapped.

"I see a way out," I said. "Maybe it's locked right now but somebody has the key."

"You'd never be able to get it from el Piojo. Go home now before he or someone else catches you here."

"Where does he sleep?"

"There's no way to get it from him. Do you hear me? If he ever caught you, he'd do unspeakable things to you. Unspeakable. And I wouldn't be able to help you. Go home where I know you'll be safe. Please."

"What makes you think," I said with feeling, "that at home I'll be safe?"

Awareness dawned a moment too late and though his arm shot out from between the bars, I'd already stepped outside his reach.

"Lotte, no," he cried.

I looked at him with calm detachment and walked out of the tent, ignoring the frantic tone of his voice as he repeatedly called my name. I don't know why I was so certain in my resolve but for some reason, I knew what I had to do. Strangest of all was that I wasn't afraid. That would come later. On silent feet, I slipped through the grounds, examining darkened tents only to find that no one used them for sleeping. It was behind the Big Top that I saw the ghostly images of the wagons, slumbering quietly in the moonlight and realized that they must be where the people lived. I approached, tiptoeing up and down the rows, inwardly despairing of ever finding the right one. Still, I noticed that many of them had painted scenes adorning their sides. The full moon made it possible for me to see them. I passed by one with a stately representation of elephants in the jungle and knew it to be el Moco's. I passed others depicting animals or circus acts and even a few with voluptuous women in – what seemed to me at the time – highly unlikely poses. One wagon in particular made me think more of a church than a circus what with its depiction of hundreds of naked baby angels playing wrestling games in the clouds. Their little bottoms were unexpectedly plump – and rosy as if they'd been spanked. It wasn't until I'd circled around to the other side that I saw another rendition of the fateful monarch, emblazoned on the door. I was surprised to find it on that particular wagon as I would never have taken el Piojo for a religious man. But the familiar orange and black design convinced me. The wagon could belong to no other.

Suddenly nervous, I held my breath and walked up to the door, putting my ear to it and listening until I was certain I could hear the sounds of snoring. Even then, I hesitated. The moment was upon me and the terror I hadn't felt before came rushing in with double strength. Clasping my trembling hands together, I considered going home and forgetting the whole thing. But no. I knew Erik was waiting for me. He wouldn't rest easy until he knew I was safe and I couldn't bring myself to face him empty-handed. So I grabbed hold of my courage and tried the door. It opened at my touch but the long drawn-out creak that accompanied the movement seemed loud enough for Erik to have heard it all the way back in his tent. For one heart-stopping moment, the snoring was arrested. I stood motionless, afraid to breathe until the comforting sounds resumed.

Slowly, with one hand still holding the door, I groped with the other for something to keep it wedged open. That way I wouldn't have to close it and risk waking el Piojo a second time. The first thing that came to hand was a very familiar black cane. I fumbled with it and with the door, finally able to prop the handle beneath the doorknob and the point in a juncture where two of the wooden strips in the floor were joined. I accomplished it all without making a sound. Somewhat heartened I crept toward the sleeping figure, wincing at every creak of the floorboards. The atmosphere within was close and rank, smelling of dirty laundry and a body gone too long without a bath. Yet I scarcely gave it any thought. For some reason I pictured el Piojo wearing Erik's key on a chain around his neck the way I wore the key to my house. That of course meant I would have to search him as he slept. My skin crawled at the thought. But before I even came within reaching distance of my goal, my feet became entangled in something that was lying on the floor. I floundered and windmilled to no avail, falling to the floor with a thud. At the same moment, the cane came loose and the door slammed shut with a bang. The sleeping figure snorted and sat up. I remained just as I was, tangled up and on the floor, willing myself to blend into the shadows. There could be no further doubt that I'd found the right wagon. Even in the darkness, el Piojo's astounding bulk was recognizable. Laboriously, he swung his legs around and placed them on the floor so that he was sitting on the edge of the bed. "Who's there?"

I could tell by the tremor in his voice that he was afraid but forced myself even so, to remain silent and motionless.

"Erik?" he whispered. But when there was still no response, he reached toward the floor, right at my feet, and grabbed onto whatever it was hobbling me. He felt my foot almost at once and immediately began scratching and striking me until his two hands found my throat. As I tried to pry loose his strangling grip, he lifted me by the neck and wrestled me onto the bed, using the suffocating volume of his own body to restrain me.

"Who are you?" he asked, blasting my senses with his foul breath. I remained mute and he looked me over carefully, slowly beginning to laugh, relaxing his hold on my neck and using his hands instead to pinion my arms above my head. With his face inches from mine, he took a deep breath, raked my cheek with the spines on his face and snuffled deep into my neck and hair. In another moment he'd transferred my wrists to one hand and was using the other to grope and to pinch me.

"Unbelievable," he muttered. "Unbelievable. You actually came to me. Do you have any idea how delicious you are, my little thief?"

He began to cover my face and neck with slobbering kisses and painful bites, a paw-like hand clamping over my mouth when I tried to scream. I was entirely trapped beneath him except for my fettered legs which jingled every time I kicked. Annoyed by the sound, el Piojo paused long enough to unwind the tangled fabric from my feet and toss it aside. "Trying to get into my pants were you?" He chuckled and his cruel hand returned to its work.

The pants hit the floor with a final jingling sound. One corner of my mind realized that the key was in the pocket. For a moment I redoubled my efforts to escape, my goal so tantalizingly close it seemed impossible I couldn't reach it. But when the groping hand moved lower, I understood that the key was the least of my worries. With one final burst of strength, I tried to kick myself free. He smothered my efforts as if they were nothing, tucking my legs firmly beneath the crushing weight of his body. I turned my face away with a sob, closing my eyes in one last attempt at denial.

It was then I heard the creaking of the door hinge and a sound like that of the floorboards protesting. I opened my eyes and was just in time to witness the feral leap of a lithe, dark figure that landed on el Piojo's back. Suddenly the weight that was suffocating me increased. With a choked cry, el Piojo released his hold on my arms to claw frantically at his throat, a dark line appearing even as I watched. Abruptly, his frenzied cries ended and his huge body began thrashing like a fish. Still caught beneath him, I tried desperately to extricate myself, struggling every time his frenzied jerking afforded me the opportunity to withdraw a little further. Bit by bit, I pulled myself out until, with one final wrench, I dropped onto the floor. Looking back, I saw what appeared to be a much smaller figure straddling that of el Piojo, pulling back his head at what seemed an extreme angle. I leaped to my feet, pausing only to grab the discarded pants before bursting out of the door and into the night. Even with the certain knowledge that el Piojo couldn't follow, I ran, filled with a dread of the man who'd saved me. His brutal efficiency left me with the conviction that if he decided to come after me I'd never get away. As if in justification of my fears, I heard a distant sound that could easily have been the creaking of el Piojo's door. Still, it was toward Erik's tent that I flew, unable to forsake him after all my efforts and hoping that if I let him out, he might somehow be able to protect me.

Without slowing, I rolled under one canvas side, came up neatly on my feet and dashed to the front of his cage.

"Erik," I cried.

There was no response and I realized he was gone.

It was then I saw that the door to the cage was open.

And I understood he'd been capable of leaving at any time. I threw down the pants with the unnecessary keys still inside as unbidden, snippets of el Moco's words returned to me: *reign of terror . . . no mercy . . . hates anyone born with a normal face . . .*

Why had I been so quick to discount his advice? An unexpected twinge in my shoulder reminded me of the remorseless strength at Erik's command. He'd been toying with me all along, using the bars of his phony prison to gain my trust. But now the game was over and he was out. He could be anywhere, lurking in the shadows, lying in wait . . .

Suddenly spooked, I ran. As I exited the tent, something black peeled away from the deeper shadows. My fear gave me a fleetness I hadn't known I possessed and carried me into the hills. When I'd crested the summit and could see my own house below, I dared to glance behind me, spying something so gray and vague that it could as easily have been a pursuer as a figment of my imagination. Fearful that it might be the former, I hurled myself down the hill, losing my balance and rolling the rest of the way. My fall was arrested by a stone projecting from the ground like a jagged tooth. Stunned, I looked up, still cross-eyed and woozy, and discerned the blurred but unmistakable silhouette of a man outlined against the rapidly lightening sky. Oblivious to any hurts, I dragged myself to my feet and sprinted toward the house. Familiar fences and trees flashed by me as I closed the distance and leaped to catch hold of the windowsill.

I'd underestimated the distance.

Sliding back down to the ground I tried again, fingernails breaking as I scrabbled against the wall to find purchase. A third time I leaped but was unable to reach even as high as before. Knowing then that my time had run out I spun to confront my fate and found instead nothing. The night was as calm as it had been when I left. The branches of the trees still rustled. The cool breeze played about my hair and caused my overheated body to shiver. I hugged myself, eyes still rapidly shifting back and forth, searching in vain for the source of my terror. But there was nothing. *Nothing.* For what seemed an eternity, I remained in that vibrant state. But my punished body was unable to keep up the physical demand and gradually allowed my heartbeats and breathing to slow. As the scene before me continued unchanging, I even began to indulge in the luxury of thinking, daring to wonder if I'd somehow imagined the pursuit.

At last, I even began contemplating the various strategies I might use to get back into my room. I'd gone so far as to step away from the wall to drag some pots up to my bedroom window when a motion at the very edge of my vision caused me to freeze. In silence, a figure stepped away from the concealing trunk of the tree and started hesitantly toward me. With a powerful jolt, my heart rate tripled. I whirled to face the danger, covering my mouth with my hands and backing away.

The advancing figure halted.

"Lotte," said the familiar, dulcet whisper. "Don't be afraid. It's only Erik."

"Stay away," I cried, my voice a harsh croak and my back making sudden contact with the wall.

"I'm not going to harm you, child." His voice took on a tone of pleading. "I only followed so I could be certain you made it home safely."

"How did you get out?" I demanded.

"With a harp string."

It was unclear what he meant but sounded suspicious. "Why didn't you do that a long time ago then?"

"I suppose I could have," he said. "Once before, I unraveled the coiled metal from the lowest string and bent it to fit the keyhole. But after several days of trying, the mechanism still held and all I'd accomplished was the maiming of my harp."

He knelt on the ground and extended one hand toward me. "Come to me, Lotte, please. You never feared me before. Why do you shrink from me now?"

His voice broke on the last word and my heart melted. But as I took my first step toward him, I heard once again the voice of el Moco hissing in my mind: *He'll lurk in the shadows. He'll pretend to be your friend. He'll destroy you.*

"You're not making any sense," I whimpered, halting. "Why would you try to pick the lock again tonight if you thought you couldn't?"

"Because of you," he said. His yellow eyes were shining, intense and frightening. "You meant to take the key from el Piojo and I knew what would happen if he caught you. Dear God, Lotte, I had to get there before you were harmed. I had to get out."

His passionate vehemence and frantic need for my understanding made it impossible for me to doubt him any longer. A lump formed in my throat as I closed the remaining distance between us. "It was you," I said in a choked voice. "You were the one who made him stop."

Unconsciously I put my hand to my throat, recalling the dark line that had appeared on el Piojo's.

My gesture caused Erik to flinch and turn away.

"A harp string?" I asked.

Only when he didn't answer did I realize he was weeping. Unclear as to exactly how it happened, I discovered a moment later that my arms were wrapped around him, my cheek pressed against his averted head.

"It's all right, what you did," I whispered, fighting to keep hold of his trembling frame. "He was hurting me."

As I refused to let go, it was possible for me to sense the moment of his surrender. Taut muscles loosened until the full weight of his torso sagged against me, his breathing still punctuated by intermittent sobs. Even so, I was unprepared for the suddenness with which he whipped back around, a moan escaping him as he crushed my body to his chest. Overwhelmed, I didn't react immediately, final awareness coming only slowly with the realization that someone, for the first time in two years, was embracing me. Only then did my own tears begin to flow.

At first, he merely continued to hold me, but after a time it almost seemed as if he were drawing strength from my weakness. His hunched figure straightened. His weeping stopped. And although I cannot say exactly when the transfer took place, at some indeterminate time, the one I'd meant to comfort took it upon himself instead to comfort me. At first he murmured to me in soothing tones, coaxing me onto my knees and encouraging me to rest my head on his chest. I felt one of his hands begin to stroke my hair. His voice slipped into song. I closed my eyes and allowed myself to become enveloped once more in the warmth and beauty of his music. For his audience of one, he chose a haunting lullaby. It was a song I'd never heard before and so much softer and more intimate than the song of the circus that it reduced me to a blind, clinging creature, capable only of listening and of experiencing the rapture. There could be no room within me for pain or regret, only the warmth and well being that his singing engendered. Even the coldness of his touch was forgotten. And when at last he was quiet, I discovered that my tears and my pain were both gone.

I looked up at him then. "You're like an angel."

He laughed a little, not the loud, self-deprecating bark I'd known previously, but a pleasant, calming rumble. "I thought the same thing about you," he said. "You came into the tent with the light in your hair and you looked like an angel with a halo of gold. At first I thought it an optical illusion. But now I understand that the vision was true. My pretty Lotte, with her sunshine hair, is the angel who has set me free." Briefly the hand he'd rested on my head came to life, smoothing my thin, flaxen tresses. "Like silk," he murmured. The fondness in his eyes almost caused me to start weeping again.

Before I could react, he set me gently aside and clambered to his feet. Only in the absence of his touch did I become aware once more of the outside world and of the fact that sunrise was only minutes away.

"I must go." He sighed and held out a hand to help me rise. "If they catch me now, this will all have been for nothing."

I nodded and tried to swallow the lump that was again developing in my throat.

"Here," he said, crouching slightly. "Put your arm around my neck and I'll lift you up to the window."

I hesitated, a new, exciting idea occurring to me only at that very moment. Studying his eyes once more and noting the absence of even the slightest hint of adult superiority or malice, I asked, "Couldn't you take me with you?"

"Ah, Lotte, if only I could." His tone of voice again became wistful. "I think I would be happy anywhere as long as you were with me. But what kind of life would that be for you, sleeping out in the elements with a repellent monster and murderer?" He straightened. "Impossible."

Still I could see he was considering it. He clenched and unclenched his fists, walked a short distance away and then returned. I watched him, praying that he would say yes and that I could go away with him. But when he stopped in front of me once again, I saw the anger on his face and I knew even before he spoke that the decision had been made.

"It might have worked," he said, "if there were only just the two of us in the equation. I would take good care of you. I would find us a pretty little house with a garden where you could grow up. I would teach you anything you wanted to learn. Oh, how I would love to teach you. How wonderfully educated you would be. No one could be a more devoted teacher than Erik to his little Lotte."

He grew silent, and I could see him struggling to contain his rage and frustration. When he continued it was in a voice so harsh and unlovely that I barely recognized it. "Unfortunately, there's the rest of the world to consider," he said. "They would never consider a freak such as myself a fit guardian for one such as you. The two of us together would be nothing less than an affront to their precious sensibilities. They'd hunt us down. We'd be forever on the run, you and I. The authorities, the bullies and all the other weaklings would forever be just a step behind us. I would *try* to protect you. I would do *anything* in my power to keep you with me. But what if one day I made a mistake? What if they snatched you away and hid you where I couldn't find you? I know those meddlesome fools all too well. They'd rather leave you to rot in some miserable orphanage than allow *me* to care for you properly."

He'd worked himself into such a fury that I regretted having said anything at all.

"Erik, please." I spoke softly, tugging on his sleeve without much real force, yet the tirade broke off as abruptly as if I'd slapped him.

"Oh, Lotte."

"I'm sorry," I whispered. "I didn't mean to upset you. It's just that I thought . . . It's just that . . ." It was so hard to put words to my jumbled thoughts. "Oh Erik," I cried. "I wish you didn't have to go. I'm going to miss you so much."

"And I you." A long sigh escaped him. "You know I'd take you with me if I could. Still, no matter what life has in store for me, no matter where in the world I may wander, you will always be with me here." He crossed his hands over his heart. "Perhaps one day, if you're sad, it will comfort you to know that someone, somewhere, is thinking fondly of you and wishing you only the best."

I was moved beyond words.

"Will you think of me too, sometimes? he asked.

I swallowed hard. "Of course I will." My voice was husky with threatened tears. "Last night I even dreamed of you. I know I'll dream of you again."

Flabbergasted, I saw the light of hope dawn for perhaps the first time in his eyes.

"Yes." He began nodding slowly. "Yes. I can do at least that much for you."

All at once he cupped my chin in his hand and turned my face up to meet his gaze. "Look into my eyes," he commanded.

The next thing I knew, the sun was well above the horizon and he was carrying me back toward the window. I realized I'd been speaking but could recall none of my own words. Confused, I looked up at him but whatever I might have said was forgotten when I saw the look on his face. His chin was raised at a proud angle. The cadaverous hue of his skin gone, replaced by the faintest hint of pink. His eyes, those frightening, unnatural eyes, were filled with a look of quiet exhilaration. And I understood that for some inexplicable reason, he was happy.

With the greatest of care, he settled me on the ledge.

"I love you, too," he said and squeezed my hand with fingers grown suddenly warm. "And now, I will always be with you, like a guardian angel. Every night when you go to sleep, I'll be waiting there for you in your dreams."

The lump in my throat made speech impossible. I busied myself instead with climbing back inside. I wanted more than ever to give him something to demonstrate that which I couldn't express in words. But the sun was rising ever higher and I knew he'd already stayed with me longer than he should have. It was then I remembered my violin.

"Wait," I cried. "Please wait. Just one more minute." And without stopping to see that he obeyed, I dove onto the floor and pulled the violin out from under the bed. In another moment, I was handing it out the window to him. "Take this," I said. "Maybe you can use it instead of your harp."

He received the black case and took my empty hand before I had a chance to withdraw it. For a moment I thought he would kiss it. But all he did was brush the backs of my fingers against the side of his face where the teeth didn't show. Then he let me go. "Thank you, dearest Lotte," he said. "Take good care of yourself."

And then he was walking away, the black case with my violin inside tucked beneath his left arm.

Chapter Five

Although Erik the man walked out of my life that fateful morning, Erik the angel took up residence in my dreams. His love and his magnificent voice were an endless source of joy and inspiration. I lived each day in anticipation of going to bed at night.

Though I never truly regretted having given him my violin, there were times I found myself missing it. The music that filled me demanded to be given voice until voice became precisely what I gave it. Embarrassing at first in its wobbling thinness, I broadened it and strengthened it, using the angel's music as guide. Always there, the moment my head touched the pillow, he encouraged me to be bold, to experiment, to soar in ever more unique and daring ways. There came a day when, all alone in a field, I started to sing and astonished myself at the power and resonance of the tone that emerged. It was hard to believe that my eleven-year-old vocal cords were physically capable of creating such sound. I devoted time every day to my continuing advancement.

By the age of thirteen, I'd developed a degree of control I wouldn't have believed possible only a few years before. It was during that year I spotted a young woman at a faire who sang for the coins people dropped in her bowl. Years older than I, at least seventeen, her voice compared to mine was like the squeak of a mouse to the roar of a lion.

Impressed by the number of coins she'd collected, I set myself up at the farthest outskirts of the faire, using my apron instead of a bowl. I sang. People gathered around me. They listened, they clapped and they gave me their coins. With the realization that survival wasn't limited to the crumbs my father sometimes remembered to throw me, I wandered ever farther from home, singing on street corners and in town squares. For almost a year I made increasingly distant forays, sleeping in strange haylofts or under the stars. One day, in midsummer after several such weeks, I decided not to bother going home.

It was shortly thereafter that I landed my first job at a tavern in Sarcelles, singing, dancing and waiting on tables. Presented each time as "Lotte, the little girl with the great, big voice," my singing turned out to be very good for business, especially with the addition to my repertoire of a number of bawdy songs the patrons couldn't resist, joining in with their off-key whiskey voices and transforming the dingy tavern into a jolly island of warmth and light. In time my shyness with the clientele gave way to a bantering familiarity. "Sing me a song, Lotte," became the phrase with which many patrons greeted me.

And I would sing. A smile and a wink during the course of the song toward the one who requested it would win me a *sou* for my pocket. But "Give me a kiss, Lotte," was more lucrative still. And as the next few years rolled by – my flaxen hair dulling to an indeterminate brown and my body undergoing those pleasing shifts in proportion – became the more common request.

At the time, though, I was less concerned with the increased liberties the workmen took with my person than by the realization that I was no longer "Lotte of the sunshine hair." What if Erik were to return one day and my darker coloring somehow caused him to love me less? Most other men, however, seemed to love me more, showing their appreciation in silver. And so it was that with care and a frugal lifestyle, I was able to convert those gratuities into a small cushion between myself and destitution that made it possible to sleep with an easier mind. It wasn't really so hard to be thrifty. What did I need with meat, after all, when bread and potatoes were every bit as filling? What did I need with heaping portions of coal when my blanket and dreams kept me warm on cold nights?

So I put up with the men and their lewd propositions, playing along to a certain degree for the sake of the money. Still, I always stopped short of "the back room" where several of the other girls earned the best tips of all. For some reason – and here el Piojo still comes to mind – the thought of lying in the arms of some dirty stable hand for a few extra *sous* was utterly repellent. True, I sometimes felt the desire for physical closeness, retaining that inexplicable need I'd had even as a child to be loved. But Erik had loved me and my angel continued to do so. Perhaps this spiritual love wasn't quite enough for the renegade desires of my newly developed body. But compared to the alternative of a quick impersonal groping, my angel's love was a refuge.

The end result was that I retained my virtue. For a time.

Chapter Six

It was during that same period I encountered the second turning point in my life. I was already in my twentieth year that fateful evening in December, belting out a lusty drinking song from my place atop the piano, when I spotted a rag-covered figure that appeared to have blown into the common room along with a flurry of snow. My heart gave a mighty leap at the sight of the black violin case he carried under one arm and without giving myself or my situation any further thought, I hopped off the piano and headed toward him. The uncharacteristic single-mindedness of my purpose was a windfall for the patrons at the tables. More than a few of these workmen murmured suggestive endearments as I passed them. One in particular, Lowell, who shoveled manure at the livery stable, had the cheek to stand up and grab my breast. Normally, I'd have boxed his ears for such an action but at that moment I didn't even slow. Not even Monsieur Bernard, the tavern owner, could stop my headlong rush. I pushed past him and knelt beside the hooded figure with the violin case who'd collapsed on the floor.

"Erik?" I whispered.

He gave no sign of having heard me.

I placed my hand on his shoulder, leaning in closer so that only the fabric of his hood prevented my cheek from touching his. "You found me, my angel. Everything's going to be all right now. Don't you recognize your own little Lotte, all grown up?"

A moment later, a bloodless hand emerged from the folds of clothing, pulling back the hood and revealing the bespectacled face of a stranger. It was pinched and pale. He was obviously starving. I gasped and drew away.

"I'm sorry," I stammered. "I thought you were someone else."

"Help us," he moaned in a thick northern accent. "My little daughter is dying."

He opened a corner of his cloak to reveal the face of an emaciated child who I feared might already be dead.

"Is this a friend of yours?" Monsieur Bernard asked from behind me.

"No." I looked away and swallowed hard, willing myself not to lose my composure. How my heart had leapt when I'd thought him to be Erik. How bitter now, the disappointment.

Stepping in front of me, the owner addressed himself to the crumpled figure. "Do you have any money?"

"No sir," the man answered. "But I beg of you, have pity on a poor starving child."

"There's no place for you here, old man."

"Sir, I beseech you."

I laid a restraining hand upon Monsieur Bernard's when he reached down to drag the man to his feet. "It's all right," I said. "Go ahead and let him have whatever he needs. I'll pay for it."

But it was still early in the evening and he only laughed at the few *centimes* I was able to offer him from my pocket.

"I'll give you the rest later," I promised.

"I thought you said you didn't know him."

"I don't."

"Then put away your pennies, foolish girl, and get back to work."

Had it truly been Erik, I'd never have acquiesced. He'd have either stayed in the tavern or the two of us would have braved the storm together. Unfortunately for the shivering vagabond, I wasn't yet ready to make such a sacrifice for him. And so, however reluctantly, I turned my back on the pair and started toward the piano at the other end of the room. By the time I'd reached it and turned back around, the man and his daughter were gone. I felt a stab of remorse but it wasn't long before I was caught up once more in the whirl of music and work and flirtation that constituted life at the tavern. Only when we closed and the employees began leaving through the back entrance did I think again of the man and his daughter. As the other girls and I stepped into the alley that ran behind the building, a ragged figure emerged from beneath a snow-covered pile of garbage. It accosted us in a broken, barely audible voice. Immediately I recognized him, hooded once more, the shape of the child that he hugged to his chest visible beneath the folds of his cloak. But the night was bitter cold and most of the girls brushed by him as if he were invisible. I myself paused only a moment, though I confess I was equally impatient to get home.

"Follow me," I said, the irreversible decision made in that brief instant without the benefit of forethought or consideration. I emphasized my words with one quick beckoning gesture and then hurried away, the sound of his footsteps behind me the only indication that he followed. In fact, I didn't look back until I reached my flat, already regretting my impetuosity and hoping somehow that I might have lost him. But since my miserable little room wasn't far from the tavern, the stranger, as feeble as he seemed to be, had managed to match my pace. Indeed, he was the first to enter when I opened the door. No less biting than that of the frigid air without, the chill that greeted us within obliged me to pause only long enough to light the lamp before turning my attention to the ashes in the stove. I added a few lumps of coal and stoked the embers into an evenly burning flame.

While I was busy, the man seated himself close to the stove on the hard planking of the floor. Once the fire was doing well, I brought him a folded blanket upon which he could sit and wrapped another around his shoulders. I returned to the stove and reheated a pot of leftover stew and boiled some water, noticing through frequent glances in the direction of my guest, that as the delicious warmth and good smells slowly radiated out into the room, his shivering diminished. He began rocking the child he clutched possessively to his breast and murmuring words in a language I couldn't understand. This continued until I was able to hand him a cup of tea and a bowl of stew. He roused the girl even before tasting it himself and spooned the broth into her mouth.

I sat on the floor beside them, another bowl of stew in my hands. "What's her name?" I asked.

"Christine."

"Why don't you let me hold her? I can feed her while you eat."

He seemed reluctant to let her go.

"It's all right," I said, extending my arms to receive her. "You'll need your strength too, if only to care for her."

He hesitated a moment longer but passed her to me with a solemnity that made it clear he was entrusting me with his most precious possession. Her eyes were open but glazed. Once she was in my arms, I discovered that her entire body had been so tightly swaddled in miscellaneous dirty strips of cloth that her blood flow surely must have been impeded. Casting a sideways glance at her father, I came to realize how distracted by desperation he must have been to have wound the rags so tightly. Quietly and without drawing undo attention to the fact, I removed some of the tourniquets from her little body, freeing her arms and readjusting the hood to reveal a startling cloud of flaxen hair.

With the loosening of the constricting fabric, her breathing came more easily and her eyes began to focus. I began to spoon the warm broth into her mouth, adding bits of potato and onion as she became increasingly aware and speaking soft words of encouragement all the while. Another glance at the father showed that he'd relaxed, satisfied that his darling was in capable hands and had begun to apply himself to the stew with a voracity that was mildly disgusting. Christine, too, had begun to slurp greedily and I did my best to keep up with her. But then, sudden comprehension filled her eyes and she looked into mine with an expression of accusation. In that split second of time before her pretty face puckered and the wailing began, I understood that she'd only just realized the arms cradling her weren't her father's.

"Don't cry, little one," I whispered, embarrassed and inexplicably hurt. "Your papa is right here. He'll hold you again just as soon as he finishes his supper. Hush now, and Lotte will sing to you." And I did, choosing, in my need for acceptance, not just any song, but the most beautiful lullaby I knew, the one my angel had once sung to me. But Christine wanted none of my comfort, crying even louder, arching her back and squirming in a way that made it extremely difficult for me to hold her. At last, her father put down his unfinished meal and took her back, her tears stopping so abruptly it was difficult to imagine the intensity of her distress just moments before. His musical, foreign words were so soft and so intimate that I suddenly felt as though *I* were the intruder. As an excuse to get away, I went to turn down the bed, placing some hot coals in the pan of the bed warmer and passing it up and down between the sheets. After some time, he got up, carried her over and placed her under the covers, kissing her sleeping forehead and making sure the blankets were arranged snugly around her before returning to the fire and his cold dinner.

"Here, let me warm that up for you," I said, ladling more of the bubbling stew into his bowl.

"God bless you, dear lady, for all the kindness you have shown us," he said.

Embarrassed not only by the unexpected warmth of his reaction but also by the inner knowledge that I'd momentarily regretted taking him in, I could only look away. "I don't really deserve your thanks," I whispered. "I almost left you to die out there."

"But you didn't," he said. "There aren't too many young women in your position willing to ignore the dangers of sheltering strangers. That is why I shall pray for you. I shall ask God to watch over and protect you."

Moved by his blessing, so reminiscent of another blessing I'd once received, I couldn't immediately respond. Instead, I reflected upon his words, upon the warmth and contentment of the moment, and even, upon the singular nature of my dreams. "You know," I said, "I think in a way, maybe He does watch over me."

The man studied my face. "You're right, of course. God cares for us in countless ways though very few are wise enough to recognize them."

I nodded, serving myself the remains at the bottom of the pot.

"A year ago," he resumed, "I thought myself the most unhappy of men. My poor, dear wife, Thérèse, passed on, God rest her soul, and then I lost the title to my land. All within a few weeks. Christine and I were forced to leave our home with nothing but the clothing on our backs."

"And your violin," I interjected, that particular item not easily forgotten.

"Yes, my violin. It's how we earn our living. I play and Christine sings. She has such a lovely voice. You cannot begin to imagine. We travel from town to town, making music for our bread. It's a hard life but I cannot complain. How many other men in this world are lucky enough to have their daughters always by them? I look at her some mornings, asleep in my arms, and I thank God for giving me the life that he has."

"But how will you make it through the winter?"

"I don't know," he said. "I'd heard the winters this far south were milder than those of my native land. But even so, a man and his child cannot survive a winter even such as this without some sort of roof over their heads."

"So you're not from here."

"We're from Skoteloff."

I shrugged.

"Near Uppsala."

Though he spoke that foreign word as if any child would know it, I, who hadn't seen a map since last attending school, was unable to guess at the country where those exotic-sounding towns might be located. Fearful he'd discover my ignorance, I asked instead, "What's your name, monsieur?"

He looked up then with an embarrassed little smile that was quite endearing. "Forgive me, mademoiselle. My rudeness is inexcusable. I'm Samuel Daaé."

"People call me Lotte," I said.

"From Charlotte?"

I nodded.

"And your family name?"

There was a pause.

"I can't – " I looked at him helplessly. "I mean . . . it's been so long."

Realization dawning, he pat my arm. "It doesn't matter, Mademoiselle Charlotte." And then with compassion, "You've been on your own a long time, haven't you?"

The kindness in his tone caused my eyes to sting and my throat to thicken. Looking at him, I realized he must have once been an attractive man. I also saw that he wasn't nearly as old as I'd thought. True, his sparse hair was the color of old ivory and lines of worry were etched deep in his brow. But the condition of his skin, so tight and resilient around his neck, gave the lie to the illusion of age. He couldn't have been more than forty, though given the extreme youth of his child, I secretly believed him to be less.

"Who is Erik?" he asked.

"Erik?" My stomach jolted at the mention of his name. "What do you know of Erik?"

"Only his name, mademoiselle," he said. "You called me Erik when you came to me in the tavern."

"Oh."

"You need not tell me if it causes you pain."

"It's all right." I sighed. "Erik was once a dear friend, a very long time ago, now. He had to leave me and there was nothing I could do except give him my violin to remember me by. That was the real reason for my mistake, you know. I saw you with your violin and thought for a moment that he'd finally found a way to come back to me."

"I'm sorry to have disappointed you."

"I was foolish to imagine such a thing. I don't even know if he's alive anymore – the way most people are alive, anyway – but I'm glad I was there when you needed me."

"She would have died tonight had it not been for you." The eyes that met mine were burning with gratitude and once again I found myself looking away. "I know we've burdened you unpardonably," he said, "and I wish I had something to give you in payment. But we have nothing, Mademoiselle Charlotte. I promise you, though, that we'll leave on the morrow and trouble you no further."

"Where will you go?"

At his hesitation, I looked up. This time it was his gaze that evaded.

"Why don't you stay here for a few days?" I said, my own mood brightening at the thought. "I'm all alone, as you know, and it's good to have company sometimes."

No answer.

"Do it for Christine," I said. "Let her have a few days of warmth and some solid meals before she has to face the cold again."

In the end, they stayed the whole winter.

Chapter Seven

That first night, Monsieur Daaé was shy about sharing the bed with me and tried to sleep on the floor by the stove. It was only after I suggested placing Christine in the middle that I was able to persuade him to remove his filthy outer garments and join us under the covers. Even then, I found that by morning, despite the narrowness of the bed, there was a good-sized space between the two of them and me. I looked upon their sleeping forms with fascination, noting the way her blond head was pillowed on his chest, the way her right hand rested so casually on his abdomen, the almost possessive tension of his two arms, holding her against him in a slumbering embrace. I found myself wishing I might sleep thus, cradled in the arms of someone who loved me. But I feared it was a sensation I would never know and got up quickly so I wouldn't have to keep watching them.

After the first few days, when Christine's little face lost that hollow, hungry look and her bone-thin legs began to support her weight once more, I saw that she was older than I'd originally assumed: nearly four. Quite simply, she was the most beautiful child I'd ever beheld with her fairy tale hair and enormous blue eyes. But I soon discovered that her looks were the least of her blessings. Quite to my frustration, little Miss Daaé turned out to be – with one very notable exception – the most musically gifted person I'd ever met. Not yet four years old, and she'd already developed perfect pitch, taking down in dictation, anything her father could play on his violin. Not yet four years old and she'd already surpassed in knowledge of music theory everything I'd struggled to learn by the age of seven. Not yet four years old and she was able to sing with a disdainful lack of effort the most complex solfège her father could notate.

"She is extraordinary," I admitted to him late one night after returning from the tavern.

"Oh yes," he agreed, his eyes lighting up at the broaching of his favorite topic. "One day she will be the greatest soprano the world has ever known."

"You're sure about that," I said dryly, annoyed and maybe even a little offended at his dismissal of my own small talents.

He turned to me then, eyes brilliant with religious fervor. "Absolutely."

"But how can you know she'll be a soprano? She could just as easily end up a contralto."

"No," he replied with aggravating self-assurance. "She'll be a soprano. She is so like her mother in every other way that there can be no doubt she'll have inherited *the voice*, as well."

"Are you saying she already *looks* like her mother?"

"Just like," he answered. "Thérèse was an angel. It's no wonder God took her back so soon. But how can I complain when He, in his divine benevolence, saw fit to leave me with her living, breathing likeness."

Our gazes were drawn to the lovely child, slumbering so sweetly, her startling hair fanned out about her head like a halo of light. I couldn't help running my fingers through my own mop of mouse brown. "Does she have her mother's hair?" I heard myself ask.

"Oh, yes," he answered proudly. "Her mother was one of those fortunate few whose hair never turns."

Turns.

"Believe it or not," I responded without intending to sound as pettish as I did, "*mine* was once that color. But as you can see, I was *not* one of those fortunate few."

He looked at me with belated understanding. "Mademoiselle, I wasn't making any kind of comparison."

I could feel my face flushing. He was right, of course, even if he'd gone more than a little overboard in his praise. "I'm sorry," I said. "The hair, I suppose, is a sensitive topic. Whenever I look at Christine I'm reminded of myself, the way I used to be. And of a time when I was happy."

"I didn't realize you were unhappy."

"Well – " I thought for a moment. "Perhaps 'unhappy' isn't the exact word to describe it. But there's an emptiness. And I guess it makes me sad to realize that if something were ever to happen to me, nobody would care."

"I would care," he said.

I looked up at him then, knowing that my eyes were pleading and my expression one of naked vulnerability. But emboldened by his words, I dared to let him see. For one moment, our gazes locked, though what I saw reflected in his eyes wasn't the concern he'd professed, but rather an inexplicable flicker of fear, quickly hidden as he turned away.

After a time, we settled into a sort of routine. In the mornings the three of us would take a walk – as if we were a family – the Daaés bundled up in the warm new coats I'd bought for them. On clear days, he would bring his violin with him and set himself up in the town square in the exact spot where I'd once sung. I still remember the first time I heard him play out in the open, bearing down with a boldness that wouldn't have been appropriate within the paper-thin walls of my flat. At first his playing had a rustiness that made me wince, but he continued, showing a complete lack of self-consciousness until he'd achieved the breathtaking fluidity that I would come to know as his trademark. Even that first time I had to acknowledge that I was in the presence of a master. The sweet voice of his instrument, combined with inspired phrasing and flawless technique made his simple music a joy to experience. It wasn't until I became aware of Christine's inscrutable gaze upon me that I realized I was grinning most foolishly. Immediately shifting her gaze from mine, her eyes met those of her father. A silent exchange passed between them. And she began to sing.

Her voice, fully opened for the first time in my presence, was everything her father had said and more. Her acute ear and supreme control made possible a subtle and haunting blend of sounds. Achingly beautiful it was. Yet I was bothered by her intrusion in a way I couldn't then explain and yearned to hear the violin alone. By then, though, Christine and her father were as oblivious to me as they were to the large group of people who'd gathered around them. The pair seemed alone in their own little world, one that excluded all others but that afforded its two inhabitants a vibrant ecstasy, painfully visible upon their faces and in their locked gazes. There was something disturbing in that intensity. The performance made me increasingly uncomfortable until I could no longer stay. As I made my escape, however, I threw a few coins in the empty violin case, knowing they had no coins of their own to seed the till and give the tourists the right idea.

They arrived back at my flat, a few minutes before I had to go to work. I'd halfway expected them to return laden with groceries, as their music had been so extraordinary and the people gathered around them so numerous. But Daaé carried nothing but the familiar black case and Christine, a porcelain doll. It was the sort of toy I would have loved as a little girl but for which I would never have dared to ask. Completely forgetting myself, I knelt down in front of her and touched one of the velvet and lace sleeves. "Oh Christine," I cried, "Where did you get such a pretty doll?"

Her reaction was to look me straight in the eye, draw her lips inside her mouth and bite down hard, a refusal so overt that it took me a few moments to believe what I was seeing. Yet even when realization dawned, I didn't blame her, but myself, for bombarding her with an intimidating and overly effusive greeting.

"I'm sorry," I said, forcing my voice to sound even and pleasant. "I didn't mean to speak so loudly. I was just so excited about your new doll. Have you thought of a name for her yet?"

Silence and huge, blue eyes staring into mine were her only response.

"I had a doll when I was a little girl," I continued, nonplused but still babbling. "She wasn't nearly as pretty as yours and was only made of rags. But I did love her so. *Her* name was Anabelle."

But having suffered me long enough, Christine jerked the doll away and ran to hide behind her father who could only shrug and smile apologetically. Unable to think of anything else to do, I gave up and left for work.

There'd been a time when I lived my whole life for the sole purpose of getting through the day. Nothing mattered but the glorious nights spent in the company of my angel, listening to his voice, so impossibly sweet, reveling in the certainty of his love and acceptance, discussing any subject under the sun, with particular emphasis on my own musical progress. I dreaded only the coming of morning and the commencement of yet another day of meaningless emptiness. But though the joy of being with him could never be diminished, I found, with the coming of the Daaés, that my waking life had taken on a new dimension. It was no longer so difficult to get out of bed in the morning, the pleasure of preparing breakfast for them making it easy to rise upon waking. Daily tasks no longer seemed the drudgery they once had, for I took pride in knowing that the two were clean and well-fed, that their clothing, like mine, was spotless, pressed and mended. But the best part of all was returning home at night, after work, to find a warm room and a kindly face awaiting me. Daaé rarely went to bed before I arrived though he always made certain that Christine was asleep by eight o'clock. Only at night were he and I truly able to talk. Even so, throughout the course of that winter, I believe we left very few topics unexplored as we sat side by side in front of the stove taking simple pleasure in each other's company.

That particular night, however, I was interested only in discussing Christine and her continued refusal to speak to me.

"She's shy," he said dismissively. "Give her some time and she'll come to trust you."

For some reason, I didn't share his confidence. He seemed completely ignorant of the unrelenting suspicion with which she watched my every move, making me feel as if I were guilty of some heinous, though unremembered crime. Inexplicably, I couldn't bring myself to enlighten him. When two more weeks went by and Daaé remained as devoid of helpful suggestions as he had at the onset, I tried on my own, to find ways to show her that I wanted to be her friend. My secret penchant for chocolates caused me, at one point, to believe that such a gift might sweeten her outlook as well, prompting the outrageous expenditure of a portion of my hoarded savings on a box of confections. The gesture was, of course, useless. Undaunted, I bought her a pad of heavy paper and a box of paints, sitting down with her to show her how to use them. After painting a few orange and black butterflies, I found myself telling her the legend of the monarch, discovering to my surprise that – though she refused to look at me – she was listening. So thrilled was I by this perceived breakthrough that I didn't even become angry when I returned home that night to see her artistic expressions all over the walls of my flat. Despite everything, though, the sad truth was that I was no closer to winning her trust than I'd been at the beginning.

At the time it never occurred to me to ask myself why her approval was so important to me. I'd always needed acceptance from everyone, so I guess I didn't see anything particularly extraordinary in needing hers. Still, there were other worrisome thoughts stirring within me that should have sounded the warning bells and didn't. For instance, I couldn't but compare the sort of life the Daaés lived and the life that Erik and I might have shared: the man and the child traveling the countryside, devoted to each other and to their music. It was as if they were living the life that should have been mine with Daaé treating Christine so similarly to the way I knew Erik would have treated me, that seeing the two of them sing together was often more than I could bear. Sometimes when I watched them, I had the disturbing impression of standing outside my own life and observing it from a distance. When that happened, I often wondered if *I* were not really just some character in a drama with the actress playing my part somehow changed. But if Christine had taken over *my* life, who did that make me? Or more importantly, *what*?

As this was my state of mind, perhaps it is not surprising that I began to associate Monsieur Daaé – at least in his current role as Christine's father and protector – with Erik. The unhappy result was that I lost my heart to him before I even knew what was happening. Maybe if I'd perceived the full significance of his relationship with Christine I would have realized earlier that my heart was the last thing he wanted. Still, it wasn't as though I had any illusions about ever being first in his affections. It wasn't as though I didn't understand that he loved her best and always would. But subconsciously, I think, I must have believed that despite his consuming obsession with the girl, there had to be some small place in his heart for a person who cared for them both as sincerely as I did.

Chapter Eight

One night toward the end of February, the men at the tavern seemed to be in rare form. They reached out to grab at me and the other girls every time one of us walked by and requested kisses even more frequently than normal. We attributed it to the full moon, the weeks of idleness caused by the weather or perhaps even the promise of spring soon to come. Whatever the reason, Lowell in particular was outdoing himself. At one point he even swung me onto his lap and whispered a very lewd suggestion in my ear. All evening he remained a nuisance, becoming drunker, meaner and more demanding until at last, Monsieur Bernard put him out. I'd expected that to be the end of it, though I made certain to exit at the end of the evening with a large group of other girls.

It was only after the last of them had gone their separate ways that I become aware of the shadow that moved when I moved. A moment later, as if to ensure the fact that I knew I was being followed, a guttural voice slurred with drink began suggesting vile and disgusting things from the darkness. I meant to make a run for it but he was already upon me, seizing me from behind, kissing the nape of my neck and mauling my breasts with his callused hands. Pulling my arms forward to protect myself, I gave him a donkey kick in the shin. But instead of winning my freedom, my defense served only to enrage him. With frightening ease he spun me around and drove his fist into my face.

I awoke sometime later, immediately aware of the grunting, sweating presence on top of me. Shock came a moment later when I realized that I was naked, that cruel hands were pinching and kneading and that something was pounding again and again into the most private region of my body. Appalled, I began to struggle, unable to control my frantic flailing even when the fists reappeared.

The next time I awoke, I was alone, my mind so muddled that for a time I could only lay where I was. But then, inevitably, memory returned and with it the physical pain. I reached down to touch the area where pain was greatest and realized by the glutinous wetness that I was bleeding. It was then I was hit by the real impact of what had happened to me. With a moan, I covered my face with my hands and succumbed to an incoherent agony of humiliation and loss. *Who will ever want me now?* In the midst of this grief, a wave of disjointed memories flooded my mind. Once again, someone was effortlessly pinning my struggling body to the ground. Again I saw my father coming at me in a rage. Again my person was being violated.

I cried out as I was hit a second time by the significance of the attack and in that half moment of clarity, I heard unnatural sounds like the half-strangled mewling of some dying animal. Only belatedly did I realize they were coming from me. Before I could react, I was back in Écouen, running down the hill at night with a demon in pursuit. I was playing my violin. I was being beaten again for having given it away. I was wandering, lost in a gray no-man's-land. I was frantically searching for something I couldn't find.

A loud thump startled me back into awareness. Another caused me instinctively to struggle to my feet despite my disorientation and the leaden torpor of my body. Only a rising sense of urgency somewhere within, gave me the strength to remain standing. With a jolt like a blow to the head, I rediscovered my nakedness. The fog lifted from my brain and I remembered everything. There was another blow from the opposite side of the wall against which I was leaning. I had no idea what was causing it but imagined a beefy man, like the stake-drivers from the circus, using one of those huge wooden mallets to break down the last protective barrier between us. I shrank back, crouching in a corner and hugging myself in silent anticipation. But instead of a continued frenzy of blows ending with the wall giving way and some monster of a man bursting forth to claim me, everything quieted.

For a while I could do nothing but remain cringing where I was, afraid to breathe. The muscles in my legs, unused to squatting for such a period of time began to cramp but still I couldn't bring myself to rise. Even when my rational mind had reasserted itself so that I realized I was going to have to do *something*, I found that I couldn't immediately initiate any kind of motion. It is hard to say how long I thought about moving before actually doing so but because of the darkness and because my eyes were nearly swollen shut, I was effectively blind. I knew I'd have to explore my surroundings with my hands. I told myself that I would count to three and then feel the ground to my right but even then, it took several tries before I actually succeeded in doing it. Strong in my mind was the image of something grabbing or biting me before I could bring my hand back to the core of my body. In the end, I discovered nothing more threatening than more straw, the same as that upon which I was crouching. With a measure of relief, I brought back my hand, counted to three, took a deep breath and felt the ground to my left. Almost at once I encountered a shoe, and then a lump of wadded fabric that proved to be my dress. It took a great deal of courage to struggle back into my clothing but I managed.

After that, it was no longer beyond my capacity to straighten up. And so I tried. But as my legs were numb from having supported my weight in such an awkward position, they were not immediately able to hold me. Before I'd completely stood, my right leg gave out and I fell against the wall with a thump. Immediately, there was an answering bang from the other side punctuated this time by an earsplitting whinny. And with that whinny came the realization of where I was. A good deal of my fear fell away, enabling me to drag myself forward, find the door that was directly in front of me and fumble open the latch. Thus I exited the stall into which I'd been thrown. The moonlight that entered from a high window illuminated the central aisle of our town's livery stable. The horse in the stall next to mine, disturbed by my presence, continued to kick the walls even as I limped toward the side exit and let myself out onto the street.

The sharp blast of cold air cleared the last of the fuzziness from my brain. I headed homeward wondering if I would find the Daaés there, anxiously awaiting me, or if perhaps they'd become worried enough to begin searching the town. I prayed I'd find them. I didn't think I had the strength to tend my own hurts and feared I'd lose my mind if I spent much more time by myself.

Luckily, I didn't have far to travel and was soon in front of my own door. I searched the remnants of my dress for the key but it was gone. I knocked. The subsequent wait seemed endless. I thought at first that my impatience was making the seconds drag by and then, with increasing desperation, that no one was home, that the Daaés were out searching for me, that despite my condition I was going to have to wait for their return on my own doorstep, exposed to the elements and at the mercy of anyone who might be passing. Without much hope, I knocked again and then again, finally collapsing to the ground and hugging myself against the chill. Only then did I hear the sound of footsteps inside, the striking of a match, the squeak of the rusty lantern and finally, the bolt being slowly pulled back. Daaé in his nightshirt appeared, standing above me, the lamp in his hand. From my place on the ground, I watched him look sleepily into the night. The expression on his face surprised me. There was no sign in it of anything being amiss, only a sort of neutral blandness as he looked first to the left and then to the right. Seeing nothing and never once thinking to look down, he began to close the door.

It was the first time I saw him clearly for what he was: a fool. But it wasn't my discovery of his foolishness that turned my surprise to bitterness or my self-pity to rage. It was the sudden realization that my failure to make it home had concerned him so little that he'd been able to sleep that night with an untroubled mind, that contrary to my imaginings of the two of them frantic at my absence, they'd been lying there, sweetly dreaming in their borrowed bed while I – the person who'd made that peaceful refuge possible – was being beaten, violated, discarded. None of it had mattered to any living person, not even to the people whose lives I'd saved.

The door closed in my face.

My rage gave me a power I didn't know I had. With a strength that belied my condition, I delivered a series of blows to the door that probably awakened everyone in the next building over. Immediately the door reopened and this time Daaé saw me.

"Lotte," he cried. His familiar use of my name without the prefacing "mademoiselle" had a stupefying effect on my wounded psyche.

Without another word, he put the lamp down and lifted me in arms grown strong after two months of proper nourishment and adequate shelter. He carried me to the bed and laid me down, seeming so shocked and so stricken at my condition that I was at a loss as to what to think. He left me briefly to stoke the fire and heat some water. In his absence I wondered if he could truly be so simple as to never imagine the possibility of anything happening to me. I was still not ready to forgive him but unbidden thoughts filled my mind of the way he'd been unable to accumulate money despite his steady earnings and a lifestyle virtually free of expenses. I couldn't help remembering the way he'd lost his farm, the way he'd irresponsibly roamed the countryside, the way he hadn't even given a thought to the oncoming harshness of winter until it had overtaken him. Angrily I called him a fool again in my mind but the rage was waning. Without wanting to, I found myself thinking that people weren't fools on purpose. Blaming a fool for his simple-mindedness was as unfair as blaming my angel for his face.

I resisted that line of thinking, perhaps because the similarities I'd seen between Daaé and Erik were the reason for my situation in the first place. But as my mind continued finding logical explanations for Daaé's behavior, my heart became increasingly frustrated at not having a good excuse for being angry with him.

It was then that he returned with a basin of warm water and began, very gently to clean away the blood from my nose and mouth. I saw him hesitate for several moments and then with determination, part my shredded garments and do what he could for the other wounds he found. I saw his eyes widen as he recognized the bite marks and I, in humiliation, turned my face away so as not to read his reactions. As he moved lower, I was unable to refrain from whimpering. Like a dog. The mortification at what he was soon to discover was more powerful even than the physical pain itself. I was completely incapable of holding back the tears that leaked from the corners of my eyes and little Christine began to stir in her sleep beside me.

"I'm sorry," Daaé whispered. His voice was thick with emotion.

For the first time since I'd known him, he placed his hand on my averted cheek in what was unmistakably a caress. With that, the last vestiges of my anger towards him left me, expelled as suddenly and irrevocably as the departing spirit from the body of someone who dies. I started weeping in earnest. As if some final barrier had been broken, he gathered me into his arms with the same sheltering possessiveness that characterized his handling of Christine and began pressing kisses to the top of my head.

"My poor Lotte," he whispered, rocking me. "My poor child."

Christine thrashed out suddenly and began talking in her sleep.

Again Daaé lifted me, settling with me on the floor in front of the stove and sheltering me against his body as if I were a little girl. He continued to hold me long after the sobs had become intermittent, as if for that one space in time, he had no other obligations and we two were alone in the world.

"Christine is very lucky to have you." I said at last, my head still resting against his shoulder. "My own father never much cared for me you know, especially after my mother died. I remember sometimes when I was alone, I used to play a little game and pretend that I was my mother and that Anabelle was me. The two of us would have the most wonderful conversations and even though she didn't know very much, she knew she could ask me anything she wanted because I would never make fun or be impatient – " Suddenly hearing myself, I looked up to see how he could possibly be reacting to such a confession. "Forgive me," I whispered, "I'm a fool."

Were those tears in his eyes?

"Never you, Lotte," he said. "The fools are the ones who abandoned you. How could anyone forsake such a beautiful and loving child?"

My arms tightened infinitesimally around his torso.

"It wasn't her fault, Monsieur Daaé. My maman couldn't help it that she died. I know she would have stayed with me if she could. That's why I used to tell myself that when I grew up, I'd have a little daughter of my own who I'd love just as much as my maman loved me and that then, maybe, everything would be all right."

"Yes," he replied thoughtfully. "I agree with you. When the time comes, your own children will be the ones to make you whole."

There was a pause during which I pondered his words. "I'm not as certain of that as I once was," I said at last. "I used to believe that love and kindness were all that really mattered but now that I've seen you with Christine, I've come to understand that there is much more involved in raising a child than I ever realized. Perhaps my father did the best for me that he could. Perhaps, in his place, I would do even worse, for surely, I am twice as ignorant and three times as poor as he ever was. Any child of mine would be entirely without a future and completely at the mercy of the world, for I could never afford to give her any kind of education."

"But you could school her yourself," he said.

"I don't think so."

"Why not?"

"Because," I felt my face growing hot with shame and was unable to look at him when I whispered, "I barely remember how to read."

My admission evoked from him an actual, physical start. He looked for a moment as though he were ready to say something but then thought better of it. Instead, he eased me back onto the floor, rose to retrieve a blanket from the bed and returned to wrap it around me. Then he sat back down at my side.

"Were you ever instructed at all?" he asked.

"I went to school until I was seven but after that, my papa couldn't afford it anymore."

"But what of your music? Surely you've been taught more recently than that?"

"Not *taught*, exactly."

"But your voice," he insisted. "It is the product of years of development. No one can produce and control such volume and tone without extensive training."

I was quiet for a time and tried to decide whether or not I should reveal my secret. But I'd had such uncharitable thoughts and he'd been so good to me despite them, that I found it impossible at that moment, to deny him anything. "I've never told this to anyone, Monsieur Daaé," I said. "Please promise me you won't laugh."

"I would never laugh at you."

Closing my eyes and praying I was doing the right thing, I said, "I dream of an angel who comes to me every night." Looking quickly at him, I saw how eagerly he was leaning forward.

"Go on," he said.

"When I'm especially lonely or sad," I said, "he speaks to me, just as if he were a real person. But most of the time when he comes, it's to sing. For over ten years now, I've worked with my voice every day, trying as hard as I can to make it sound more like his. I'll never succeed of course. Not completely. But even so, all the years of trying have brought about certain – well – changes. Sometimes when I sing, I don't even recognize myself."

He caught my hand so suddenly and with such strength that I gasped. "Is it true?" he asked, his voice betraying what I felt to be excessive fervor. "Are you truly visited by an angel of music?"

"I don't know if 'visit' is the right word. It's more as if his image is always in my mind, but only surfaces when I'm asleep."

"And this image," Daaé pressed, "What is it like?"

Immediately, my mind conjured the figure of my angel. The angel who was my first and best friend. The angel I loved. What words could I use to describe him: Twisted face? Suppurating skull? A hole where others have a nose? I couldn't bring myself to speak those words, as if giving them voice were a betrayal, their mere utterance a lie, evoking an image of ugliness where, in fact, only beauty existed. "His presence is like a warmth all around me," I said at last. "I don't think that most people would be able to see or comprehend his beauty."

"So he cannot be seen?"

I considered for a moment, remembering a long ago circus and a man in a cage. "He would choose not to show himself, I think. He would prefer only to be heard."

Daaé nodded, apparently overlooking the oddness of my wording. "Will he come to you, tonight?"

"If I can get to sleep." My words were not intended as a dismissal but he interpreted them as such. He released my hand and returned to the bed where he carefully lifted his daughter's sleeping head to remove the single pillow we usually shared.

"Perhaps his coming will help you heal," he said, placing the pillow beneath my head. "Good night, Lotte. I'll pray for you."

He'd already stood and was heading back toward the bed before I realized in a sudden panic that he was leaving me. "Samuel," I called weakly, daring to use his first name in the aftermath of our closeness.

He paused.

"Don't leave me."

He returned but I immediately noticed a stiffness about him and a wariness that hadn't been there before. I'd been wrong to call him Samuel.

"There's nothing to be afraid of," he said. "Nobody here will hurt you."

"I know," I said. "But once you stop talking to me, I'm going to start thinking about everything. And I'm afraid if I do, I'll go mad."

"Then I shall sing you a lullaby so you'll go right to sleep." And he did, poor simple fellow, imagining that a child's lullaby could erase the effects of rape. Still, I closed my eyes and listened with all my might, willing myself to sleep so that all would be as he said. But when he'd finished, I was still awake. And when he got up that second time to return to his bed, I felt it would be better to let him go. Alone, I tried to keep my mind on the words of his song. I tried to think about all we'd discussed. I tried to think about my angel. But hard as I forced my mind to remain active, short, sharp flashes of memory interrupted my sweeter thoughts, causing me to flinch where I lay.

With no one to keep the demons at bay, they encroached with growing strength until I could no longer ignore them, reliving the rape again and again in my mind, remembering more vividly this time, the details of my disgrace, each wound I'd sustained the result of an individual, bestial act. Flinching and writhing with each remembered brutality, I began to see each wound as something filthy, as some stain not just upon my body but upon my soul. It gave no comfort to realize that most of the hurts would eventually heal because the one that was most important never would. I'd been irreparably damaged. I was no longer whole. And with that thought came a wave of self-loathing that filled my heart and never again entirely departed. I was contaminated. I was used. Like a garment, worn every day and never washed. Like a leftover crust of bread, gnawed, stale and discarded. And although I wanted nothing so much as for the angel to come and comfort me, I was too ashamed to call him. How could I ask an angel to have anything to do with a stained and filthy creature such as I? I wept, no longer worthy, in my mind, of the love I so desperately craved. But when at last I fell asleep, my angel was there waiting for me.

"Do you remember what I told you a long time ago, about what you should think when you were sad?"

I looked at him mutely.

"I said that it might comfort you to know that someone, somewhere would always be thinking fondly of you and wishing you only the best."

"But I'm *ruined*," I wailed in an ugly, distorted voice. "How could anyone think kind thoughts of a stained, filthy creature such as I?"

His laughter was that jarring bark that once, long ago, had frightened me. "What nonsense," he exclaimed. "Who *is* it exactly, that you think you're talking to? Who do you imagine me to be that I would quibble over 'stained' or 'filthy?'" He knelt down then in front of me, extending his hand as he often did when he was calling me to him.

"No," I said, resisting the call. "I see what you're trying to say but it's not the same. You were born the way you are. You never did anything to make yourself that way."

"And what did you do," he shot back, "to make yourself the stained and filthy creature you suddenly claim to be?"

"I didn't – "

"We're the same," he interrupted with uncustomary heat. "We are both victims of miserable humanity, blameless for our condition yet abhorrent to all."

"Abhorrent?" I was shocked despite myself at his wording.

"Not to me," he answered with feeling, gesturing again for me to approach. "Come here, Lotte. Let me show you that there is no difference between us. Perhaps we are abhorrent to the world but let us not be abhorrent to each other."

I hesitated.

And so he turned his right cheek toward me, revealing more skull than flesh, the small amount of remaining skin gangrenous and festering.

I gasped despite myself for I'd never seen his condition so deteriorated. "Or could it be," he asked, giving me a meaningful look, "that *I* am abhorrent to *you*?"

"Never," I cried, running to his kneeling figure and taking his wounded head in my arms. "You're my angel," I whispered. "You're my love. How could you think I could ever find you abhorrent?"

The shocking spread of disease in his body could have easily given the lie to those words had they been spoken by someone less needy or less stubborn than I. Even as things stood, his condition had so worsened that I didn't doubt he was testing me. But that was a test I could never fail, incapable as I was of denying him no matter how bad the physical became. So after a frantic interval during which I reaffirmed by means of desperate kisses and caresses, the truth of the words I'd spoken, he rose up of his own accord, gripped me by the shoulders and forced me to look into his eyes.

"All right then," he said. "If I am your *angel*, how can you expect any less of me than you do of yourself? If you can still love this," and he gestured toward his face, "how can you imagine that anything anyone did to you could somehow cause me to love you less? What sort of angel would that make me?"

I'd insulted him. It was the last thing I'd ever have done intentionally. I took a breath, determined to explain myself. But he placed his index finger against my lips. "I am a part of you, Lotte," he said. "I am no less and no more than you are yourself. As long as you want me, I will be with you. As long as you love me, I will love you. That was the nature of my gift to you. Nothing that you do and nothing that is done to you in the outside world can ever make a difference to us here. Do you understand?"

I was so close to tears that I dared not speak. Instead, I nodded.

He nodded too, apparently satisfied. "Then come," he said in a lighter tone, putting his arm with easy familiarity over my shoulder and leading me onto a lush spring meadow. "Wouldn't you like to sing with me a little?"

Chapter Nine

As a result of my dreams, I awoke the next morning to a feeling of provisional peace. It gave me strength to know that despite the level to which I'd sunk, my angel was still with me and apparently always would be. Even so, the reality upon rising was that I was so swollen it hurt to move and my bruises so purpled I couldn't bear to look in the mirror. Thus, I wasn't fooled into complacency by my angel's acceptance. I knew that to the rest of humanity I was now fatally flawed and that the consequences of my damage wouldn't always be easy to accept.

The first of many such consequences wasn't long delayed. Christine awoke, took a good look at me and recoiled with an expression of repugnance. After her first shock, she refused to come near me and Daaé, who'd originally thought to have her stay and assist me while he went in search of a doctor, was forced to abandon that plan when the neighbors on either side of us began banging on the walls as a result of her full-throated wailing. His altered decision to bring her along shut off the tears as effectively as if they'd never been. The two of them exited hand in hand, conversing amicably and looking as if they were going for a stroll.

As it turned out, they were gone for several hours and a ghost of the anger I'd known the previous night returned. Still, what I felt wasn't so much self-righteous indignation at being forgotten as it was annoyance at Daaé's inability to keep from being distracted. I reasoned that something must have caught their attention. A shop window, perhaps, or a fortuneteller. Eventually I grew disgusted enough with my inactivity to drag myself to my feet, make the bed, tidy the flat and start preparing the midday meal. When I'd done everything I could possibly do and they still hadn't returned, I began experimenting with the heavy stage makeup that I owned but seldom wore in an attempt to cover the most livid discolorations. The end result, though masking the bruises, did nothing for the puffiness and succeeded only in making me appear as though I'd been born with some facial deformity.

"We are the same," my angel had said. "We are both victims of miserable, humanity, blameless for our condition yet abhorrent to all."

He was more right than I cared to admit. Any illusions I may have had on the subject were destroyed when Christine, entering unannounced just ahead of her father, caught sight of me and started to scream. Mortified, I turned away, listening as Daaé comforted the hysterical child and using the time to remove the offending makeup. When at last he'd coaxed her onto the bed and her initial reaction had been reduced to a few intermittent sobs, I heard him approach me from behind.

"What were you trying to do?" He sounded almost angry.

"Just make myself presentable for work," I said.

"You're not thinking of going to work tonight, are you?"

"I had to try."

"Nonsense," he chided, though the sting was gone from his words. He took my hand and led me the few steps to the bed. "Come here and let me apply the poultices the apothecary gave me. He said they would help."

"Weren't you going to bring a doctor?" I asked, surprised that a mere trip to the apothecary would have taken so long.

"I intended to," he said, "but he was unwilling to make a house call to this part of town for the amount I was able to offer him."

With a squeak, Christine scrambled off the bed to cower resentfully in the corner. With her gone, I was able to lie down and abandon myself to his ministrations as I had the night before. Christine began whining from her corner as if she had some sort of pain until Daaé was obliged to go and kiss away the imagined hurt. He'd returned to me for less than a minute when her fussing became even more adamant so that when he went to her yet again, I decided it was time to sit up and take care of myself. When I'd finished, I went ahead and tried to serve them the soup I'd prepared but they'd already eaten at a nearby inn. In the end, all my activity must have convinced them I was out of any danger and they probably thought it prudent to go out and earn some money. They left the flat again, this time with the violin. Before closing the door behind him, Daaé promised to stop by the tavern and tell Monsieur Bernard I was ill.

It was several days before the bruising and swelling went down enough so it was possible to cover what was left with the makeup and go back to work. But with the semblance of normality restored, I found it impossible to make mention of my misfortune. Monsieur Bernard seemed concerned when he saw me. He took me aside and asked what had really happened. Perhaps if he'd come to me earlier, I'd have told him. Unfortunately, by the time I'd healed enough to return to the tavern I'd already come to the conclusion that my scars, unlike those of my angel, were internal, that the abhorrent part in me could remain forever hidden as long as I didn't reveal it myself. And so, despite having to deal with Lowell's new smugness, it became impossible for me to mention his crime. In time I couldn't even admit it to myself.

Eager for every aspect of my life to return to the way it had been, I resumed accompanying the Daaés to their place in the square every morning. Still, although Daaé seemed to look upon me with excessive compassion and treated me always with the utmost kindness, it wasn't long before I realized that things between us had not returned to normal. Of course I could never be entirely certain but I attributed the growing gulf between us to his knowledge of my disgrace. It was only years later that it occurred to me that my calling him by his first name that night had perhaps drawn his attention to the significance of taking me in his arms. Made aware at last of his feelings for me, maybe he'd felt it necessary for Christine's sake to put some distance between us. In any event, the intimacy of "Lotte" was never repeated. Nor did he ever call me just "Charlotte" alone, unaccompanied by the obligatory precursor "mademoiselle." And as the days continued to roll by at an alarming rate, I had to admit to myself that the two were going to leave me very soon. That even my pathetic need for them to be with me would have insufficient power to detain them once the time came. Determined not to become a spectacle when the moment was upon me, I forced myself to watch them at night, nestled together like resting spoons, cruelly asking myself what it was that had made me think I could ever play a part in their lives. The two of them were a unit unto themselves. Where was it, exactly, that I fancied myself fitting in?

Chapter Ten

As luck would have it, spring broke early that year. By the end of March, the trees were beginning to bud and only the smallest patches of dirty snow remained on the ground. The store windows too were already full of holiday displays, from baskets of assorted confections to lacy frocks and Easter bonnets. The three of us were looking at the windows on one of those pristine mornings when Christine took it into her head to run ahead of us and stop at a window farther down the street. Walking at a much more leisurely pace, we caught up with her at what turned out to be the cobbler's window. By then she was nearly bursting to show us what she'd found. On display was a pair of the prettiest little red shoes anyone could ever hope to see.

Of course she wanted them. What little girl wouldn't? Daaé began digging through his pockets but couldn't come up with anything even approaching the amount on the price tag. With a regretful shake of the head, he said something in his native tongue that could only have been an apology.

Without hesitation, she turned to me and in clearly understandable French asked, "Do *you* have enough?"

Thunderstruck, I could only stare. I'd not been completely certain she spoke French at all. Doubtless, I'd never expected her to speak it to me. But my shock lasted only an instant before I recalled myself, tearing my gaze from her impatient little face and starting to dig through my own purse. The fact remained, however, that I never carried more than just a few small coins and so, upset almost to the point of tears, I could only deny her request. At that moment I think I truly believed I might have secured her affection if only I'd been able to buy her those damned shoes.

That night, when the two of them were sleeping, I went to my hiding place and pulled out the tin in which I kept my savings. I felt a pang when I opened it, seeing how diminished it was. But I set aside my misgivings and I counted out the amount needed to purchase the Easter shoes. The following morning, I was glad I'd wasted no time. Daaé was up early, wandering ominously around the flat and gathering up his things in a way that worried me. I talked to him as he worked, telling him how good my work had been the night before, bragging about my numerous tips and mentioning that I'd received my weekly salary. I pulled the coins from my pocket and showed them to him proudly.

"Perhaps we could get her those shoes now," I whispered, "as long as it's all right with you."

He considered for a moment.

"When I was a little girl," I pressed, "I had a pair of red shoes. You have no idea how much I loved them and how carefully I cleaned and polished them. Every little girl needs a pair of pretty shoes. Please. Let me get them for her."

I could tell he was reluctant but since he could deny his darling nothing he finally relented.

"Come, Christine," I cried, perhaps a bit too joyful. "Let's go for a walk."

She eyed me dubiously.

"I have a surprise for you," I said, jingling my handful of coins.

Immediately her eyes brightened and her face broke into the sunny smile I'd often seen her bestow upon her father but never, until that moment, upon me. "My shoes?"

I nodded, speechless as she ran to me and took my hand as easily as if she'd done it a hundred times. In a state of awe over her simple willingness to accompany me, I still sensed the expression of disapproval focused upon my back as we went out. Once the door closed behind us, though, Christine and I walked to the cobbler's shop without disturbance. It was like we were mother and daughter. Considering my own looks at her age, my having a little daughter like her wasn't completely outside the realm of possibility. I wondered if the strangers passing us on the street were mistaking us for such. The idea pleased me more than I can say. So when the cobbler referred to her as "your little girl," I didn't correct him. As it turned out, the shoes fit perfectly and I paid out a good portion of my remaining life savings in a golden glow of happiness that should have served as a warning. Christine, too, seemed to be in higher spirits than I'd ever seen her, dancing along at my side as we headed home until we reached the bakery where she stopped. She pressed her nose against the window and viewed the pastries and petitfours on display.

"May I have one?" she asked sweetly and looked at me with those limpid blue eyes.

Who could deny such an angel? My heart already having melted the moment she took my hand, there was nothing for me to do but buy her a pastry and a cup of chocolate to go with it. Afraid she might spill on her new shoes, I suggested she sit down at one of the little tables inside the bakery. Readily agreeing with me, she took the seat I indicated and daintily tucked her feet up beneath her.

I sat down across from her and watched her eat. She did so as if she had all the time in the world and I imagined the joy of being able to watch her just so, every day for the rest of my life. But we didn't speak. And after a time I found the silence starting to weigh heavily. More in an attempt to make conversation than for any other reason I asked, "Do you like staying with me, Christine?"

She took a long moment to respond and I was almost afraid she'd remembered she didn't speak to me. But then she looked into my eyes, very matter-of-factly, and stated, "I wish I had my own bed."

I nodded, having wished the same thing on more than one occasion. "Would you like me to get you one?" I asked, my mind casting about for inspiration regarding the financing.

"Could you get it today?" she asked, looking hopeful.

"Not today," I answered. "But soon. Very soon. I promise."

Casually, she dropped a piece of pastry into her mouth from above. "Papa says we'll be leaving tomorrow."

Stunned, I couldn't respond. I sat there in shocked muteness as the bottom dropped out of my stomach and tears began forming in my eyes. I knew that if I did nothing to halt this course of events, I was going to start crying and that if I did, all would be lost. So with a strength and willpower born of fear, I swallowed the lump in my throat and forced the tears back. "Wouldn't you like to stay?" I asked once I was certain I'd mastered myself. "You wouldn't have to worry about being caught outside in the cold anymore. You'd always have a nice warm room to sleep in. And your own bed too, as soon as I can manage it. I'm sure your papa wouldn't mind staying longer if he knew how much you liked it here."

She shrugged.

"I would be very sad if you had to go away."

This elicited no response at all but she began to fidget. The last vestige of rational thought told me to let it be. But desperation screamed that Daaé was already decided. Christine was my last and only chance. If I couldn't somehow convince her to stay, the two of them would walk out of my life the following morning and leave in their wake an emptiness I didn't think I could bear.

"Christine," I pleaded, throwing away any dignity I might have had, "Tell your papa you want to stay. Please. In these months that you've been here, I've come to love you just as if you were my very own daughter."

The look she turned upon me could have brought back winter. "I'm not your daughter."

"No," I said, in growing despair. "But I love you just as much as if you were. I want to take care of you, Christine, and watch you grow up. I want to be like a mother to you."

"No," she shouted, loud enough to attract the attention of people around us. "You are not my maman."

With a look of distress on that little face, she leaped off the chair and ran out of the bakery. I ran after her, calling to her. But she never even slowed. I pushed myself, surprised that I had to when running after such a small child. And of course I caught her. There'd never been a question of my catching her.

"Let me go," she screamed, shocking me with a kick to the shin.

"Christine, please," I cried, hugging her struggling form.

"Let me go."

"I will," I promised, holding her even tighter. "But only if I can be sure you won't run away."

Instead of responding, she bit me.

The surprise of the attack caused me to loosen my hold and in that split second of confusion, she got away from me. My flat was so close I was unable to catch her a second time. She was there already, pounding on the door and screaming for her papa in a wild, hysterical voice. Almost immediately, the door was flung wide and in another instant her father had caught her up in his arms, sparing me only one sharp look of resentment before turning away and carrying her inside.

Unable to face him, I stayed outside, leaning my forehead against the wall. My body spasmed with sobs and hot tears gushed forth. How had I managed to make such a mess of things? I'd never meant any harm. I'd felt sorry for them, two lost souls, forsaken by humanity. Had pitied them as I pitied myself. Had cared for them the way I'd always secretly wished that someone would care for me. I had loved them . . .

Only slowly did realization dawn. They'd been helpless. They'd been at my mercy. And I'd taken advantage of their situation to foist my own contemptible needs upon them. They never asked for my love. They never wanted it. But until the weather improved to such a degree that they could survive in the open, they'd had no choice but to grit their teeth and endure my pathetic, fawning advances.

Inside my flat, I could hear Christine speaking through sobs nearly as powerful as my own. I even heard Daaé's voice in soothing response, speaking to her, as always, in a language that had excluded me from the very first. Ironically, the months of repeated exclusion had rendered those foreign words more intelligible than I'd realized. I understood when she said, "She is not my maman." I understood when he replied, "No my treasure, she is not your maman." And this cursed understanding served only to make my isolation complete.

After a long time, he came out alone and closed the door without locking it. "What happened?" he asked. His voice, though calm, held no warmth.

It took me some time to get myself under control and even then, I was unable to look at him. "I didn't mean to upset her," I said at last.

"I'm sure you didn't," he responded, "but that doesn't change anything. What, exactly, did you say to her?"

Looking down at my hands I noted that the bite mark was very obvious and realized a moment later that he'd seen it too.

"I told her that I loved her," I said miserably, hesitating for a long time before finding the courage to add, "and I said I wanted to be like a mother to her."

"Don't you think that's something you should have discussed with me?" he asked, suddenly so distant and aloof that it seemed impossible the same man could have held me once so tenderly in his arms.

"I didn't mean to say it." My voice was full of pleading. "Christine told me that you were leaving tomorrow and it came out without my meaning it to. I'd had no idea you were planning to go away so soon. Oh please, Monsieur Daaé."

He didn't respond and I knew I'd said too much. The only thing left for me to do then was cry. He stood there for quite a long time, observing my grief with a coldness I couldn't quite bring myself to believe. He couldn't *really* hate me after all we'd been through together. He couldn't possibly be as unmoved as he seemed by the affliction of one who'd never shown him anything but kindness. I longed for him to take me in his arms, to bestow upon me a forgiving embrace. Even a touch would have sufficed, a warm hand grasping my shoulder in commiseration. But at last he turned and went inside, no olive branch forthcoming, to emerge a few minutes later with his violin and Christine. He didn't spare me another glance though she turned around to look at me with her big, solemn eyes. Realizing that she was watching, I wiped at my face and tried to muster a smile.

In response, she stuck out her tongue.

Once they had turned the corner, I went back inside, laying down on the bed and crying myself to sleep. I awoke again in a groggy haze that afternoon noting, though not really caring, that I was late for work. Surrendering to the torpor that made my body feel so uncharacteristically heavy, it was far easier to continue lying there than to consider any other option. Still, time passed and despite any reluctance

I may have had, my mind began to take in its surroundings. Suddenly I realized that I was alone at a time of day when I should not have been. The Daaés hadn't returned. A surge of panic brought me up and out of bed in the time it would have normally taken me to open and close my eyes. But in the next moment I noted that all their things were still littered about, just as they'd been in the morning. Once up, I shuffled to the basin and splashed some water on my face, ran a comb through my hair and found myself going through the motions of preparing for work.

In fact, work turned out to be just what I needed to bring me back to the land of the living, the immediacy and the petty problems of dealing with the clientele and fighting off Lowell forced my mind away from the desolation that had nearly consumed me. Still, the yawning chasm awaited, and when, all too soon, my shift ended, I found I didn't want to go home. Deep down, I suppose, I knew what awaited me there: a cold, dark room, empty except for my own belongings. The reality, when the moment of truth could no longer be delayed, proved almost an anticlimax. The vacancy that greeted me was so exact in every detail to what I'd imagined that I felt almost as if I were looking upon the scene for a second time. I can admit to a measure of astonishment only with regard to one, unanticipated detail. A thorough search produced no letter or note of any kind. I teetered then between possible reactions during a period of numbness that couldn't last. I might have chosen self-pity, moping about and fading away, allowing the colossal demonstration of uncaring to ruin my life. But then my attention was caught by the talentless repetition of what was meant to be orange and black butterflies still adorning my walls. And I chose instead, rage.

It descended upon me like a poisonous red cloud, burning my face and causing my hands to tremble. Running to my secret hiding place, I pulled out the tin with my life savings and opened it to reveal the few centimes that remained, warm coats, extra coal, food for three over a span of four months, chocolates, paints and a certain pair of red shoes had decimated the nest egg it took me seven years to stash. Suddenly blinded, I flung the tin against the wall, my mouth erupting in curses that had never before been a part of my vocabulary. The pennies fell jingling around me. The next thing to hit the wall was the poker, then the pot and soon I couldn't even identify the things that I hurled, screaming obscenities in a voice I wouldn't have recognized as my own. Soon the neighbors, awakened from their precious dreams, added their protests to the din, shouting and banging against the walls. My flat was suddenly too small to contain the magnitude of my fury and I burst out into the night.

I didn't stop running until dawn, though by then I was halfway to Paris. Far from exhausted, I felt more alive than I had in years. My heart beat fiercely with a power I'd never known. All the detritus of my guilt and moral upbringing burned away in the flames of my passion. Like the monarch, reborn from the ashes of its own cremation, I was better, stronger and above all, free.

And I vowed then and there, on that desolate road, that no one would ever hurt me again.

Chapter Eleven

I arrived in Paris with the fury of a natural disaster. Homeless, penniless and unemployed, I sang with all my might, danced with abandon and warmed the bed of anyone who would pay me. I no longer cared what sins I committed. Already abhorrent, I couldn't imagine what difference it would make. As a result, I never once spent a night on the street, never went without a meal and within two weeks, had found permanent employment as a singer, dancer and serving girl at a bar called Le Chien Blanc. It was there that the illustrious Maestro Pedicini, professor of music at the Conservatoire Nationale, asked for a private introduction. The introduction was ostensibly to complement me on my "truly magnificent instrument." He took the opportunity while he was at it, though, to insinuate his hand beneath my bodice. Still, the world doesn't judge a man by his behavior in private but by his accomplishments in life coupled as always, with his ability to serve one's own interests.

Taking the world view, myself, I allowed him a tantalizing sample with the understanding that he would have full right of access only after giving me a *real* singing lesson, to take place in an actual rehearsal room at the conservatory, just as if I were a regular tuition-paying student of music. It wasn't long before this became a permanent arrangement. Plump, sweaty and prone to gout, my maestro became so worried about my eventually finding a better situation elsewhere that I'm pretty sure I received more than my fair share of professional help and attention. Eventually, I even became the recipient of a full scholarship, contingent of course on the continued good reviews of my maestro. Said funding made it possible for me to study not only vocal technique and repertoire but also music theory, music history, piano, Italian and German.

When, after four years, I received my certificate of completion, Maestro Pedicini suggested we celebrate by spending the summer in his native Milan. I wasn't particularly interested in spending the next three months in his flabby embrace but that was before he informed me that he'd arranged for my audition with the company of the Teatro alla Scala.

The next thing I knew, I was drinking *caffè espresso,* eating *pollo alla cacciatora* and practicing my Verdi.

The audition turned out to be very similar to the competitions in which I'd sung at the conservatory, the exception being that there were far fewer people scrutinizing my performance. My slight nervousness at the beginning evaporated the moment I heard my own voice issuing forth with its usual power and effortlessness. I wasn't shy in demonstrating my extensive range, in excess of two octaves, nor my precise control in coming out of a perfect tremolo. I allowed my voice first to reverberate throughout the house and then to fade to that exquisite, high pianissimo that I knew to be the envy of every soprano at school. When I'd finished, I was almost sorry to be concluding the audition but remembered to sink into the deep, stylized curtsy I'd practiced before a mirror.

Ignorant of the odds against my being selected to join a major company straight out of conservatory, I was annoyed beyond measure that as the result of said audition, I was admitted only as a member of the chorus. I demanded immediately that my maestro take me back to our cottage and teach me whatever it was I'd failed to learn, forcing him to continue working me until he surely must have regretted bringing me to Milan. With fierce determination, I worked for the rest of the summer, heedless of the torturous transformation my once delightful rehearsals had undergone. My teacher too, made miserable by the demands I imposed not only on myself but on him, begged me to ease up. But his feeble protests only goaded me to stricter measures. I fully expected him to be relieved when August came and he had to return to Paris, so I must say I was more than a little surprised when he came to me, bags packed, and asked me to return with him.

"Why?" I asked. "Wasn't the plan for me to get a few years experience here?"

"You don't need experience," he said with an odd desperation in his voice. "You're ready now. There is no one, anywhere, who can sing as you can."

His expression was that of the hopeful spaniel. It was this, I think, that put me off. If his face were any indication, I was pretty sure he'd have stooped even to calling me beautiful or professing undying love if he thought it would get me to return with him. The question of his actually loving me didn't once cross my mind – though I've wondered about it since. At the time, I still saw myself only in terms of my disgrace. No man could ever love a creature as abhorrent as I – not even one as greasy and sour-smelling as my maestro. What did occur to me was that he might want me because none of the other whores he'd approached could be coerced into servicing him as thoroughly or with as relative good will as I did. This vision of myself – that I imagined to be his – sickened me. And so my response to him was, "If my singing were really so all-bloody wonderful, why are you just telling me now? Why not before, when it might have meant something?"

"Your progress," he stammered. "You're twice the artist you were in June. I'm certain you'll be able to get a leading role in Paris now. As a member of the chorus, your talents here would be wasted."

His words were sorely tempting but that desperation in his eyes made me doubtful. When I tried to look into his face, he shifted nervously away.

"Experience is never wasted," I said. "My position here at La Scala is assured. I'd be foolish to give it up in favor of some pipe dream. I choose to stay, Maestro."

His expression was comically tragic. His mouth turned down into his sagging jowls in an exaggerated parody of grief. I halfway expected tears. As it was, I came close to laughing out loud at the maudlin extent of what I perceived to be his phoniness. He did catch me off guard, though, when he reached toward me with his hand and instead of grabbing and twisting, only cupped my face very gently in his palm. "Good-bye then, my little Charlotte," he whispered. "I wish you nothing but the best."

My arms had risen in a protective gesture across my chest the moment I saw him coming at me. But it seemed he really was just trying to say farewell. I lowered my arms and gave his cheek a reciprocal pat. "I wish you all the best, too," I said.

Within a week, I'd found a new teacher. Within six months, our resident diva's pregnancy became visible and within eight, I'd taken her place. "Charlotte," so difficult for the Italian mouth to get its tongue around, became officially "Carlotta," and by the following summer, Maestro Pedicini found, with his return to Milan, that his little Charlotte was no more, that in her place stood a proud and pitiless creature, the culminating result of years of determination and training, of repeated exposure to indifference and degradation, of habituation to the use of sexual favors as currency: the new reigning diva of La Scala: La Carlotta.

Chapter Twelve

My instincts couldn't have served me better. They kept me out of France at the commencement of the Franco-Prussian war and out of Paris throughout the Commune. In addition, I discovered that La Scala was considered by many to be the foremost opera house in all Europe. What better experience could one have? During my first few years there, I wouldn't have so much as considered signing a contract elsewhere. Even the renowned Academie Nationale de Paris would have seemed like a step down. This, as I have said, was my initial opinion.

But by the time I completed my fourth season, I began to feel the itch to move on. Much as I loved Italian opera, I found myself wanting to tackle the works of some of the German composers with a greater frequency than that afforded any diva at the very Italian Teatro alla Scala. Therefore, my fifth season was characterized by numerous absences during which I sang at opera houses all over Europe. Signor Bonifacio, La Scala's manager at that time encouraged these forays as long as they remained within specific parameters. He even told me once that my becoming an international celebrity would be that much more of a draw when I went "home" to La Scala. I vividly remember the night he invited me to a private dinner, the last course of which I felt certain would take place in bed rather than at table. I couldn't have been more wrong. Bonifacio was all business, making use of paper and pen to map out what he called my "public persona." As my name was Italian, he wanted me to pretend that *I* was Italian for as long as I was abroad.

"And what's wrong with being myself?" I asked.

"You belong to us, to La Scala, to Italy," he said. "Think of how the Italian people love you. Think of all that Italy has done for you. When did the French ever care what happened to their little Carlotta, all alone in the world? Why should they have the glory of claiming you now?"

"What nonsense," I said. "It's bad enough you uneducated Italians can't correctly pronounce my name without attempting to deny me my nationality as well. I would have thought better of you, Signor, than to come up with such an ill-conceived notion. Imagine *me,* with my French accent and tripping over your damnable grammar, claiming to be Italian. You know as well as I do that I'd be revealed as a fraud within minutes of meeting a real Italian. Then where would we be?" Piqued and choosing not to hide it, I purposefully used the strongest language that came to mind. It was disconcerting when his reaction was nothing more than a slow, reluctant nodding.

"You're right," he said after a pause. "I fear we'll have to make you Spanish."

"I beg your pardon."

"Yes," he continued, "Spanish would most definitely do. We could say you were born in Barcelona but came to Milan at an early age to study music. *That* would explain your deplorable command of the language. All you'll need is to dye your hair black, learn a few Spanish *maledizioni* and roll your R's."

"I haven't agreed to any of this," I said.

"You want to tour Europe, don't you?" He looked into my eyes like a predator sizing up prey.

"But – " I looked ceilingward for divine intervention. There was none. "If I say I'm Spanish, then Spain will try to claim me."

"Bah." He waved a dismissive hand. "There is no opera in Spain."

"But I speak no Spanish at all. All I'd need would be to run into one Spaniard abroad . . ."

"There have been no Spaniards abroad since the defeat of the Spanish Armada."

Although el Moco and el Piojo had both been from Spain, I doubted his narrow-mindedness would count Gypsies as Spaniards.

"Your choice is simple," he continued. "You're either a Frenchwoman in Italy or a Spaniard abroad. But I'll be damned if I'll let the French claim you when it was we, here at Il Teatro alla Scala, who took in this little frog and turned her into the queen of our national opera."

I slapped him and walked out but he had me and both of us knew it. It was therefore without surprise that I received a package from him on the morrow containing a bottle of black hair dye, several books about Barcelona and a long list of Spanish words and phrases accompanied by a curt note that they be memorized at once. The whole thing proved a shameful farce but if the subsuming of my *self* were the price I had to pay in exchange for the opportunity to play the great houses of Europe, then I found myself, if not willing, at least resigned.

It wasn't long before I learned to roll all my French and German R's to say *Dios mío*, instead of "my God," *gracias*, instead of thank you, and plenty of other nonsense that no Spaniard with even the most rudimentary grasp of German or French would feel the need to say in his native tongue. Still, I must admit that my new dark hair – brown, not black – pleased me greatly. It was so striking when contrasted with the dishwater hue of my natural color that it almost made up for the fact that when I looked in the mirror I could no longer find even the slightest remaining trace of the little Lotte whom Erik had loved.

I couldn't, however, admit to regret. Or not much regret, in any case. My angel, albeit slightly transparent, still came to me. Sometimes. When I dreamed of taking a bow on some foreign stage, he would be there in the shadows where I could feel his presence. When I dreamed of sitting on a marble bench in a midnight garden, he'd be standing just behind me. But when I truly felt alone I would call to him and call to him as I walked the twilit alleys of some abandoned dream city. And if I screamed loud enough and long enough and if I wept while I did it and if my heart felt like it was tearing open inside of me, he would step out from some nearby shadow and take my hand. Then we could talk as we had always talked. Like mentor and student. Like adult and child. Always I awoke before having the chance to say all that I needed to and

I think he may have had something to do with that. Please stay with me, I would think. Or, why can't I live here with you forever? Or I'd look into his eyes and *see* how much he loved me and reach up to kiss or caress him. And awaken.

One thing, though, above all else I knew: in time of direst need he'd be there for me. And whenever I missed him enough to put myself through the soul-wrenching agony of his summoning, he would come to me. And comfort me. And be with me.

In my dreams I was forever Lotte. And Erik was forever my angel.

So what difference if my outer, waking shell had changed? Carlotta was, after all, a very handsome shell. Men all over Europe said so, sending expensive gifts with letters so sugary sweet that reading them set my teeth to aching as much as any chocolate.

The next two years saw me all over Europe, from the Prinzregententheater in Munich to the Royal Italian Opera House in Covent Garden. At the Vienna Opera, I had the opportunity to work under the direction of the great Hans Richter, discovering that my voice not only had the power and endurance to shine in Wagner but also the flexibility and range to sparkle in Mozart. At one point my journeys took me as far north as The Royal Opera in Stockholm where I found I understood a great deal more Swedish than I would ever have expected. I managed a little side trip to Uppsala, only forty-five miles to the north and to Skoteloff, which turned out to be nothing but a little hamlet next door. I walked through the cultivated fields, wondering which had once belonged to Samuel Daaé.

L'Opéra Monte Carlo precipitated a bout of homesickness with its opulent decor, caryatids and masks, so reminiscent of the new Paris Opera House – still under construction when last I'd seen it – that I wasn't surprised when I learned that the architect for both had been one and the same: the famous, or perhaps infamous, Charles Garnier. It was also the first place I sang Gounod's *Roméo and Juliette* in my own language. It was probably no coincidence that just three weeks later I received an invitation to sing *Faust*, another great work by Gounod, very near that other great palace of Garnier.

To my supreme disappointment, the grand new opera house was yet unfinished and the official Théâtre National de l'Opéra de Paris was still on the Rue le Peletier. Be that as it may, my reception there was so warm, I almost imagined it a joyous homecoming. Such a privilege it was to be able to sing in French again, such a relief to purchase a pastry without having to struggle for the words, such a novelty to be treated with obsequious respect by the same people who'd once turned up their noses, that when my contract with La Scala came up for renewal, I chose instead to accept the offer of employment extended to me by the management of the new Paris Opera, officially opening on January 5th, 1875, to sing at the inaugural performance and to remain henceforth as the company's resident diva.

When I moved back to Paris – a much more complicated procedure than leaving it had been – I was able to immediately purchase a small house on the Rue du Faubourg-Saint-Honoré, thanks to the tidy savings I'd amassed during my six year sojourn abroad. Back in my native element, my status as international celebrity, combined with my willingness to perform at various grand *fêtes* and intimate *soirées* around town, helped me start a little auxiliary account in addition to my regular savings. It was by virtue of this fund that I began to earn special favors by quietly bailing out anonymous members of the titled nobility. I would take care of certain debts in exchange for the deed to some rental property in the city or a parcel of cultivated farmland.

Gentlemen, too, helped advance my situation. Philippe, the Count de Chagny, actually gave me a carriage. He was a good man, if a little cold, introducing me within the proper social circles and sometimes, when the wine had been flowing, inviting me to demonstrate my uncanny ability to shatter glass. Discovering my penchant for chocolates, he was forever giving me boxes of them so that over the next six-year period, I gained enough weight to require several new wardrobes and ended having four of my back molars pulled. By then, of course, Philippe had discovered the slender young dancer, La Sorelli. Regardless, the chocolates still arrived every once in a while, as did he himself when La Sorelli was in a snit. In daylight the count and I always greeted each other most cordially and the carriage he'd allowed me to keep – in all good will – remained as useful as ever.

One might expect that after a lifetime of poverty and near-starvation, this arrival of financial security would bring with it a measure of happiness. Indeed, during the greater part of my six years at the Paris Opera, I experienced a contentment I hadn't known at any other time. Still, I can only believe that "happiness" as such, is rarely the lot of any diva. There are just too many practical jokes and cruel pranks at her expense, too many catty remarks and whispered secrets followed by loud cackles of merriment and surreptitious glances in her direction, too many wolves disguised as understudies, chorus members and swings, watching her with narrowed eyes and bated breath, waiting, hoping, praying for her to falter.

Even so, I wasn't without my own defenses. I was, after all, "La Carlotta," a phenomenon of versatility and range known throughout Europe. I had, over the years, developed a merciless sense of humor and a sharp tongue, neither of which I was afraid to use. I did, at that stage in my life, sing with laughable ease, the most difficult roles ever written for the soprano voice, a feat none of my younger and hungrier rivals had yet been able to match. Despite all that, or perhaps because of it, the animosity against me during my time at the Paris Opera grew decidedly more acute than it had been anywhere else I'd performed. I sometimes imagined that the very walls and the air I breathed held some sort of grudge against me.

And then of course, there was the ghost. I'd actually heard of several ghosts throughout my travels, the one at La Scala supposedly appearing in the form of a beautiful lady with dark hair and a white gown, haunting the corridors in the darkness before dawn. The Royal Opera House in Stockholm, too, had its resident spirit: a stagehand who'd plummeted to his death from a catwalk nearly a century before, who would offer a sip of grog to an unwary newcomer only to disappear with a malicious chuckle when the victim brought the cup to his lips, swallowing air. Despite being more than a little superstitious myself, I never saw so much as a trace of these aforementioned apparitions and eventually came to the conclusion that the story-tellers, like my old friend el Moco, had invented such tales to frighten children.

The uncustomary boldness of the Paris Opera ghost, dubbed by the employees as "the Phantom of the Opera," made skepticism more difficult. From the beginning, there were times when the temperature in the room would suddenly drop and the hairs on the backs of my arms would rise. Whenever that happened, tacks would mysteriously appear on my chair. Buttons, buckles and belts from my costumes would disappear at the very moment when they were most needed. At first I chalked it up to the more virulent spite of my Parisian competition. But even when I was most definitely alone, whenever the air in the room became fetid and clammy, items I'd placed on my vanity only moments before would vanish the instant I looked away, to be found only after much searching wrapped in a kerchief at the bottom of a drawer. I remember once, things in my dressing room started moving around so quickly that I practically saw them changing positions on their own at the edge of my vision. Seriously unnerved, I refused to finish putting on my makeup until the management changed my room, right then and there, causing the performance to be delayed by forty-five minutes.

All of this aside, though, I strongly believe that I didn't start out as the ghost's primary target. The pranks he played on me were more nuisance than threat. Such however, wasn't always the case. A good example to the contrary was the incident in which, according to Jammes, one of the many *petit rats* whose noses were into everything, the ghost took over the body of Gabriel, the Chorus Master who, in front of several witnesses appeared to bounce himself off the walls of the stage manager's office, crush his own fingers under the lid of the piano and then throw himself down a flight of stairs. Later still, Joseph Buquet, a stagehand, was found strangled. The powers that be, in all their stupid arrogance, pronounced his death a "natural suicide," despite the fact that those of us more familiar with the strange happenings around the Palais Garnier, knew it to be no such thing. Previously, La Sorelli had placed a lucky horseshoe on the table in the doorkeeper's vestibule, letting it be known that all company employees should put their hand on it for protection before entering the house. Said horseshoe was the cause of more than a few jokes at La Sorelli's expense. Everyone laughed. No one entered without touching it.

Chapter Thirteen

One day, perhaps six months before my retirement, my own turn came to see a ghost. Despite the fact that it was as visible to the others as it was to me, I'm certain I was the only one to recognize it as the creature of chaos and destruction that it was. Standing in the wings during rehearsal, nineteen or twenty years old at most and with the flaxen hair of a towheaded child, this was the ghost from my past, now in the full flower of womanhood. My stomach gave an ugly lurch in recognition. But as drawn to destruction as I've been throughout my life, I was helpless to do anything except introduce myself in as polite and aristocratic a manner as my pounding heart would allow. Blushing furiously and behaving for all the world like any one of my numerous, tongue-tied admirers, she was incapable of response.

"What's your name, *mi hija*?" I prompted with honeyed condescension.

"Christine," she finally managed. And then in a rush, "Oh señora, it is such an honor to finally meet you in person."

"Not at all. Not at all," I clucked with exaggerated munificence. "The honor is mine. After all, you are the legendary Christine Daaé, are you not? The child destined to become the greatest soprano the world has ever known?"

"I am Christine Daaé," she responded, the sudden suspicious narrowing of her eyes so odiously familiar that I couldn't quite believe the last time I'd seen it had been – *¡Dios mío!* – almost 16 years before.

"I knew it had to be you," I continued with outward amiability. "Carlotta never forgets a face. Or a slight. So tell me, *cariño*, how is your *papá*?"

A look of pain crossed her face. "You knew him?"

"Knew him?" I began slowly, as if considering my answer. "Perhaps not. Let us just say that there was a time when I was his friend. And believed him to be mine."

The suspicious look was back. "Well, he's dead now."

An invisible sledgehammer struck my gut though I cannot say whether it was due to grief or gladness. Still, I retained enough presence of mind to spot the look of vulnerability in her eyes. "Such a pity," I retorted, aiming at that vulnerability with a tone of lofty indifference and gratified beyond measure when she turned away too late to hide the tears.

I doubt most people would feel I was justified in holding against the young woman a crime she'd committed at the age of three, but that, *que Dios me perdone*, is just what I did. I hated the girl with an intensity that was almost incapacitating, she who'd taken everything I had and then thrown me away like a piece of stinking garbage. Afraid I might do something I would later regret, I left her and returned to rehearsal, vowing in my black witch's heart, to make her life miserable for as long as she chose to stay within my domain.

In the following weeks, I was often privileged to hear, in the most minor of roles, the superbly unexceptional singing that was Mademoiselle Daaé's. It pleased me beyond measure that all her father's dedication, hard work and shameless boasting had borne such mediocre fruit. Her thin voice and excessive vibrato resembled nothing so much as the bleating of a nanny goat and I wasn't the only one who thought so. It did my heart good to overhear one afternoon Meg Giry – another of the *petit rats* – comparing the voice of my pretty angel to a rusty hinge. No one could understand how such singing had won her a place in our company in the first place, let alone anything higher than a position in the chorus. It made no sense and there was endless conjecture and whispering on the subject. At last it came to light that one of the Opera's most powerful patrons, the Count de Chagny no less, had used his influence to help her along. So there was a touch of scarlet in our little princess after all. Oh how I hoped the spirit of Samuel Daaé was seeing this.

What surprised me, though, was that I never once saw Mademoiselle Daaé in the company of the count. Outwardly, at least, he was still fetching and carrying for La Sorelli – not that any such thing would preclude a secret liaison. But as was my wont, I left the logistics of this unusual *ménage* to the imaginations of those who specialized in such matters. My concern, as always, was for my own reputation and career. My old nemesis cozying up to my old patron was a little too much like handing them both the book of my life along with a pair of shears.

Always one to pay well for information, I learned one day, even before it was announced, that Mademoiselle Daaé was being slated to play the part of Siebel – to *my* Marguerite – in the company's next production of *Faust.* Incensed, I went to the managers.

The two of them began their act of bowing and scraping the moment I entered the office, taking my wrap, holding my chair and offering me a cup of tea. Their behavior reminded me of two naughty schoolboys trying to weasel out of a punishment.

"What is this I hear about Christine Daaé being given the part of Siebel?" I demanded.

They glanced at each other before responding.

"The cast for *Faust* hasn't yet been announced," Monsieur Poligny replied. "What makes you think that Mademoiselle Daaé has any particular role?"

"Can you deny it, monsieur?" I asked.

He sputtered something. Heaven knows what. But I continued as if he'd remained silent.

"You know as well as I do that the girl doesn't have the voice for such a role. *Por Dios,* her lower register is completely undeveloped, her upper register is harsh and her middle register lacks clarity. What on Earth can be accomplished by casting her opposite *me*?"

"We believe she has great promise," ventured Monsieur Debienne, an old fool who wouldn't have known an aria from a recitative.

Poligny silenced him with a gesture. "One must look at the big picture señora, not just the merits, or lack thereof, of any single performer. Much as I myself would prefer pure art at its highest, this company is a business and the interests of the patrons who, incidentally, pay *your* salary must be taken into account if we are to continue in our necessary service of providing quality music to the people of Paris."

"Quality, pshaw!" I returned. "Let's see how the big picture looks if your prima donna takes her voice back to Italy."

"You can't do that," Debienne cried, leaping out of his chair. "You have a contract."

"And what can my contract do, Monsieur, if I develop laryngitis or bronchitis or some other condition that makes it impossible for me to sing?"

Debienne had turned pale. "You wouldn't . . ."

"Monsieur, it's not a question of what I would or wouldn't do. I'm simply reminding you that these things can happen all at once and without forewarning to any member of your company, even its star. And as you surely know, there's nothing to do for such debilitating ailments except to take oneself off to warmer climes."

"I'm sure that will not be necessary," said Poligny.

"That's music to my ears, monsieur," I responded.

It came, therefore, as a most unpleasant surprise when the postings a few days later still showed Mademoiselle Daaé in the role of Siebel. I tried to speak to the managers again but they were unable to see me and my letters to them went unanswered. For a time, I strangled on my rage as rehearsal after rehearsal, Christine's Siebel bleated words of love to my Marguerite. But I held my bile, waiting until opening night to play my ace. It was then I sent a message to the management, barely an hour before curtain, to the effect that I was suffering from a bout of bronchitis and would be unable to perform. I heard later that my sudden absence provoked quite a scramble and that the box office was forced to give numerous refunds.

Unbelievable as it may seem, Christine remained in the role.

Time to tighten the screws. I sent a message once again on the night of a very important gala performance in which I was to sing the prison scene and trio from *Faust.*

My absence that night proved to be the biggest mistake of my career.

Not content to sit at home and soak my feet, I dressed as a Parisian lady, no Spanish veil or tiara that night, and managed to enter the Opera anonymously, as a regular ticket-holding patron. The show itself, viewed from a seat directly beneath the spectacular chandelier, seemed bigger than life with its impressive lineup of celebrities. Gounod, Reyer, Saint-Saëns, Massenet, and Delibes were all there, each conducting his own work. Marie Gabriele Krauss and Denise Bloch also had been invited, the former winning a standing ovation with her rendition of the bolero from *Sicilian Vespers,* the latter doing no less with the brindisi from *Lucrezia Borgia.* The next name in the program was mine and I watched with some interest as the master of ceremonies reappeared upon the stage. I was prepared for some apology and explanation with regard to my indisposition. Instead, he announced that the part of Marguerite in *Faust,* scheduled to be sung by me, would be performed instead by a promising new soprano: Mademoiselle Christine Daaé. My groan was echoed throughout the auditorium and the poor man was nearly booed off the stage.

But the opening of the curtain effectively silenced the crowd, revealing as it did the celestial image of Mademoiselle Daaé herself, reclining in all her languorous, bare-armed splendor, upon a bale of hay that was the only prop. Faust and Mephisto entered singing though I doubt anyone was paying them the slightest attention.

"Marguerite," Faust sang, *"Marguerite."*

And then she began.

The first note out of her mouth as she slowly rose up was all I needed to realize that I was in very serious trouble. Gone was the bleating vibrato and nasal tone. Gone was the mealy-mouthed pronunciation and sullen stage presence. Radiant, as if she could already see the gates of Heaven, she allowed the music to use her as its joyful instrument, vibrating with intensity as it channeled through her, bursting forth the way light bursts forth from the sun. Love was there too, and longing and pain and hope, like a promise of redemption. With a simple sincerity that couldn't have been feigned, she gifted us all with the miracle of sublime sweetness, blessed us, each in our own imperfection, with one perfect memory of absolute beauty, ennobling us through glory that should have belonged solely to the angels and to God. Only once before had I known such music. Erik's music. And the remembrance nearly brought me to my knees. But instead I was required to surge to my feet with the rest of the crowd, paying her enthusiastic homage as the music came to its triumphant conclusion.

It was in the absence of her bewitching siren's voice that I was finally able to regain enough independent thought to begin wondering how such a transformation could have occurred. Still mindlessly applauding, I realized that she must have deceived me right from the beginning. Artistry such as hers didn't become what it was in a day. I deemed it more likely that she'd used her own stupefying technique to *imitate* mediocrity, laughing up her sleeve and biding her time. In the end, it had been child's play to lull me into unsuspecting complacency, affording her just the opportunity she needed to both save the day and burst forth in all her revealed splendor like a monarch from the flames. All around me, ladies and gentlemen alike were dabbing at their eyes with scented handkerchiefs. The very sight caused my blood to boil. I knew very well the girl had no heart. How could she possibly be singing as if her very soul were lousy with love? She was an impostor, a phony, a superb actress. This I knew. But with that single performance she had the entire public besotted with her. And then, at that moment she managed to upstage even *my* poison thoughts when, in a brilliant touch of theatricality, she did a dying swan, banging her head convincingly against the hard wood of the stage. Much as I often pretended otherwise, I doubted not, in my mean, shriveled heart, that the faint was real. *No one* could do what she'd just done without its taking a tremendous, physical toll.

"Poor child," the lady on my right said. "She really gave us everything she had."

Other snippets of conversation proved that the rest of the audience was equally solicitous.

"She's exhausted, the dear. Anyone would be after such a performance . . ."

"I hope she's going to be all right . . ."

"I wonder why we've never heard of her before. She's quite extraordinary . . ."

"How fortunate that Carlotta was ill tonight . . ."

I was so sickened that I feared I might vomit. And in the morning, when I learned that she'd been made my understudy, I knew it was the beginning of the end. All she would need now would be another one of those fortuitous "accidents" attributed to the opera ghost, whereby Carlotta fell through a trap door, or was hit on the head by a piece of falling scenery, or was set fire to, or mysteriously hanged, or drawn and quartered, or chopped into a hundred tiny pieces, and the way would be free and clear for the new diva, Mademoiselle Christine Daaé. She herself treated me thereafter with such exaggerated courtesy that it was obvious she knew exactly where she stood. No longer content to merely pass me in the halls as if I were invisible, she sought me out, wishing me a cheery good afternoon, or complementing me most kindly on my dress, my hair or my performance. The increasing magnitude of my impotent rages were in strict contrast to this new, self-assured demeanor of hers and made my subsequent attacks upon her seem even more excessive and outrageous. At wits' end, I decided to call out the heavy artillery.

Throughout the years, I'd accumulated a number of people in high places who were beholden to me, businessmen, journalists, the nobility. Never having truly expected to be in need of these resources, I was suddenly grateful for their existence. Without apology, I called in my favors. I visited people who, by the looks on their faces, had hoped never to see me again. I launched a program that in plain language could only be called a ban. Newspapers and journals no longer ran any kind of review in which the name of Mademoiselle Daaé was mentioned. Miscellaneous titled patrons of the opera took to visiting the new managers Monsieur Armand Moncharmin and Monsieur Firmin Richard, who'd taken over the administration of the Paris Opera shortly after Christine's triumph. My friends did their best to exert their collective influence, ensuring that my nemesis was given no leading role. Even Count Philippe, who was unable to help me in this particular matter, stuck his neck out much further than I would have expected, confiding, during a brief moment of candor, that he was *extremely* disappointed with this Daaé person who was playing some cat and mouse game with his younger brother, Raoul. His confession of annoyance was the closest thing to support that he could give me. But it was enough. By telling me that, he was letting me know he'd do nothing to impede the machine I was setting in motion.

As a final precaution, I hired a private investigator to keep an eye on my target and find out, if he could, where she lived and with whom she was studying. It wasn't long before I learned that Christine had become the adopted daughter of a Professor and Madame Valerius after her father died and that she was living with the professor's widow. I also discovered that although she claimed to have no teacher, she was visited in her dressing room each morning, at eight o'clock sharp, by some mysterious person who gave her lessons but who could never be caught either entering or leaving. Intrigued, I went there one morning with the hope of listening at the door and learning for myself who the elusive maestro was. Would that I'd never become involved with that cursed girl. Eight-ten in the morning found me walking toward her dressing room, following the magnificent thread of her unmistakable new voice. Just as I arrived at the door, she stopped singing and her maestro demonstrated a particular phrase.

All it took was that first note, that first single voluptuous note and I became as a victim of paralysis.

It was impossible. It was the final insult. What more could anyone do to me that they had not already done? For, God help me, I knew that voice. I knew that voice better than I knew my own name.

"No," I whispered, my throat so tight that I feared I would choke. "Not that. Please not that."

"But, Angel," she whined, "I don't understand."

"You will, my darling," came his patient reply, "Just take it again from *Je ris . . .*"

I realized numbly, that they were rehearsing Marguerite's Jewel Song, normally my part. But it hardly mattered. I listened in open grief to the beloved voice that had guided me and comforted me since my childhood, teaching her everything she would need to usurp me. Somehow, she'd managed to steal even that. She'd robbed me of my Angel of Music.

For a time, I couldn't leave. It had been so long since I'd heard his sweet voice outside my dreams that I clung to the sound of it even though it wasn't directed toward me. I barely comprehended the words but the tone brought back fresh to me that night, twenty-seven years before when he'd held me in his arms and promised to visit me forever after in my dreams. With inexplicable vividness, I remembered the feel of him as I returned his embrace, the smell of him as I rested my head in the crook of his neck, the warmth of him enveloping me despite the unaccountable coldness of his skin. I remembered that he'd told me that he loved me.

I almost forgot to hide myself before she was due to come out, remembering to scurry away only at the last possible moment. Even so, I was back there far sooner than any sane person would have considered safe, pushing open the unlocked door to her dressing room with shocking boldness, his long ago words to me giving strength when I'd thought I had none. "Just let me know that it's you and you'll be safe, for I could never intentionally hurt you."

"Erik?" I whispered, closing the door behind me. "Erik, it's me, Lotte. Don't you remember?"

I barely recognized my own voice, so tiny, so vulnerable, so young. Anyone hearing it at that moment couldn't have failed to recognize the voice of little Lotte lost for so long within the bovine bulk of the woman she'd become. But no one was there to hear. I turned up the gas, just to be sure, recognizing the interior of the same dressing room from which I myself had been chased, not long ago, by the antics of an ornery opera ghost. There was however, no sign of him at that moment, no change in temperature, no musty smell of the tomb. I might even go so far as to say that the walls of the opera house, normally so full of malevolent eyes, had somehow become quite ordinary. Just walls. And I felt certain that a pin or a broach placed on the vanity right then would still be at hand even a minute or so later.

It was the thought of the vanity that drew my gaze initially. But it was the fateful flash of orange and black that held it there. With eyes opened wide I approached what looked to be a crystal sphere on a wooden stand. Embedded in its heart was the butterfly of my dreams. Only once in my life had I seen a real monarch and even that had been while in the thrall of Erik's enchantment. It was the reason the monarch was so dear to me. It was also why I'd come to think of it as some mythological creature, more akin to dragons and unicorns than to the actual world of flora and fauna. Yet there it was, in Christine Daaé's dressing room, frozen eternally at the center of a paperweight, denied its God-given right to rebirth by flames. I lifted it up, overcome by emotion, imagining a kinship between the creature and myself. Each of us had been denied, each of us thwarted, each of us helplessly ensnared in the same spider's web. In the end, I couldn't bear to leave it behind. And as no one was watching, neither ghost, nor angel, nor yet, even a simple, human person, my thievery escaped detection.

I must say that the jewelers and tinkers all eyed me strangely when I presented my paperweight and asked them if they could remove the butterfly intact. Even so, it was one of them who eventually pointed out the inscription on the underside of the wooden stand:

Mariposa Monarca
México

Without a doubt then, it had been a gift from the Count's younger brother, Raoul, who'd won some small fame as a mariner and who must have brought the thing back after one of his voyages. Such a gift hinted at slightly more than a nodding acquaintance between singer and nobleman. I was surprised in retrospect at having achieved Philippe's promise of nonintervention. But as I'd never been one to question the motives of the nobility, I gave it not another thought, returning to the business at hand. What could I do after all, beyond leaving the bauble with the tinker and attempting to pick up as many of the pieces of my shattered life as I could after the astounding revelations of that morning?

I suppose that in a former life I might have gone home and made myself sick with crying but there seemed to be no point. Such an indulgence would only put me at risk of missing another performance. If nothing else, I refused to play so easily into their hands. As things stood, the situation was still salvageable. I was still diva, after all, and I wasn't as helpless and without resources as I once had been. My plans were all carefully laid. My people were in place and I had one other ace in the hole on which my enemies were not counting: Christine didn't remember me. Or if she did, she hadn't yet recognized her would-be stepmother beneath the phony accent and the sixty extra pounds of lard. Knowing this, I decided on a desperate scheme: to enlist her aid as my unwitting messenger. To this end, the next time I passed her in the hall, I gave her as exaggerated and cheery a greeting as ever she had given me.

"Why good afternoon, *cariño,*" I effused.

"Good afternoon, señora," she answered brightly, "You're looking well today."

"As are you, *mi hija.* By the way, say hello to your teacher for me. We are old friends, you know."

She stopped dead in her tracks, all pretense of amiability gone. "I have no teacher," she said, eyeing me suspiciously.

"Of course you do," I answered, cheerful as ever. "You meet with him every morning at eight o'clock – don't frown so, *cariño,* you'll give yourself wrinkles before your time. I know it's supposed to be a big secret but you needn't worry about Carlotta. *I'd* never tell. Just say hello to him for me . . . and tell him that I miss him."

"You can't know him." Her agitation was deeply gratifying.

"Oh, but I do, *mi amor.* You see, I too, was once visited by the Angel of Music."

I was unaware that human eyes could actually bulge. Oh how I wish I'd had a mirror with me. She was still standing there making that ridiculous face when I walked away.

Chapter Fourteen

The next afternoon, Christine came to my dressing room, a gloating smile marring the normal, angelic vacuity of her features.

"He says you're a liar," she said, not bothering with any of the social niceties and obviously relishing the excuse to repeat such a thing to my face.

"How so?" I asked, unruffled.

"He says you're nothing but a singing machine, not a real artist at all and that an angel would never visit the likes of you."

"Tut, child," I said. "He obviously didn't know who you were talking about. You told him that Carlotta sent her greetings, didn't you?"

"What else would I say?"

"You should have said little Lotte."

She winced and looked away. When she replied, still not meeting my eye, it dawned on me that she was beginning to suspect who I was. "I know that story," she said. "Little Lotte thought of everything and nothing. A bird of summer was she, who soared through the rays of the sun as golden as her own blond curls, crowned in springtime. Her soul was as clear and as blue as her eyes. She loved her mother dearly, was faithful to her doll and took good care of her frock, her red shoes and her violin. But above all else, she loved to go to bed at night because in her dreams she heard the voice of the Angel of Music."*

¡Santa María, madre de Dios! My eyes must have been saucers. "Your father told you that?"

"Everyone knows that story."

"I don't think so," I said. "And anyhow, it didn't happen that way."

"How would *you* know?"

"Because I was there, *mi hija*." Lord, I felt sick. "Just tell him next time that it's Lotte who greets him."

"*I* am little Lotte now." The way she said it, there was no doubt anymore that she knew me. That she knew what she'd taken from me. And was reveling in her triumph. *Why didn't I leave her and her simpleton father to freeze in the snow?* My mind conjured for me the image of Samuel Daaé's gentle, foolish face and I felt a pang at my own malignant thoughts. Christine must have sensed that moment of weakness because it was then she looked me straight in the eye and said, "*He* calls me little Lotte. So does Raoul. And my father did too when he was alive."

That caught my attention. I don't think she realized, though, when she looked at me so unflinchingly what it was she'd just revealed. I set aside for the moment the significance such revelation had for me. Instead, I met her challenge and focused on the significance for her. "Interesting," I said. "Your *father* called you little Lotte?"

She gave me a tight, smug grin.

"When exactly did he call you that?"

"At odd times."

"I'll wager that's what he called you when he held you in his arms at night, wasn't it. How old were you, by the way, when he finally stopped doing that? Or did he ever stop? Were you already a big, grown girl like you are now when he kissed you and caressed you all alone in some loft?"

Her face flushed red as a ripe tomato. "Shut up, you evil woman," she shrieked. "How dare you speak ill of the dead."

"I speak only the truth, *mi hija*. Deny it if you can."

She fled, leaving me alone with the other half of my realization. I walked to my dressing room in a pensive state. So Daaé called her little Lotte. I mustn't have been quite as disposable as I'd assumed. With an exquisite little thrill, it occurred to me that I'd become for him, what the angel had become for me: a recurring phantom of the mind who revealed itself only in dreams. For all the good it did me, I understood that when Daaé embraced his daughter, mine was the face he imagined and mine was the name he repeated, over and over, as he held her. Far from forgetting me, he'd turned me into a legend that would be passed down long after I was dust. How could it be that such an extraordinary occurrence would have no bearing at all on the miserable situation in which I found myself at present?

But I knew full well it didn't. Christine was little Lotte because the angel came to *her* now.

It had been years since I'd actually been impatient to go to bed. Calling the angel was so emotionally draining anymore that I always awoke the next morning with a headache and nausea. That night I didn't care. I needed so badly to speak to him that the thought of being laid up even for a week didn't daunt me. I went straight home from my performance and directly to bed. I called to my angel with all the desperation in my heart. I screamed until my voice was gone. I beat the stone walls until my fists became bloodied. I wept until my very soul was spent.

But he didn't come.

The following morning, my headache was nothing compared to my black mood. I rang for the maid who, as was her custom, brought me my mail and a cup of hot chocolate. One item in particular, addressed in red ink, immediately caught my attention and for some reason, my heart began pounding even before I was able to read its contents. Neatly slitting the envelope with the dagger-like opener, I removed the enclosed missive, unfolded it and read:

*If you sing this evening, fear not but that a great misfortune will strike you the moment you begin . . . a misfortune worse than death.**

It was unsigned, of course and the deplorable handwriting was unfamiliar. Yet I knew, as surely as I was sitting there in bed, from whom the letter had come. Doubtless, Christine had gone running back to her teacher – as she used to run back to her papa – bawling at full volume as a result of the heinous abuse she'd received at my hand. And Erik – so protective of his little Lotte that he'd once even killed for her – couldn't help but be whipped into cataclysmic fury. I knew him too well to expect anything less than full retribution.

Well, we would see, wouldn't we? Even if Erik hadn't a clue as to my real identity, just hanging about the opera should have taught him Carlotta wasn't the type to ignore a challenge. The sight of a hearse passing by my window just then made me more than a little nervous however and so I summoned all my friends to the house. Once they were assembled, I made a grand display of the letter and explained, for the slower ones, that my absence would mean that Mademoiselle Daaé would sing in my place. Next, I proceeded to paint a vivid picture of the plot that had been hatched to further her career at the expense of my own, the message, in my opinion, being proof positive that her supporters were willing to resort to the very lowest and most uncouth forms of persuasion.

" . . . And to think that the arts are supposed to be ennobling," I raged. "The problem is, too many people with no talent at all still feel the need to stand before multitudes. And if they can't rise on the strength of their merits, they'll use whatever other means they find at their disposal."

I waved the letter in the air "I *will not* be cowed. I will not give in. And so, I'm sure, they'll do their worst. Help me. If enough of you can attend the performance tonight, perhaps these cowards will be afraid to show their faces."

As if on cue, Monsieur Richard's secretary was announced. He entered, obviously surprised to see such a crowd in my sitting room and said he'd been sent to inquire after my health.

Meeting the gazes of several of my supporters, I turned back to the secretary and asked, "Why would Monsieur Richard be so suddenly preoccupied with my health?"

"It seems," the poor man said, tugging at his collar and looking nervously about, "that the management received an anonymous letter this morning advising them to prepare Mademoiselle Daaé to sing on your behalf tonight. Because you'd be ill."

The loud exclamations that broke out all around me drowned out whatever else he said. But what had been heard was quite sufficient.

More than sufficient, in fact. I myself was shaken. Still, if ever there'd come a time to rally the troops, this was it, and with a show of righteous bravado, I called out for quiet.

"Tell Monsieur Richard," I said, "that I would perform tonight even if I were dying."

Cheers and applause filled the room as I sent the bewildered fellow away with my message. Shortly thereafter, the rest departed, each of them squeezing my hand and promising not only to attend my performance but to bring along any number of friends as well. If nothing else, I knew that whatever the evening's outcome, everyone of any importance in Paris would be there to witness it.

I spent the rest of the afternoon pampering my voice, drinking tea with honey and avoiding any drafts. At five o'clock, the maid came up with two items that had just been delivered. One was a white cardboard jewelry box. The other was a letter. Assuming at first that the two were together, I reached for the envelope, stopping short at the sight of the red ink used to address it. My heart lurched, but I was too angry to allow my fears to get in the way. I slit the seam of the envelope with my dagger and ripped out the contents.

*You have a cold. If you are sensible, you will understand that wanting to sing this evening would be madness.**

I laughed without humor, sang a few notes, just to be sure, and wondered what diabolical punishment he had in store for me. Yet even as I pictured one possible scenario after another, I folded the letter carefully and pressed it between the scented pages of a book of poetry. That letter, and its companion of the morning were probably the only tangible gifts I would ever receive from *him* and so I took care to preserve them.

Secretly, I found myself hoping that my "misfortune" would somehow involve his coming to me himself, prepared to do whatever harm he'd planned, only to recognize me at the last moment as the little girl who'd once saved his life. Christine said the angel called her little Lotte. Was it possible I'd been a phantom in *his* mind as well?

That Erik – the *real* flesh and blood Erik – had remembered me with fondness through all the intervening years?

With a sudden twist of perception, everything honed into vivid focus and I understood precisely what had happened. He loved blond-haired, blue-eyed Christine, because she looked like me. Not Carlotta the diva of course, with her fake hair, fake accent and the haunches of a Belgian draft horse but "Lotte of the sunshine hair," as she would have been when she reached the age of twenty had circumstances not so physically changed her. Worse yet, Christine had been nicknamed "Lotte" and knew all about the monarch and the Angel of Music. If he truly had loved me for all of that time, how could he possibly have resisted so many coincidences? Remembering my own ordeal with Samuel Daaé I clearly understood how even fewer coincidences than that had been necessary for *me* to become hopelessly smitten.

So excited did I become at this train of thought that I began to tremble and for a brief moment, indulged in a flight of fancy, imagining him coming to me, his eyes lighting up in sudden recognition, his arms spreading wide to receive me. But then I shook my addled head and snorted. Since when had things ever turned out like that?

"What if he no longer cares who you are?" asked a nasty little voice in my head. "You've been standing outside, looking in on your life for so many years that perhaps this time you really *have* lost your place."

Indeed, what if Christine really had become Lotte? What if Erik knew, but no longer cared that a substitution had been made? What if he despised me for the shallow, selfish creature I'd become and had chosen her not because she was *like* me but because she was better? I knew all too well the savage brutality of which he was capable, my shoulder still aching at the memory. What if, despite everything that had come before, I'd made him my enemy? What if, having thwarted his will and become his target, that rabid strength and blind rage were turned, full bore, upon me?

"He has no conscience," el Moco had said, "No mercy. And in the end, he will surely destroy you."

My trembling increased and I found myself tempted to curl into a tight little ball. I resisted the temptation. What's more, I took a good look at myself from the outside and was disgusted with what I saw. I would not be intimidated. So, with an angry snarl, I pulled myself together, my attention only then returning to the remaining parcel. Still believing that *he* had been responsible for both, I took a deep breath and stole myself for something nasty, picturing one by one in my mind, the most horrible objects I could imagine fitting inside the box. Only when I'd come to terms with the possibility of a springing mousetrap, a leaping spider or some bloody, severed piece of anatomy did I knock off the lid with a poker. But the sight that greeted my eyes was none of those things. It was so welcome and, in that instant, so thoroughly unexpected, that I could do nothing for several moments aside from releasing a sigh. It was the monarch, forgotten after recent events, laid out lovingly upon a piece of cotton batting, freed at last from its crystal prison. I drew in another breath and bent down for a closer look. More beautiful than I'd ever imagined, I couldn't help marveling at the delicacy of its antennae and the strange, almost velvety texture of its body. It held my attention as perhaps nothing else could. But even as I examined it, my initial delight transformed into something much less pleasant. I was contemplating a corpse. The thing was *dead*. For some reason, I'd expected it to recommence its interrupted cycle once it had been set free, returning to life in a triumphant explosion of flames. But this, apparently not being the case, disturbed me more than I was able to consciously admit at that time. Perhaps, I told myself, the cycle was longer than I thought. Perhaps they only came back after a certain period of time. Perhaps being stuck in the sphere for so long had affected it. Perhaps I needed to help it along.

I should burn it.

And with that thought came another – a sudden ultimatum that I would surely have retracted if only it had been possible for me to do so.

"If I burn it and it is reborn," said the voice in my head, "then everything will turn out all right in the end. But if, when I burn it, it's only consumed, it will mean that the angel was a dream, nothing more, and that all I believed in my life was a lie."

Why on Earth had it been necessary to think such a thing? Berating myself for all kinds of a fool, I knew it was too late. The notion, once conceived, couldn't be forgotten. Quickly, before I could change my mind, I scooped up the insect and threw it on the fire, crouching to witness the sealing of my fate. It ignited at once, the tiny carcass so dry that it caused a brief, spectacular tongue of flame to shoot up, identical in every way to the one that had burned so long ago, in the palm of an angel's hand.

All at once, I was turning away, was walking out of the room, was closing the door behind me. I couldn't stand to watch it. I couldn't bear to know.

Unable to stay around the house any longer, I went to the theater, arriving much earlier than usual, and completely aware, as I alternately paced the floor and lounged about in the isolation of my dressing room, that I was making myself an easy target. Still, I might as well have taken a nap for all the extraordinary occurrences I witnessed during that time. Not so much as a single tack materialized on my chair throughout the entirety of my toilet. All my preparations proceeded with a dreamlike facility that was, in itself, ominous. He was up to something. This I knew. If only I'd guessed at the preparations that were occupying him elsewhere, this story might have had a different ending. I might have saved the life of that poor woman, crushed to death under the great chandelier when it fell. I might have found my way to the attic where Erik was doing whatever it was he did so that great brass and crystal monstrosity would drop on cue. We might have looked at each other in the flesh for the first time in twenty-seven years. I might have spoken his name. And he, mine.

But I knew nothing then of his plans.

More time was spent, pacing up and down until at last it was a quarter past seven. Relieved, I set myself to warming up, carefully putting my voice through the normal routine of exercises until it was at its accustomed level of suppleness and fluidity, only to find, upon finishing, that I'd achieved that state of readiness in half the usual time. At a loss once more as to how to occupy my time, I renewed my pacing, singing a phrase or two every now and again to keep the instrument at optimum flexibility. Suddenly, right in the midst of an aria, an idea occurred to me that I realized at once was my chance at salvation. I could sing something that Erik would recognize, something that only Lotte would know, something that would, at long last, penetrate the stubborn fog of unawareness that seemed to be clouding his brain. I would sing the song that he'd sung to me in that faraway place such a long time ago.

With an unfamiliar thrill of excitement, I began to sing his own lullaby, remembering, as I continued, the sound of his voice when first he'd sung it.

Superimposing in my mind the sounds I was making with the sounds I'd heard then, I gradually narrowed the frame of my consciousness until the two voices became one. With eyes shut and soul opened wide, a new sound began to emerge, bigger, rounder and yet infinitely sweeter than any music I'd ever made before. Hearing it, I wasn't entirely certain that it was coming from me but my whole body was vibrating with the effort and I could feel my vocal chords responding to the demands being made on them.

It *was* me.

After nearly a lifetime of striving, I'd finally learned to integrate my body, my mind and my soul, had finally found the way to use that newly unified whole as a conduit for all the love and beauty in the universe, had, at long last, discovered the glorious rapture of sound for which I'd so endlessly searched. And at this, the eleventh hour, I came to understand that the effort had been wasted. Exhausted, I understood why Christine had fainted after her much longer ordeal. But the real difference wasn't in the duration but in the setting. Her renaissance had occurred on a public stage for all the world to see. Mine had taken place all alone in a dressing room from which even the ubiquitous opera ghost was absent.

A knock on my door, and my well wishers were upon me with bouquets of flowers and boxes of chocolates. Some of them who'd perhaps heard a few final phrases drifting down the hall, commented upon my being in good voice that evening. I nodded, smiled tiredly, and thanked them from the bottom of my heart. A good number of them remained with me up to the five-minute call. I was beyond exhaustion and knew I'd been foolish to exert myself so extensively before a performance, especially this particular performance. But because Marguerite doesn't sing in the first scene of *Faust*, I knew that if I forced myself to relax and paced myself carefully, I'd still have the stamina to pull off a triumph.

I'd almost forgotten about the collective presence of my faithful admirers in the audience until, during the second scene, the four paltry lines that Marguerite sings elicited from them a wild ovation that was quite over the top and succeeded only in embarrassing me. Other than that well-meaning, if misguided disturbance, there was no interruption of any kind. The only other circumstance that might have been deemed odd was the presence of the managers, who almost never attended a performance, seated together in the third box on the grand tier.

It wasn't until I was once again offstage that it occurred to me, that with those four insignificant lines, I'd beaten the prophecy. The message had said that my misfortune would occur at the moment I started to sing, yet I'd successfully survived the entire first act without suffering anything even remotely "worse than death." During the interval, and just as I was beginning to breathe a little more easily, there came a knock at the door. I could tell by the buzz of excited conversation on the other side that it was a pair of my friends, though it was highly unusual for them to disturb me between acts. Nevertheless, I let them in.

"It's going to happen during 'The King of Thule,'" Mlle. Elizabeth declared.

"Yes," replied her mother the Comptess with the air of one who knows all. "The second scene in Act I didn't count."

Well-meaning busy-bodies though they were, it was unusual for them to so forget their upbringing as to burst in with news before putting all of us through the normal ceremony of proper salutation. Their state of upset frightened me more than their actual words. "Have you heard something?" I asked.

"Well, it stands to reason," Elizabeth said.

And though the response proved that in reality they knew nothing, I found myself, nodding. "You're right." I replied. "It does stand to reason."

"You see?" Elizabeth said, elbowing her mother. "I told you we should tell her."

"You're right," I repeated with a growing, sickening conviction. "That's when he would do it, so that Christine could sing 'The Jewel Song.' That's the one they were rehearsing. Oh . . ." Unconsciously I began to twist my hands, recalling myself only when I saw their wide-eyed stares. Swallowing my near panic in the face of these observers, I forced the tension from my jaws, shoulders and hands, even finding the strength to smile at them reassuringly. "Thank you for telling me," I said. "Now that I know, I'll be ready for them."

"You can count on us too," Elizabeth said. "We won't let anyone by us."

"Thank you."

They left me in a bustle of self-importance with many parting words of encouragement. And then I was alone again, facing the possibility that they were right, and that the trial, which I'd thought over had in reality not yet begun.

Extremely aware of everything with the commencement of Act II, I noticed not only that Christine, singing Siebel's "Flower Song," had gone back to her bleating, former self but that Count Philippe, up in his box, was looking exceedingly annoyed and that if posture were any indication, Philippe's brother Raoul was weeping. I made my entrance to more wild cheering and before I knew it, the dreaded "King of Thule" aria was upon me. Terrified, I fear I sang little better than Christine. But when I finished and no bolt of lightning struck, I dared to hope. "The Jewel Song" also came and went without incident and with the over-enthusiastic ovation that followed, I found I was suddenly filled with a burgeoning joy. My pathetically limited imagination could supply no reason for my combined success with Christine's unaccountable return to the ranks of the mediocre except that *he* had come to a new decision. Reasoning that since the only possible basis upon which he could have made such a decision was his having heard me, I concluded, with a surge of excitement, that he'd finally recognized me, that he knew who I was, that it couldn't be long before he returned, at last, to me. From then on, I feared nothing, allowing myself to bask in the adulation of my admirers, tossing my head and strutting upon the stage with the arrogance of a peacock. I was no longer Marguerite. I was Carmen.

In such a frame of mind, I reached the famous love duet.

At that point, Carolus Fonta, the famous baritone who was playing Faust that night, knelt and sang:

Laisse-moi, laisse-moi contempler ton visage
Sous la pâle clarté
Dont l'astre de la nuit, comme dans un nuage,
*Caresse ta beauté.**†

And I began with my response:

> *O silence! O bonheur! ineffable mystère!*
> *Enivrante languer!*
> *J'écoute! . . . Et je comprends cette voix solitaire*
> *Qui chante dans mon coeur!**†

But I never made it past that point. At the moment I reached the word *"coeur"* I heard an obscene bodily sound like a cross between a belch and a croak. It was so loud that it overpowered the strength of my own singing. The audience rose up as a single unit. The orchestra faltered and I looked around, only to discover that everyone, including Carolus, was looking at me. Only then did I understand. They believed that hideous sound had issued from me, that after all these years of perfect reliability, my voice, my faithful instrument, had finally, somehow, betrayed me. In a horrible vision of clarity, I comprehended Erik's plan. His intention had never been to cause me physical harm but to utterly destroy me as a diva, to ruin my career, to make a fool of me in front of *Tout-Paris.*

Right there on stage, I began to cry.

"Not this," little Lotte whispered. "Oh please, Angel, not this."

"Go on," a voice cried.

I looked up in confusion to see an ashen-faced Monsieur Richard leaning right out of his box.

"Go on," he shouted again.

I'd already realized the direness of my situation. But in that moment I also realized something of equal importance. Despite what happened the next day, despite what happened even in the next five minutes, right then, right there, I was *still* diva. My hands began to tremble and my body was suddenly infused with a rush of power, the likes of which I'd known only once before, as a force that had blasted me to Paris in a single night of fury. I would not be shamed. I would not let that cursed impostor take my place.

With a physical wrench, I pulled myself together, wiped my nose on the sleeve of my costume, and told the conductor to take it from *"O silence!"* admonishing him to keep the orchestra going no matter what happened. With that, I began again. The croaking recommenced as well, but I was ready for it, singing at maximum volume so that people could realize I wasn't its source, that indeed it was the very disturbance we had feared. For several painful stanzas, there took place a macabre duet in which each voice tried to prevail. His was formidably loud but I had exceptionally good pipes of my own and in a fair fight, with the power of my rage behind me, he couldn't have dominated me for long. Then at last, there was one sweet moment during which the croaking stopped and there emerged in triumph, the crystalline, bell-like tones of a perfect soprano voice.

And then the great chandelier came crashing down, right into the midst of the audience.

I think I would have continued still, such was my determination. But the music had stopped, chaos reigned and no one was paying me the slightest attention. Whether or not I cared to admit it, the battle was over and I had lost. Belatedly, I understood that his all-consuming need to put his darling in my place had been the only thing that ever really mattered. To that end, he hadn't balked at committing the most monstrous of acts, murdering innocent bystanders just so *I* could never redeem my shattered image. Having sorely underestimated the ferocity of his passion, I saw too late that the seeds of the disaster had been sewn by my own hand. Fighting him had been a mistake. But it was, by and large, an insignificant one when seen in the light of my foolishness, twenty-seven years before, in setting him free – was well nigh nonexistent when compared to the lugubrious, fawning trust of one unbelievably stupid little girl, welcoming the implantation of his image, like an infection, within the moist, dark recesses of her mind.

"Angel! Angel!"

The cry was so guttural, so frantic and so loud that I didn't recognize the voice as Christine's until she dashed out onto the stage. I watched her as she ran from stage left to stage right, straying so close to the edge that I thought she'd end in the pit. Without once slowing her madwoman's pace, she veered off at the last possible moment and fled, still screaming, into the wings. The sets, the curtains, everything passed by me in a blur before I realized that I, too, had left the stage at a run, that indeed, I seemed to be following her. We left the wild crowd behind us, she and I racing down the empty corridors. Not once did she look back. Her distress, combined with her continued shrieking – which, incidentally, couldn't have been doing her voice any good – apparently made her insensible to the possibility that anyone could be following.

When she reached her dressing room, she paused only long enough to slam the door behind her. The solid wood only partially muffled the continued sounds of horrible, throaty screeching. Having no honor left to lose, I knelt down to watch her through the keyhole, discovering that the muted thumping sounds that had commenced a moment earlier were the result of her fists pounding against the mirror on the wall. There was no doubt this was a genuine expression of grief, overdone to be sure, but painfully consistent with her habitual, no-holds-barred manner. Yet I was at a loss to explain what had provoked it. She seemed to believe the catastrophe had somehow harmed her angel. How could that be possible when he'd caused it? Slowly it dawned on me that she was unaware of the connection. She truly had no idea of the crimes her "angel" had committed on her behalf. She was just one more innocent pawn in the game that Erik was playing.

I cannot in truth say I was moved to pity at this revelation but I confess I was bearing off in that direction when a new sound, added to the din, suspended further thought. A plaintive, moaning wail rose up all around her, sweet and melodic, yet easily overpowering the obnoxious noise of her unconstrained hysterics. Abruptly, she quieted, listening in rapture as the music grew louder, transforming at last into words sung so tenderly that I was as caught up as she. His voice had never been more beautiful and very quietly, the sobbing began again in me. As I watched, the mirror swung away, revealing a dark passageway beyond, and she, seemingly in a trance, drifted toward it. From my vantage point I could see to the very end of the tunnel, spying before she did, the figure dressed in black, the figure that could only be he. With silent yearning, I watched the hypnotic grace with which he extended his arm and raised his head, realizing only then that he was masked. And as the mirror slowly began to close, effectively cutting off my final glimpse of him, it came to me that she'd never seen his face.

Epilogue

The following morning, it was Monsieur Moncharmin's secretary who came to call, bringing with him a bank draft for an extraordinary sum he explained was the amount required to relieve me of the remainder of my contract – as if there were even the slightest chance that *I* could ever sing again. My music was as dead to me as if it had never existed. My thoughts were dominated instead by disturbing, nightmare images that refused to give me peace: images of my Erik, shamefully masked, images of a three-year-old Christine, recoiling in disgust at the sight of my battered face, images of a future in which, despite his most careful precautions, she sees his face and reacts with predictable horror and loathing. All the love and kindness he has shown her since the beginning will be as nothing to her then, for she will leave him as easily and with as little remorse as she and her father left me on that day when my own mask finally slipped. Her rejection will kill him. I know this with the same certainty that I know the blow he dealt me was also a mortal one. I am haunted even now by the grossness of the sound he used to bring about my ruin. Nothing could have better illustrated the contempt in which he must have held me, *he* who was my beloved, my inspiration and the sole reason for my existence.

Just this morning I read in the paper that Count Philippe was found dead in one of the cellars beneath the opera house and that Christine

Daaé, her foster mother and Raoul the new Count de Chagny have all mysteriously vanished. I know what this means of course, even though the detectives may still be sniffing footprints and examining the paneling with their magnifying glasses. It means that Christine has seen Erik's face. It means she has forsaken him with loud exclamations of revulsion. It means she's run off somewhere with her pet count, though I must say I'm impressed she thought to take along her foster mother as well.

And Philippe? He was a hard man. But essentially descent. There are many other noblemen much crueler and less fair in their dealings and it saddens me that if one of that ilk had to go, Philippe would be the one. He must have got in the way, poor man. No doubt he caused Erik some annoyance and was summarily swept aside just as I had been.

How ironic that Erik and I had been in the same opera house for six years and never recognized each other. How strange that at times we had even been in the same room without knowing it. Perhaps at some point we even touched. Though, dear God, if I pursue that train of thought I know I'll go mad. It wasn't until I saw Erik open the secret door behind Christine's mirror that I realized the cold and damp I'd always associated with the opera ghost's presence in my dressing room was in truth, the draft from a hidden doorway leading to the cellars. He'd opened a door and come inside. He'd been there with me, moving my possessions, stealing my clothing and putting those damnable tacks on my chair. I know his talents as a magician and hypnotist are such that it would enable him to do those things without my being aware of his presence. But for him to do it six years running and never realize the identity of the person he tormented? To have him there with me all of that time and never even sense that he was near? It seems impossible yet I know it to be true. And I also know that now he is dying. Indeed how ironic that I can sense his death throes here in my heart when before I couldn't even sense his presence when he stood not three paces from me.

Oh, Erik.

What misery must you be facing now, all alone in the darkness? Are you thinking perhaps of your own little Lotte, who saw beyond your poor face to your heart and was able to love what she found there? Can your memories of her at least help in some way to ease your final agony? Do your dying lips utter her name one last time?

I for my part, no longer see my angel, no matter how my soul cries out for him, no matter how my heart is breaking. He left though he promised he wouldn't. He left without saying good-bye. And now my nights are empty and gray. I spend them roaming the bleak no-man's-land of my dreams, forever searching but never finding that for which I seek.

*Any passage ending in an asterisk is from Gaston Leroux's, *The Phantom of the Opera.*

†Barbier, M. Jules and Michel Carré, lib., *Faust,* with music by Charles Gounod. First performed March 19, 1859, Théâtre Lyrique, Paris.

The Portal

Prologue

Madame la Comtess de Chagny, formerly known as Mademoiselle Christine Daaé, the famous soprano, was accustomed to being treated with the respect and admiration befitting a diva of the Paris Opera. It therefore became quite tiresome when her in-laws took to treating her as something less than themselves. Her manners, it seemed, lacked a certain polish and her speech pattern was not without a quaint provincial turn of phrase the noble family found "charming." The countess soon came to understand that each compliment was an insult, each smile, a sneer. Family gatherings became ordeals to be endured. Her face, formerly known for its beauty, started to take on a sour cast. Count Raoul couldn't comprehend the morose cloud that had descended upon his young wife and seemed oblivious to the censorship being visited upon her.

At last, she herself brought it to his attention.

He replied that she must be imagining things and reminded her that she was still new to her position in society. He tried to console her with the promise that in time she'd become more comfortable with the social graces and no longer feel out of place. This observation, implying that the former prima donna was lacking in social grace, was as insulting as it was true. Her mortification couldn't have been greater had he slapped her.

So she left, tears of outrage spilling during the long trip from the de Chagny country estate to the city of Paris. She returned without remorse. She returned with the confidence of the prodigal son finding his way home. She swept through the front door of the great Opera House as if it belonged to her and strode without apology to the poorly lit passages in the back.

Alone at last, she knelt upon the floor, giving way to the anger and self-pity that threatened to consume her. She allowed her misery full rein. No attempt was made to muffle the sobs that grew steadily louder and more frantic, feeding upon themselves and gradually transfiguring into mindless ululating wails, reverberating throughout the back passages of the Opera. This orgy of grief continued until she'd completely exhausted herself. It was then she took to scratching feebly at the wall, begging for admittance in a poor broken voice, hoarse from her screams.

And he came. As surely as a demon must come when summoned, he came. Without question. Without resistance. And though he hadn't spoken, she knew he was there. She could sense his presence on the other side of the wall. Her hand reached up to caress the stone as if it were the face of a lover. Her hot forehead rested against the unyielding coolness. In this attitude, she poured out her sorrows. Anyone watching would have thought her mad.

"Help me," she whispered. "Please help me."

"I will help you," the voice said. "I will take you away from the suffering of this world. I will build a great house for you and for me, a house of many windows so you may always have sunshine, a house of dark corners so I too may find peace, a house as a portal between our two worlds, a house where at last we can meet."

That was how my mother and father came together at last. After so much sorrow. After so many ruined lives. But love must have its way and the diva of the Paris Opera doubly so.

Yet, this isn't so much their story as mine. How I was born to the Countess de Chagny even though she'd lived estranged from the count for several years. How frightened she was for me to meet my real father. How she dillied and dallied until it was almost too late.

Settle down now. Stop pulling your sister's hair. I promise you this is the strangest true story you're ever likely to hear. The story of how your own Grandmaman Lotte came to meet the Phantom of the Opera back when she was just a little girl, no bigger than you are now. Yes, the Phantom was my father, hard as that may be to believe.

Hush now, and listen.

Chapter One

It started with the music. That wondrous music I heard so many times at night after Maman tucked me into bed. It penetrated my sleeping brain when I was a very little girl and insinuated itself into my earliest dreams. So much a part of my slumber was this music that I didn't come to recognize it as something existing on the outside until I was older.

I still remember the night I made that discovery. My eighth birthday was still several months off when a bad nightmare hurtled me back into consciousness. I sat up in bed, heart pounding, eyes wide. For a moment, I thought the dream was still with me, for the music was still faintly playing. It wasn't until my breathing slowed that rational thought reasserted itself. I reasoned that Maman must have awakened and unable to sleep had risen to play the piano in the music room. Still, I couldn't help noting that if indeed it were Maman, she was playing much better than she ever had before. Curious, I got out of bed and walked toward the music room.

I passed through the house, all aglow with the cold, eerie light of the moon that shone through the numerous windows. Despite the moonlight, the music room with its heavy drapes drawn, stood in darkness. The piano at center was an indistinct shape. It was also quite obviously silent.

I stood gaping at what I knew to be the only piano in the house, closed, locked and protected by a dust cover, while all around me the music still surged. My fear which had been lurking just below the surface, chose that moment to come sweeping to the fore in a nauseating wave of panic. I ran from the room, the ghostly refrain dogging my every step. Sometimes it increased in volume, sometimes it became muffled but it was always present, no matter which corridor I chose. It continued even after I'd jumped back into bed and several minutes later when my initial panic subsided, I lay there with no other recourse but to listen. The piano had been joined, though I couldn't say when, by an instrument I was unable to identify. I was confused, at first, by its transparency and sweetness. It mingled with the voice of the piano in a complex counterpoint of matching tones and clearly articulated words.

Words?

I was overcome by nervous excitement and by the realization that the new voice was a woman's. Yet no human person could possibly sing like that, with that full, echoing resonance and that insidious undertone that got into my blood and made it move faster. I kept bouncing back and forth between thoughts that I must still be dreaming and the knowledge that I couldn't be. Everything else was too real. From the clamminess of my sweaty sheets to the stale taste in my mouth.

I thought of the stories I'd read. I thought of angels. I thought of mermaids. The sirens, it was said, sang with such beauty that a mortal heart could break just hearing them. This music was very like that. I didn't want to cry but I was crying. As if some outer force had taken control of my body.

Though that couldn't have explained it either because I continued to weep long after the music ended.

The next morning, I wasted no time in asking Maman if she too had heard the singing. Immediately, she shifted her gaze away from mine and in that listless manner she sometimes had, mumbled that she didn't know what I meant. I was unconvinced and continued to pester her in growing frustration until she ordered me from the room. I left, dragging my feet along the runner and wishing I could destroy something. I pulled some of the flowers out of an arrangement and threw them on the floor. But no one was present to be scandalized by my behavior and this too frustrated me.

I went outside and wandered about, committing petty crimes such as deliberately walking through the flower beds and kicking dirt into the fishpond. Through no particular planning, I ended up in front of the stable. It was there it occurred to me that I might be able to spend the rest of the morning pushing the hay out of the loft and into the barnyard below. Remembering how hard the stable hands had worked to put it up there, I smiled.

Without further consideration, I climbed the ladder to the loft and opened the outside door. I used a pitchfork to separate clumps of hay from the nearest pile and to fling them out into space. I'd be caught, of course, before I emptied the entire loft but I hoped to go undetected long enough to make a big stack in the yard outside. I imagined myself leaping out the window and landing on that stack in a spectacular display of insolence when they finally came after me.

The more I thought about that grand exit, the more dramatic and appealing it seemed. I'd already worked up a fairly good sweat when the tine of my fork caught something hidden beneath the hay. I cleared away the concealing wisps and found I'd speared a rat trap. It had already sprung and the unlucky victim was still there, its broken spine and final throes quite ghastly to behold. It wore a twisted grimace that revealed just the slightest hint of sharp little teeth and its eyes were rolled up into its head, all white. I examined it in horrified fascination and as I did so, a diabolical plan took shape in my mind. Thrilled by its very simplicity, I gave up any thought of emptying the loft.

I removed the carcass from the trap, wrapped it up in some old burlap and returned with it to the house.

That evening, I went up to my room early, leaving Maman below in the sitting room, working on her embroidery. I placed the candle on the floor and got down on my hands and knees to withdraw the bundle from under my bed. I could smell the little corpse even through the wrapping and held it at arm's length as I walked to Maman's room.

I opened the door and stepped inside. In daylight, Maman's bedchamber was a bright and airy place. At night, as seen by the uncertain light of a candle, it was scary. The big mirror on the wall opposite the panel of windows was especially troubling. It acquired an odd sort of dimension in the darkness that it lacked in the light. Additionally, while looking at it only through the corner of my eye, I'd once or twice imagined some movement within its depths that would immediately cease when I turned my full attention upon it. For this reason, I kept an eye on it the whole time I was crossing the room. Nothing happened, of course. Even so, I didn't feel safe until I was actually inside the closet with the doors shut firmly behind me.

Inside, the closet was roomy and if all the racks, shelves, drawers, dresses, boxes and shoes had been removed, could easily have served as a small bedroom. For this reason, I had plenty of working space.

I went through Maman's hatboxes until I found her favorite hat. It was adorned along the front brim with two stuffed turtledoves. I untwisted the wire that held one of the doves in place and put the stable rat on the hat where the dove had been. I adjusted both rat and remaining bird so the final effect would be symmetrical and aesthetically pleasing. As the *pièce de resistance*, I wrapped the rat's fleshy tail all the way around the crown so that it came in contact with the feathers of the remaining dove.

Before I closed the box, I gave my creation a final once over and found I'd succeeded in creating a tableau that was darkly appealing. The two disparate figures, snuggled together so lovingly both disturbed and moved me in a way I couldn't explain. For a moment I hesitated, having second thoughts about leaving it there. I knew Maman would never appreciate the beauty of it. She'd scream and fling it away from her without even stopping to consider the finer points.

Then again, wasn't that what I wanted?

I realized I was just being silly and put everything away without further reflection.

The worst over, I needed only to leave without being detected. Like the meticulous murderer who obliterates any trace of his crime, I wrapped the discarded dove in the old burlap and placed it securely under my arm. I opened the closet door a crack to make sure Maman hadn't come in without my hearing her. Everything was just as it had been so I exited the closet and closed the door behind me.

It was that split-second delay for the purpose of closing the door – necessary if my activities were to go unsuspected – that nearly cost me my sanity.

You see, I looked into the mirror one final time.

What I saw froze me in mid stride. I was standing perfectly still and so was everything else in the room but a tall shadow was nevertheless crossing the length of the mirror. Transfixed and unbreathing, I prayed that it would merely complete its stroll to the other side and then disappear. Instead, at the last moment, it made a startled motion and stopped where it was, directly in front of me. The frantic beating of my heart became audible. My unblinking eyes remained riveted upon the dark shape that seemed to be *beyond* my own superimposed reflection.

It occurred to me then that the shadow must be standing directly behind me. That something evil was breathing on the back of my neck. That any false move would mean certain death.

Suddenly, the dark shape leapt to the side of the mirror and vanished. I, with a yelp, regained control of my body and moved so quickly that I do not, to this day, remember leaving the room, only that I was once again in the hallway, trembling outside the closed door.

I was still shivering when I got back to my room. Even the heat from the fire didn't warm me. Only as time passed did I become more confident that nothing was going to happen to me. At some point, I became aware of an uncomfortable lump wedged tightly between my arm and my ribs. I pulled it out and found the dove wrapped in burlap. I'd kept it with me all that time not as a result of any great presence of mind but only because of the panicky tightness of my stricken muscles.

I flung it into the fire and watched it burn. By then, I'd regained enough self possession to move the remains about with a poker until all of it had been consumed. By the time I was satisfied, my shivering had stopped and I was able to go to bed.

The following morning, my fear from the night before was just a memory. In daylight it was easy to convince myself that the moving shadow had been only a trick of the candlelight. By that evening, I'd grown so smug I found it hard to keep from breaking into a gloating smile every time I looked at Maman.

Even so, I did what I could to avoid entering her room alone or in the dark.

A period of waiting followed during which a more courteous, respectful and obedient little girl couldn't have been found. I knew it was only a matter of time before Maman stumbled across my little masterpiece since she often wore that hat to church. Still, as the days went by and nothing happened, my mind became occupied with other things.

The music of the night turned out to be a fairly regular occurrence, growing more potent as time wore on. At last, without really expecting much, I told my nanny, Madame Jenner, all about it. Before I could even finish my story the poor lady made the sign of the cross and whispered urgently that one should not speak of such matters. I was not angry, for I sensed that her response, however unhelpful, was honest. I'd halfway expected her to be ignorant in any case since no one but my mother and myself spent the night in our house. From the earliest times, I could remember the grand exodus of servants to the village every evening at sunset. Always in the past, I accepted this arrangement. Now, I was beginning to wonder about it.

I started listening more closely to the whispering of the various domestics.

The amazing things I learned as I spied upon the staff only fueled my curiosity. I was afraid to leave my bed at night since my scare in Maman's bed chamber. But all of it, the stories, the music and most especially the voice, had a peculiar drawing power that was becoming harder to resist. I couldn't help remembering the stories I so painstakingly read in Latin about Odysseus. He'd heard about the bewitching voice of the siren that drove men mad and tied himself to the mast of his ship while still far away. But as soon as he heard the siren's voice he became like a rabid animal, struggling to free himself so he could jump overboard and drown in the ocean. I felt very like Odysseus, lying there in bed, my cowardice acting for many a night like the leather thongs that had bound that legendary mariner.

In the end, I had no choice but to get up and follow. Despite the profound joy the voice inspired within me, I told myself that the only reason I was following the music was to discover its source. This proved impossible. The singing seemed to come from everywhere at once with the single exception of the particular spot I was inspecting at any given moment. With my ear against the wall in the hallway, I would inevitably hear the sounds even more clearly from the opposite wall. With my ear to the opposite wall, I would become certain the sound was coming from a closet. I spent many nights in this fashion, wandering the house in quest of that illusive song until at last, it would cease altogether, leaving me shivering in the darkness of early morning.

During the daylight hours, when our house was filled with sunshine, I sometimes revisited the places I'd gone at night. It was all to no avail and I came to the conclusion that the whispering servants were right. Our house was haunted.

On Sunday morning, two weeks after I'd asked my mother about the music and she'd pretended to know nothing, I was sitting downstairs, waiting for her to finish her interminable preparations so we could go to church. Just as I had the previous Sunday, I strained my ears for any unusual sounds coming from the upstairs apartments. It was just after I decided I'd have to wait another week that I heard the scream. I ran up the stairs two at a time and got to Maman's room before anyone else. I pushed open the door without attempting to hide my smugness.

The sight that greeted me succeeded in wiping the exultant smile from my face. Maman was lying on the floor, the overturned hatbox a few steps from her. She didn't appear to be breathing. With a cry, I threw myself down beside her, certain I'd killed her.

I kissed her face and called her over and over until someone who'd entered without my being aware, succeeded in restraining me. Several of the servants had come into the room, summoned by the scream just as I had been. One of the maids took my place on the floor and began slapping Maman's cheeks, rather roughly, I thought. Some of the others, in an obvious state of upset, milled about and created confusion.

It was Cook, arriving completely unruffled a few minutes later, who took charge. Ox-like, in both physical build and imperturbability, she glanced at Maman, declared that she'd fainted and sent Elise, the maid who was holding me, back down to some special place in the kitchen where she kept a supply of aromatic vinegar. In the meantime, Cook ordered two of the men to carry Maman to her bed and then sent them away.

By the time she'd done that and then loosened Maman's clothing, the maid had returned. She uncorked the bottle as Cook directed and held the open mouth up to Maman's face until her eyelids fluttered and she awoke. At first, I was beside myself with relief and stood there behind the rest of the observers peeking foolishly around and between them in a vain attempt to catch a glimpse of her. But just as the roosters in the barnyard used their big bodies to keep the smaller chickens from the grain, the gaping crowd managed just as effectively to cut me off from any sight of my mother.

Forgotten chick, left to my own devices, I soon cleared the giddiness from my mind and observed that the box was still lying on the floor. Quietly, I sidled over and righted it, catching a brief impression of advanced corruption spread everywhere. I couldn't help gagging as the smell of it reached me. A furtive glance toward the group around the bed confirmed that no one was paying me the slightest attention, so I retrieved the cover, put it back on the box and carried the whole thing out of the room under their very noses.

I went downstairs and hid it in the upper cellar where the piles of junk would camouflage it as nothing else could. It would be very easy to return after dark, bring it back up to my room and burn it in the fireplace.

I returned to Maman's bedroom to hear her frenzied raving and the servants telling her that there was no rat in the house. As I stood there watching the proceedings through the mirror, a most delicious feeling of power blossomed inside me. My prank had been successful beyond my wildest dreams and with slowly growing comprehension, I came to understand that I, Lotte, had reduced my mother to hysterics. No longer would she hide her petty secrets from me. I would pull them from her one by one, threatening her with even more horrible surprises if she dared thwart my will.

Without warning, my attention was caught, not by the reflection of the preceding drama, but by a vicious face leering back at me from the mirror. I jumped back, thinking that the shadow had returned. But the figure with the evil grin jumped away too and I realized I'd been startled by my own reflection. I laughed but was shaken.

As it turned out, scaring myself was the least of my worries. That evening, when I went back to the cellar to retrieve the box, it was gone. That night, I had the most horrifying nightmare of my life. I dreamed I awoke. But I couldn't really have awakened because I wasn't in bed. I was in a dark place I'd never seen before and was seated in some sort of vat with my arms pulled tightly behind me. I couldn't move them and reasoned by the pressure and bracelets of soreness around my wrists, that they were bound. My entire body, except for my head and bare feet, was submerged in a gelatinous substance that gave the impression of bubbling and frothing. The darkness, though, made it impossible to be sure. The sensation was disconcerting and I tried to stand up only to discover that my ankles, too, were bound. This, combined with my position and the weight of the substance was sufficient to keep me pinned and almost completely immobile.

At first, I systematically tested my bonds, trying to slip numb fingers into knots. But my own body wedged my hands against the side of the vat so securely that there was no room for me to work. At the same time, the nature of the substance was truly starting to worry me. It felt like fat, slimy little bodies with sticky feet were creeping across my belly and slipping between my legs. The more I focused on it, the more certain I became. There was something alive in there with me.

Suddenly overcome by panic, I hurled my hobbled body from side to side, pulling wildly at my fetters and realizing only then that there was nothing I could do. I was completely at the mercy of whoever had put me there and if they didn't come back I would never get out. *Never.* I started screaming. The light increased. I flung myself harder and screamed even more frantically. The living toads in which I'd been covered became frightened themselves and started jumping in all directions.

I remember nothing more.

In the morning, I awoke in my own bed, my body covered with a brownish-green slime.

From then on Maman was quite safe from any of my practical jokes.

Chapter Two

Several months later, I celebrated my eighth birthday. It was a birthday I was destined to remember for the rest of my life. That very evening, after the party was cleared away and I'd climbed into bed, Maman came to tuck me in, carrying a glass of the most noxious-looking substance I'd ever seen. She looked nervous which put me on my guard.

"Drink this," she said, extending the glass.

"What is it?" I took a tentative sniff and turned away as my stomach rolled over.

"It's medicine," she said.

"Poison, you mean."

"It's important that you drink it." The only sign she'd noticed my sarcasm was an increase in listlessness.

I wasn't convinced.

"It's because *he* wants to speak to you," she added with obvious reluctance.

This caught my attention. "Who wants to speak to me?"

She sighed. "The angel."

If I hadn't spent the previous few months chasing phantom voices around the house, I would have dismissed her reply with a snort. As things stood, I was intrigued.

"What angel is this?" I asked. "Is it that voice I'm always hearing at night?"

"I don't know what you've been hearing at night," she said, "but he can only talk to you if you drink this."

The thing is, I couldn't imagine downing the stuff. It smelled like something retrieved from the water closet and the fact that she was trying so hard to get me to swallow anything so obviously unpalatable amazed me. See, if she'd wanted to put me out of my misery, she could have made me some tea using the tainted water from the creek down the road. Any creature that drank that water died. And the beauty of poisoning me in such a manner would have been that I'd never suspect it.

All of which meant she wasn't trying to kill me.

"This had better not make me sick," I said.

Her anemic complexion drew a shade or two paler but she didn't back off. Which piqued my curiosity in a way nothing else could have. She'd definitely been respecting my warnings of late unaware, it seemed, of the special protection she enjoyed.

Amazing though it may seem, I did end up not only downing the stuff but also going to extraordinary lengths not to vomit it back up. It took a few minutes before I sensed a numbness coming over my body, starting in my stomach and radiating outward. I threw my mother a frantic look but she avoided eye contact. I tried to stick a finger down my throat but found I couldn't move. My eyelids dropped shut as if the threads holding them had been cut.

I was trapped inside my own body but my mind seemed more alert than ever. I couldn't have moved a hand or opened my eyes to save my soul but I was aware of the muted click as Maman closed the door behind her and the muffled sound of her footsteps retreating down the hall. I was also aware when the door to my room opened again and an icy draught of foul-smelling air swept toward me.

I tried to jump up but my muscles remained loose and unresponsive. I sensed that something unspeakable was coming toward me yet I was powerless to do anything to save myself. The whimpers that would have burgeoned into throat tearing screams stayed locked inside me.

My frenzied writhing was nothing more than the throes of a trapped spirit bashing itself back and forth like a bird inside a cage. Unstoppable, those footsteps approached my bedside, that sewer stink settling inside of me like a poisonous fog. I knew a creature from my darkest nightmares was standing there beside me. I imagined it slimy and corrupt like Maman's dead rat but with teeth like razors, claws like nails and possessed of a mindless, insatiable hunger.

Then, a most unexpected thing happened. My name was spoken by the most beautiful voice I'd ever heard. It was more beautiful, even, than the siren's. There was a sweetness to it and a resonance to it like nothing I could have imagined. And unlike the siren, whose tones were crystalline and high, this voice was unmistakably male.

"Lotte?" it said. "Lotte, my dear, don't be frightened. I'm only the angel of whom your mother spoke. I've watched over you ever since you were born and love you with all my heart."

He went on in that vein, speaking reassuring words in a soothing tone. I was not immediately able to come to terms with the contradictory impressions I was receiving and assumed the clammy choking stink was connected in some way to the voice. Still, as time wore on and nothing hurt me, I found myself allowing the voice to calm me. Strange too was how his almost paternal use of the term "dear," began to warm a very secret place in my heart. There was something very special about being addressed by something that beautiful in such obvious terms of affection. I think anyone who heard that voice would want to be loved by the being that possessed it.

Somehow, he was able to sense this shift in my state of mind. Although the voice remained as heartbreakingly gorgeous as it had been from the start, he changed his tack and used it instead to tell me the most delightfully irreverent anecdotes. His descriptions of the house staff were cruelly accurate. He had Cook's provincial dialect down to the last swallowed r. He used it to say very "un-Cook-like" things, supplying me with new and colorful swear words – not to mention some truly disgusting concepts – that were certain to scandalize everyone.

Seemingly encouraged, he roasted a few of the other servants, replaying what I soon understood to be their supposed reactions to some of my pranks. This, truth be told, was unnerving, for he obviously knew more than anyone should have about what I'd been up to. The longer it continued, the more uneasy I became. He, on the other hand, so caught up in his own farcical renditions of bygone events, didn't seem to realize how much he was starting to scare me.

On and on he went, speaking more rapidly, more frantically, an ugly manic edge beginning to show through the richness of his tones. Finally he forgot himself so thoroughly as to punctuate his narrative with a sinister, throaty chuckle that turned the blood in my veins to ice. He stopped short, belatedly realizing, I think, that he'd lost control of himself. A moment later, I felt him lean directly over me and I knew he was studying my useless, flaccid form.

"I do believe I've frightened you," he said, as though such a thing would never have occurred to him had he not seen it for himself. "No need, my dear, I assure you. Still – " And here his voice took on a subtle tone of menace. " – In my opinion, that nonsense with the rat was quite beneath you – not to say that the work itself was completely without its charm. But it's imperative you learn to distinguish between those who matter in this world and those who merely take up space."

With a groan, he turned away and began prowling the room, muttering curses and self-deprecations that I knew I wasn't supposed to be hearing. Every time his pacing brought him nearer the bed, my heart pounded faster. The fiery rage building up inside him was almost palpable and I waited in silent agony for a pair of blood-encrusted talons to close around my throat.

He sighed and then for the next few minutes or so made no sound at all. I don't really know how long this went on but I began to wonder, first, if maybe he'd dissolved back into the ether. And next, if I hadn't just dreamed the whole thing. I even attempted to shift my position, though that proved as impossible as it had previously been.

All at once, he moved. I barely had a chance to mentally react to a slight creak of the floorboards before he came arrowing toward me. In a moment, he was beside me again, closer than he'd yet dared to stand. I felt a slight depression in the mattress at my side and knew he was resting his elbows there. I couldn't have been breathing and waited only for death, silently praying that it wouldn't hurt too much. But close as he was, he never touched me. That beautiful voice, when he finally spoke, was weary and sad.

"It's late," he said, "And almost time for me to leave you. Don't judge your angel too harshly. He loves you more than you could ever imagine and no matter what he sometimes says or does, he could never truly harm you. Trust me, Lotte, and I will bring to you greater joy than anything you've ever experienced."

And he began to sing.

If you can comprehend how deeply that voice affected me when only speaking, just imagine what it would be like when it sang. From the very first note, I was so completely lost in the miracle of that perfect voice that it no longer mattered that my body had turned to stone. His music lifted me like a feather and carried me on the wings of melody to a beautiful place I'd never known. If I were a prisoner, I didn't care, for my heart was expanding with sweetness and warmth, my body alive with vibrant sensation. No longer trapped, my soul found the freedom of eternity, soaring ever higher in joyous celebration. Oh, what rapture my angel taught me. How close, how tantalizingly close, did he bring me to heaven.

But barely was the ultimate glory within reach, when I felt myself falling, for he couldn't sing forever, cruel angel, who only offered a taste and then denied me the cup. Fleeting and ephemeral, the notes died away, the bedroom door closed and the air around my bed began slowly to warm. And I, wretched mortal, experienced the greatest emptiness of my life. Oppressive silence filled the vacuum and the memory of the music to which I tried so desperately to cling, faded, leaving me with nothing more than the ghost of an aching, impossible beauty. My heart cried out to him, begging him to return. And I discovered, without really caring, that even paralyzed, I was able to weep.

The next morning, I thought I was going to vomit up my very organs. The viselike pressure all around my head was somehow in my stomach as well, keeping me retching even when there was nothing left inside. Maman was back, fluttering around, as ineffectual as always, trying to put damp cloths on my forehead. I dare say I was completely useless until that evening. But before I finally drifted off into the deep dreamless sleep that my exhausted body craved, I heard the song of the siren again.

I think that for the rest of the month, my mother must have felt as though she were taking her life in her hands every time she opened a drawer. True, the medicine had made me suffer. True, that guilty way she always behaved around me was maddening. But I remembered being bound in a tub full of toads and found it easier than you might imagine to resist the temptation to torture her again.

Besides, I had to admit that without the medicine, I would never have met the angel. That would have been unbearable. I couldn't think about the unique way he had of speaking to me – as if he cared about me deeply – without an inner pang and a tendency to tears. At such times I actually missed him and found the inner voice of my mind calling out to him and begging him to come back to me.

Inevitably, though, thoughts of a second visit brought back other memories, memories of corruption and cold, memories of a wicked sense of humor that crossed the line, memories of strength held barely in check, of a mind not completely under control. Always I remembered the music, both beautiful and terrible. I didn't know if I could survive such an experience a second time.

And I longed for it with such desperation that I could think of little else.

It was therefore with both excitement and terror that I viewed my mother the following month, that guilty look back on her face and another glassful of that noisome substance in her hand.

I drank it, of course. And every proceeding month I drank it again. Always I put up a token resistance. Always I capitulated in the end. The only time I was spared was when Maman took one of her mysterious trips to Paris and I, evicted from my home, was forced to spend the month with Cook in the village. Away from the house on the hill there was no medicine and no angel but immediately upon Maman's return and my reinstallation in my own quarters, the old routine began again.

The angel, during successive visits, spoke to me of many things. Though I couldn't respond, I felt as though a bond were forming between us. His ability to read me, uncanny during his first visit, seemed to improve over time. He would ramble on in his usual way and then suddenly stop, lean over me for a few moments and say something to prove that even my thoughts were not hidden from him. Certainly my actions were not. It was not unusual for him to start by telling me how clever I'd been when I'd done such and such, to so and so, hinting at some delectable outcome that I – not being able to pass amongst the servants unseen – couldn't have witnessed.

He would hint, as I said. He would begin the tale of the scullery maid walking down the steps to the wine cellar. He'd say how she put her hand on the knob and turned the key in the lock. He'd say how she started to open the door, how the lever from the trap I'd installed started to move, how the rope tightened, how a few grains of sand sprinkled from the bag. And then he'd go off on some tangent, giving me suggestions, for example, on how to better steady the apparatus so there would be less play in the rope, how to control the size of an explosion by regulating the amount of powder in the firecracker, how to wind the spring in the finger trap so that next time the stable boy wouldn't escape unassisted.

From there, he'd further digress into a whole treatise on mechanical engineering, maddeningly oblivious to my slavering impatience to hear the end of the original account. He'd go on and on, throwing in stories sometimes about an architect in Persia who'd built a whole puzzle box the size of a palace or an engineer in Turkey who'd built a mechanical man that resembled the Sultan to such a degree that it was able to conduct business in his stead. But in the end, after he'd said whatever else he wanted to say, he never failed to reward me, almost as an afterthought, with the intelligence I'd been so desperate to learn.

It didn't take me long to figure out he was doing this on purpose. It took me only slightly longer to realize that he was instructing me, casually dropping gems of wisdom that I was free to pick up or leave but never to ignore. He was so artful in weaving together the things I wanted to know with the things he wanted me to learn that I soon stopped trying to determine which was which. It was easier just to relax, to listen and to enjoy. For if nothing else, he was always entertaining.

I'm sure this eclectic approach of his was the reason I learned so much more from him than I ever did from my hired tutors. I'd always been one to enjoy learning but had little patience with the repetitive exercises they always seemed to find so indispensable. My instructors ignored me when I told them I already knew, or could do, whatever it was they were trying so hard to pound into me. To this day, I remember one particularly bad session in which Monsieur Duprès, my music teacher, insisted that I play through the circle of fifths on the piano, twenty times flawlessly. I told him I'd only do it if he did it first. There was a big argument, of course, and in the end no one played anything.

"You should have done it," the angel said a few evenings later. "You and I both know *he* never could have. But you could, blindfolded and in your sleep. Don't challenge him with words but with deeds. Your very ability to carry out whatever ridiculous instructions he gives you will be what ultimately renders him microscopic. Then too, there's always the chance that one of these days, purely by accident, he'll actually teach you something. You must never completely discount the possibility of learning something even from a hopeless imbecile."

I did as the angel described and found that this sort of revenge truly was the sweetest. As I became more adept, I embellished upon the original, confessing to M. Duprès, after playing everything to perfection that I'd neglected to practice any of the exercises he'd assigned. It was also very gratifying to watch the changing expressions on his face when I gave a cursory examination to the violin he handed me one day and then played music upon it as if I'd been practicing for months. Since the laws of acoustics were the same no matter which instrument I played, it was only a matter of understanding the mechanics of the particular instrument in question before being able to produce any melody with which I was already familiar. In the following weeks, M. Duprès brought any number of different instruments for me to try and I repeated my performance on each of them. I know he was impressed despite all his loud disapproval. In fact, I can say that everyone in the household was awed by my musical abilities except for my mother who, as far as I knew, had never heard me play.

No doubt due to the siren, as time wore on and my lessons continued, I found myself leaning more in the direction of vocal music. Just as with the musical instruments, I learned quickly. Despite my tender years, certain folk songs and lieder were soon within my grasp. Less than satisfied, I wanted to sing Mozart's "Der Hölle Rache kocht in meinem Herzen," but M. Duprès wouldn't budge in his opinion that I would have to wait until my voice matured before I attempted opera. In the end, I had to content myself with lyricism in lieu of fireworks and was not completely displeased with my interpretation of certain country airs.

Still, the day M. Duprès invited Maman to come to the music room to hear me sing I became so nervous that I actually threw up. Following that, I told my teacher that I didn't want to sing for her. M. Duprès threw a prima donna's fit of his own which only firmed my resolve. But when he saw that his tantrum was doing no good, he took me aside and spoke to me as he never had before, admitting to me, for the first time, that my talent was something extraordinary and that my singing voice, though still that of a child, was truer than any other voice he'd ever heard.

"Please, Mlle. Charlotte," he pleaded, "Sing for your Maman. She will be so surprised."

'Do you think so?" I asked, imagining her, all at once, running to me with tears in her eyes and telling me I was a good girl.

"I know so," he answered with such conviction that I allowed him to steer me unresisting to my usual spot at the curve of the piano.

Maman had brought her sewing with her and had continued working on it throughout the previous scenario. She continued even during M. Duprès' stiff, metronomic introduction and as my own entrance loomed, I began to wonder whether or not this performance were a mistake. Too late, though. I was already starting. As the angel had taught me, I tried to allow nothing to distract me. I'd chosen for my performance, the "Skye Boat Song," a simple Scottish melody that I'd always thought lovely. It was well within my range and technical grasp, so I was able to concentrate on tone quality, phrasing and the infinitesimal nuances that were supposed to mark the difference between a live musician and a mechanical box.

But as I sang, I became increasingly aware of the thinness of my voice and the forced artificiality of my interpretation. Surprised that I'd never noticed any of this before, I was still unable to deny that it had been there all along. For some reason, performing for Maman was making me more aware of everything. Never in my life had I tried so hard to create something wonderful and moving.

Never in my life had I failed so utterly.

The servants standing by the door applauded with enthusiasm. M. Duprès had an odd catch in his voice when he came around to congratulate me. They almost made me believe I'd done something noteworthy. After several minutes of this gushing profusion, I found the strength to look once more at Maman who had indeed put down her sewing. My heart leapt and for one moment, I thought I'd actually touched her. But her gaze remained averted. And in another moment I understood the reason. She couldn't bring herself to look at me.

I bit my lip because I refused to allow anyone to see me cry and left the room with what dignity I could manage. Mme. Jenner, followed me out and tried to comfort me without understanding the reason for my disappointment.

"You can't expect your mother to notice things other people do, Mlle. Charlotte," she said gently. "The poor lady has had a very hard life and is still haunted by it."

I know that to the outsider it often appeared as though my mother's head were as empty as a drum. Her disconcerting habit of talking to the walls, hiding behind the curtains and pressing her body up against that accursed mirror was bound to give people that impression. But just too often, I'd seen her eyes suddenly focus into hard points and heard her say something so exceedingly perceptive that I knew there was a sharp mind behind that dreamy façade. For this reason, I couldn't so easily explain away her inability to look at me after my performance. Though she was always denying it, I was convinced that she too was acquainted with the siren's voice. Was it simply that she was comparing my voice to the siren's – as I had – and found mine lacking? Or was it, perhaps, that nothing I did could ever move her?

I pondered both these possibilities long and hard, though since the second implied no hope, I had to put my confidence in the first. All things considered, I was a very lucky girl. After all, how many other children had the benefit of comparing themselves to the siren? I was convinced that all I had to do was learn the secrets of that voice and apply them to myself. The immediate problem, however, was their discovery. I thought my tones were true, my rhythms accurate and my pitch as close to perfect as my ear could discern. Still, there was an inexplicable "something" present in the siren's music that was *not* present in my own. I did my best to find the missing ingredients and cannot begin to describe the tortures I inflicted upon my poor vocal cords to that end.

One day, frustrated and hoarse from my own self-abuse, I finally did the unthinkable. I asked M. Duprès if there was something wrong with my singing. He took advantage of my uncertainty to give me an earful about practice making perfect and all kinds of other drivel that I mentally reduced to a dull buzz in the background. He knew nothing. But it occurred to me that there *was* someone who'd know the answer and who would make no bones about telling me straight. My angel. The problem was, I was a piece of inert meat whenever he came to me. I thought about my dilemma and about the concoction that reduced me to such a useless state. According to Maman, it was only this "medicine" that enabled me to hear him at all. But I began to wonder. And in the end I devised an experiment.

Throughout my childhood, I'd conducted many experiments. I liked to think of myself as the "mad scientist" sometimes, like Doctor Frankenstein. But in reality, my "laboratory" which I'd set up in a tiny room off the wine cellar, more closely resembled a tinker's shop. I put together little mechanical toys there, some of them nasty, like the finger trap, but most of them benign. I also enjoyed inventing machines that would do the work that people normally did. I once even scribbled down some drawings for a series of devices that could cook an egg, toast a piece of bread and deliver the breakfast tray to my room via the dumb waiter.

This time, however, the experiment wasn't for the purpose of testing a machine but rather the reliability of my mother's word. The next time I was served up the brew, I did my usual griping, waited until Maman was looking away and then poured the whole mess under the covers. It was cold and slimy but I'd known worse. After I'd curled up comfortably, she kissed me on the part of my body nearest to her – which turned out to be my ear – and floated out the door. I would almost have thought the pounding of my heart would give me away. The thrill of expectation alone made it difficult to lie still.

I don't know how long I really waited before I heard footsteps outside my door. It seemed an eternity. I had plenty of time to consider my predicament and convince myself that I'd made a mistake. What did I know, after all, about this angel? What kind of creature brought with it draughts of frigid air and the noisome stench of the grave? What could it possibly look like? For some reason, I doubted it resembled the depictions of celestial beings painted on the ceiling at church.

It was this train of thought that finally caused me to consider a possibility I'd avoided thinking about before. What if it weren't really an angel at all that came to me in the darkness? What if it were something hideous and malevolent? Unbidden, some of his more caustic remarks and that evil, throaty chuckle came to mind.

It was then I heard the footsteps. It was then the doorknob began to turn. It was then I broke into a cold sweat and decided to act as though I'd taken the medicine. The door opened and the clammy atmosphere of the tomb closed in around me. It combined with the sweat on my skin to make the hairs on my arms stand on end. I could easily imagine the hair on my head doing the same as that pestilential presence approached my bedside. It took all the will power I possessed to keep myself from gagging on the smell that filled my nostrils and penetrated my mouth.

The first sound out of him was that menacing chuckle. "Go ahead, vomit if you have to. It's the usual reaction. You'll get used to me in time, though. Heaven knows but my Christine was able to do it."

I didn't so much as cough.

"You might as well say something," he said, the pitch of his voice rising. "I know very well you didn't take your medicine tonight, you naughty girl. You think your silly attempts to hide it fooled anyone around here? Only yourself, I'll wager. You're just like Christine. Unable to resist a peek behind the curtain. Well, now you've done it, so you might as well go ahead and say something. And don't pretend you haven't been dying to answer me back with that nasty little mouth of yours, you saucy girl. I know you too well for that."

Unfortunately, the nasty little mouth in question was speechless and trembling.

Even with my back to him, I could feel his wrath mounting and I knew that if the idea of living to see another dawn appealed to me at all, I'd better say something soon. Replaying his angry diatribe in my mind, I latched onto something I didn't understand and at the last possible moment discovered a question I could ask. "Who's Christine?"

There was a moment of stunned silence.

"Christine?" he said. "Why your mother, of course. Don't you know your mother's name?"

I had the feeling my sudden stupidity was going to get me killed but after all, no one before had ever been so bold as to use my mother's Christian name. Somewhat defensively, I told him so.

"No, I suppose not," he said. "But the word 'mother . . . ' You must be made to understand . . . That particular word is repugnant to me and I just cannot use it in association with Christine."

"You were right," I began with full knowledge of the words to assuage a wounded ego. "I didn't take my medicine because I *did* want to talk to you. I've been having a problem with my . . . with Christine, and I knew you'd be able to help me."

"What kind of problem?" he asked suspiciously.

I believe at the time I thought I was going to say something about her indifference to my musical talents. What I actually said was, "Why doesn't she like me?"

To my surprise perhaps as much as to his, I burst into tears. God only knows where it all came from but I really was wailing and keening and making quite an ass of myself. After a few moments of that disgusting display, I felt a weight lower itself upon the edge of the bed. I knew he was sitting right there, inches from my back. A bony hand, as icy as death, began to stroke my hair, the smell of putrefaction so strong at that close proximity that I began retching. I can only hope he attributed it to the violent sobbing rather than his own presence, though I fear it would have been impossible to deceive him. To his credit, he continued to stroke me and to whisper my name over and over until I managed to get myself under control.

By the time the sobs had become intermittent, I found a freshly laundered handkerchief in my hand and I used it to wipe my face. He seemed to know better than to put any part of his anatomy near my nose or mouth but as soon as I was myself again, I noticed he kept one hand pressed firmly against my temple so I couldn't roll onto my back and look at him. His voice was gentle when he spoke. There was no longer any hint of sarcasm. "Oh, Lotte," he said, "You have no idea how much Christine loves you. You've been blessed with the most beautiful . . . mother any child could wish for. She would do anything for you."

"No," I said. "My mother doesn't even know I'm alive. She walks around with her eyes wide open but she doesn't see anything. If something happened to me, she wouldn't even notice."

"There you're wrong," he said. "Christine sees more than either of us. She lives on a completely different plane. She listens regularly to the conversation of angels and cannot be bothered with the normal or the mundane. But she does love you. If you heard her speak of you, as I have, you'd no longer doubt."

"Has she spoken to you then?" I asked.

"Oh yes." He sighed. "Many a night have we spoken."

"Who are you?"

But he only shushed me and promised "You will know all, child. But you must be patient and wait until the time is right."

I was tired of evasion. Up until that moment I'd felt as though I were somehow special to him. But there he was, perpetuating the big mystery, just as Maman always did. Worse yet, the two of them had been discussing me. He must have noticed my stiffening for he took the coward's way out. Rather than try to soften the blow or offer any kind of explanation he began, instead, to sing. I fought him, despite the rare beauty of his music. Infinitely more powerful, he compelled me to sleep. My eyelids became heavy and I was not aware of the moment when he removed his hand from my head.

The click of the door and the return of warm air revived me. Although my body felt oddly lethargic, I forced myself to get up and put my ear to the door. I heard his retreating footsteps. When I was pretty sure he'd rounded the corner, I dared to crack open the door and take a peek. There was no one in sight but I heard the murmur of voices down the next hallway. I crept to a place where I might stick out my head and see what was on the other side.

It was dark, though some small amount of light was coming in through the floor to ceiling windows. What I saw at first was a figure dressed in white, which I realized in another moment was my mother in her nightgown. She did look beautiful with her long flaxen hair flowing behind her, like an angel in the moonlight. Slowly I became aware of another figure standing beside her, a tall figure dressed from head to toe in black, with one dark arm around her waist. She was leaning on him slightly as they walked down the hall.

And then, impossibly, they shrank into the floor. It was as though the darkness had taken on substance and swallowed them. I ran to the spot where they'd been but the hallway was empty except for me.

Chapter Three

I believe I was up earlier the following morning than I'd ever been before or ever will be again. Dressed in my most comfortable frock even before the rim of the sun had broken the horizon, I was back at the corner of the hallway where last I'd seen the ghostly couple. So many questions were buzzing in my skull that I actually had to make a conscious effort to stop and examine each thought one by one. It was tantalizing to imagine that my maman was part spirit, as the "angel" had implied, and could come and go between our two worlds at will. Still, my more rational side leaned toward an equally intriguing if earthly explanation, namely some kind of hidden door in the corner. I examined the paneling, paying special attention to the junctures but found nothing unusual. I tapped on the wall at various intervals and discovered that there was indeed a section that had a more hollow sound than the rest. Encouraged, I narrowed my search to that portion of the wall, examining it again but still finding nothing. I started again with the tapping. With care and patience I was able to discover exactly the spot where the door must be and had I dared, could have easily outlined it in chalk. But there was no break, no hidden lever, no loosened board. It was maddening. In despair, I gave the wall a mighty kick just as Mme. Jenner turned the corner and as luck would have it, just in time for her to see me do it.

"Mlle. Charlotte," she cried, shock and indignation registering in her voice.

I looked at her sheepishly, my busy mind already concocting some rubbish about the rats I could hear, squeaking and scurrying behind the paneling. She took my hand without demanding an explanation, however, and towed me back to my room where breakfast was waiting. I noticed it consisted only of tea and broth. Obviously, Cook had expected me to be ill.

"Hurry up and eat," Mme. Jenner said without seeming to notice the breakfast I'd been served. "We're going to have to pack your things and move you down to the village before noon."

"Today?" I asked. "I thought I wasn't going until tomorrow."

"That's what we all thought," she said. I sensed that the irritation in her voice wasn't directed at me. "Your mother just informed us that she'll be leaving for Paris this afternoon."

So Maman knew. All along she'd known I wouldn't be ill and consequently that I'd not taken my medicine. Quite deflated, I sat down to my meager breakfast. At the first spoonful, my disappointment transformed into fury.

"What kind of bloody breakfast is this?" I shouted.

I believe Mme. Jenner would have slapped my face had she feared me only a little less. "How dare you show such ingratitude," she cried. "You will eat what the good Lord provides."

"I won't," I shouted back, tears in my eyes.

It had just dawned on me that if Maman had known in advance I wouldn't be sick, she could have told Cook to send up a regular breakfast. It was just like her to use the knowledge to her own advantage and leave a day early while completely forgetting about my breakfast. She never thought of me. My face felt hot and for a moment all I could see was red. I stood up, deliberately knocked over the bowl of soup and ran out in a rage. I got to my mother's room and flung open the door.

It was bright with morning sunshine and Maman, still in her dressing gown, was seated at her little writing desk. So intent was she on her project that she didn't even flinch at the sound of my violent entrance. I stomped noisily over to her table and when that also elicited no response, reached over to rip the paper from her hands. I caught a glimpse of what she was doing and stopped cold. Without looking up, she continued to copy from a red-inked manuscript on her left to the staves of blank music paper on her right. My mother was copying music. I'd had no idea she employed her time in such a fashion. Why was she doing it herself? Surely she could have paid someone. Was it her own, perhaps? Was Maman a composer without my even knowing?

I looked at the manuscript itself, my mother so oblivious to my presence that I felt as if I were perusing it in a room by myself. It looked to be some sort of piano piece, a polonaise, and though written in A major, had a haunting quality that I thought very likely to bring tears to my eyes were I ever to hear it played. Though vaguely familiar, as something only partially remembered from a dream, I was certain I'd never played it.

In the end, I decided that Maman was not the composer because the handwriting of the original was very sloppy, almost like mine, whereas the black ink copy, despite the speed at which she was throwing it down, was very crisp and painstakingly neat.

"Maman?" I whispered.

She looked up then and I realized by her focused gaze that she'd been aware of me all along.

"Yes, dear?" she responded, sounding slightly rushed, as if pressed for time.

"What are you doing?"

"Just copying over this manuscript."

"Why?"

"I'm bringing it with me to Paris today and I always feel better knowing there's a copy safe at home."

A pained expression crossed her face when I gingerly lifted a page of the red-inked manuscript to study it more closely. "This is nice," I said.

"Yes, it is." She reached for it. "Now put it back, dear, I really must finish this before I leave."

"Can I go with you?" I asked.

"No dear, of course not."

"But why not?" A whining tone was creeping into my voice and I could feel my lower lip beginning to jut.

Instead of answering, she began to fuss with my collar.

"I really wish you'd put on another frock," she said in that motherly tone I despised. "This one is so old and worn out. I'll have to tell Mme. Jenner to get rid of it. Have you packed?"

"No."

"Have you had your breakfast?"

"No." And the anger of a short time ago came rushing back. "Why didn't you tell Cook to make me a regular breakfast?"

"Because I expected you'd not want a regular breakfast this morning."

"But you knew I wouldn't be sick." My tone was triumphant. "I know you did because you already knew that you could leave today instead of tomorrow."

"I suppose I forgot," she answered, her tone perfunctory. "Why don't you run along down to the kitchen and ask Cook to make you something that you like?"

"Okay," I answered, giving her an evil grin and darting from the room with the page of the manuscript still in my hand.

"Lotte," she shouted.

I don't know why I was enjoying myself so much. I was truly angry. Even so, I laughed as I dashed down the stairs with Maman running down behind me. She looked very undignified when I glimpsed her, passing by me on the upper level as the stairs switched back below the landing. Still way ahead, I darted into the dining room and crossed its expanse, ultimately slamming into the swinging door that led to the kitchen and nearly knocking down Cook who was standing just the other side. Recovering from her momentary upset, Cook regained her balance and caught me by the wrist. Maman moved to snatch the sheet from me but I transferred it to the other hand and held it over the pot of soup that was cooling on the table.

"Take me with you," I said, "Or I'll drop it."

"You'll do no such thing," Cook said, seizing my other wrist in an iron grip.

She squeezed hard. My fingers went numb, my hold weakened and Cook caught the page just as I let it go. Maman took back the page calmly though her face was still flushed and her breathing heavy.

"Cook, please make Lotte something solid for breakfast. It seems she isn't as ill as we thought."

I stared at Maman resentfully as she left the kitchen but she didn't look back.

Chapter Four

Maman was always the last to leave on these unexplained trips to Paris. She stayed behind until the very end, making sure that everything was securely locked and that all the servants were on their way to the village. None of them ever stayed behind to take care of the house. Its infamy was enough to ward off any would-be trespassers. When Maman was gone, it always fell upon the servants to look after me. I had, throughout my childhood, spent time with almost all of them in their own homes in the village. I believe they originally took turns amongst themselves so that none of them would have to put up with me for too long. In the end though it seemed Cook had taken the responsibility upon herself exclusively.

At first, I couldn't understand why she did it. Heaven knows, she had enough children of her own without taking on an additional headache such as myself. But as time passed, I began to notice at odd times her sharp little eyes focused upon me in an expression strangely akin to pity. Granted, she never did this when she thought I was looking.

Thus, it was hardly a surprise when Cook once again accompanied me to the village. Maman watched us from the front steps as we walked down the cobbled drive and out the gate but I refused to give her the satisfaction of looking back or waving good-bye. I was in a foul temper, the morning's events doing nothing to alleviate the rancor I always felt at compulsory exile. Even under the best of circumstances, I hated the village and all the stupid bumpkins who lived there, my downward-spiraling mood usually commencing in earnest with the first sight of the contaminated creek that ran parallel to the roadway. Inevitably, there was to be found either in the water itself or right alongside, the carcass of some poor animal that had come to drink. For some reason, there seemed to be more than the usual compliment of bodies this time. Although the standard fare was chickens, that particular trip yielded a small dog as well. I was greatly relieved when at last we reached the fork in the road and were able to leave the waterway behind us.

A little later, we crested a hill that gave upon the village. Dominating the nearer part of the valley was a great candy-striped tent that I'd never seen before. Cook became suddenly animated explaining that a circus had come to town and asked if I would like to see the show along with her own children. I shrugged but she persevered, describing all the wonders that a circus had to offer: the animals, the clowns, the acrobats. I thought she must be feeling sorry for me again.

Whatever her motivation, I found myself that very afternoon, on line outside that tent, so seemingly festive from the distance, so worn and dirty up close. I stood there, accompanied by Cook herself as well as her extensive gaggle of credulous brats. They were exclaiming in wonder at all the sights and sounds, at the wrinkled elephant with its big, fake ears, at the rusty calliope wailing like a kitchenful of tuneful tea kettles. I myself remained aloof and indifferent to such pedestrian wonders and only sniffed when one of the other children directed some enthusiastic comment at me. I was determined beforehand, you see, not to enjoy any of it.

I shouldn't have worried. The circus was appalling. Even Cook seemed disappointed by the threadbare costumes and aging acrobats. The clowns were so rough and loud that they frightened some of the younger children. I myself felt a lump form in my throat during the dog and pony act. An old crone with grapelike growths on her inner thighs ran around the ring in a pink tutu, a spangled whip in her hand. She used it to cut at a shaggy, one-eyed pony any time it hesitated to jump a hurdle. I wondered what had happened to the pony's other eye. Even the other members of the audience grew restless during that one and I sensed an air of general relief when the show was over and we all got to leave.

Outside, there were several rows of smaller tents, some with signs promising a closer view of the animals seen during the show. I must admit I was interested in spite of myself. Cook seemed to have an unlimited number of coins she produced magician-like from the folds of her skirts so that I understood it was Maman financing our little excursion. We went in and out of the tents and around and about the cages, looking at black and white striped horses, gigantic, pear-headed serpents and a big, black, hairy creature they called a gorilla that looked like some sort of deformed person. It was picking its nose and paying no attention to any of us.

Despite our loud objections, Cook told us the next row of tents was strictly off limits. She hurried us past posters promising glimpses of the smallest man in the world, the legless wonder, a pair of Siamese twins and many others. The first tent in the next row had a poster depicting a tropical scene in great detail. In the forefront was an enormous crocodile with a human leg protruding from its jaws. Cook eyed the poster with uncertainty.

"What does it say, Mlle. Charlotte?" she asked.

"It says 'The African Crocodile' Ma'am," I lied, having already read it and determined for myself that this was a curiosity I didn't want to miss.

She nodded decisively and our group attached itself to the small crowd already gathered. There was a clock with moveable hands set up at the entrance, indicating that the next viewing would be at 3:45. Since none of us carried a watch, we merely waited until they collected our coins and herded us inside. This tent, unlike the ones housing the menagerie, had no cage. Instead, there was a makeshift stage consisting of a sheet hung over a wire and a big wooden block. Since we children were small, we were able to weave our way in and out of the crowd to the very front of the roped-off area. Cook, because of her size, had to remain in the rear. She sounded as if she might have been protesting but who could tell with all the noise going on? Besides, the others were already following me up to the front.

Scarcely had we elbowed our way to the wire when a seedy showman with a matted beard came out from behind the sheet and began spinning some foolishness about a missionary and his wife who'd traveled through the deepest jungles of the Congo. Supposedly, the man fell into the water during a river crossing, his pregnant wife watching helplessly as a gigantic crocodile tore him limb from limb. This incident was such a shock to the poor lady that her child was spontaneously aborted, having inherited the characteristics of the monster that had eaten its father. The storyteller went on at some length, his eyes shifting from face to face in the crowd as he delivered the tale in a sonorous, theatrical voice. At some point he must have deemed us sufficiently softened, for he reduced the volume of his speech so we all had to strain forward to hear.

"With us today," he began, in the most tragic of tones, "is the living proof of this incredible story, the creature born prematurely yet surviving to adulthood through the ministrations of the native woman who found him and took him in.

"Ladies and gentlemen, with the greatest humility I offer you . . . the Crocodile Man."

All at once, the shadow of someone, or something could be discerned standing behind the sheet. There was a collective gasp as it revealed itself, naked except for a pair of trousers slit up the sides. In truth I was only able to get disjointed impressions of the thing as it moved past, for my eyes had fogged and I was suddenly unable to breathe. What I thought I saw was something resembling a man in that it had a head, two arms, two legs and wore clothing. Other than that, who could say? It was scaly, like a lizard and its body was covered with strange eruptions resembling yellow cauliflower. The head was maybe twice the size of a human head and so lumpy and asymmetrical that I was unable to find the face. It passed quite close to where I stood gaping, close enough for me to smell its reeking body.

It was this, I think, that was my final undoing. I knew that stench. It had become all too familiar in the months that the "angel" had visited me and I found myself choking. Was this what the "angel" looked like? Was this the creature that came to me in the night? Was this the thing that had sat on my bed, caressing my hair with its filthy claws?

I covered my face and crumpled to the ground. No one else seemed to notice. Vaguely I was aware that the thing had mounted the wooden block. There was the distant sound of a whip cracking as I struggled for air. The people seemed to be booing and whistling. Objects were flying over my head in all directions as the room began spinning and my vision grayed. All at once, I heard a horrific scream. It took me a moment to realize it was coming from me. Once I'd started, I couldn't stop and went on and on and on. My hysteria seemed to act as a catalyst, evoking similar reactions from others around me. The agitated crowd trampled my prostrate figure, inadvertently kicking my face and stepping on my hands. I tried to crawl away like some miserable dog, a forest of legs swirling around me, my head bobbing up and down and my crinkled face dripping with tears and sweat. Instinctively, I headed towards the light, but before I reached it, I felt an arm pass underneath me and pull me up.

"Come," said a woman's voice.

A hand closed around my upper arm and someone began pulling me along. We were outside the tent and hurrying across an open expanse. I got the brief impression of a large, enclosed cart before I was hauled up some steps and propelled into darkness. Someone sat me down upon the floor. Someone was bathing my face and wiping my nose. Slowly, my eyes adjusted to the gloom and I became aware of a lady sitting cross-legged in front of me, holding a rag to my nose and urging me to blow. She seemed quite young, little more than a girl herself, though I noticed she was balancing a baby on one of her legs, a baby who was, apparently, nursing. The girl noticed that I was looking at her and smiled.

"Better now?"

Her voice was as sweet as her face.

I nodded dumbly and became aware of other figures approaching us.

"You shouldn't have brought her here," said someone behind her. The speaker revealed himself a moment later as a child of perhaps four, who was smoking a cigar. I know I jumped at the sight of him for he smiled ironically, revealing full-sized, tobacco-stained teeth and I realized with a jolt, that I wasn't looking at a child but at a full-grown man so small that his head would have barely passed my waist.

"What's your name?" the lady asked, ignoring him.

I swallowed once, and returned my attention to her. "Lotte," I whispered.

"That's a nice name," she said, speaking to me as if I were a much younger child. "My name is Christabel."

I don't t know what came over me, exactly, but her voice was so gentle, her eyes were so kind and she seemed so normal after all that had happened that I found myself embracing her. She returned the embrace awkwardly, as she was supporting the child with her other arm. I closed my eyes and rested my head on her shoulder. She stroked my back. The cigar man continued his harangue about her impetuosity putting them all in danger but she replied in soothing tones meant for me as much as for him.

For some time I ignored him. I couldn't remember anyone holding me the way Christabel was. None of the servants – certainly not Maman – would ever have held me like that. But like a bothersome fly that won't go away the cigar man's voice kept on buzzing in my ears till it hurt. I opened my eyes and looked toward him.

Had it not been for Christabel's soft cheek pressed against mine, had it not been for the feeling of utter well-being that her hand upon my back produced, I think I'd have gone mad then and there. But she *was* holding me and I felt protected to such an extent that I was able to look at the rest of the company standing behind the cigar man. Every one of them was what the world might call a human oddity: a man without legs, a boy with pincers instead of hands, a man nursing a baby – no, a woman with a beard! Until that moment I never imagined so many different things could happen to people. They studied me even as I studied them. At last I drew back from Christabel and sat up.

"Hi," I said to all of them, feeling unusually shy.

Some of them greeted me in return. I don't know why that surprised me. I looked towards the cigar man and said, "I didn't mean to cause you any trouble."

The deeply engraved lines of his scowl became somehow less pronounced and in a much gentler voice he said, "Such a polite little girl. No, it's not you who are the trouble. It's them." He nodded toward the door. "I don't expect most of the people out there would take kindly to your being abducted by a freak."

"I wasn't abducted," I began and then stopped. "Freak?" Deep in my heart, I think I already knew to whom he referred. How odious he was to me then. "What freak?" I demanded, not wanting to know. Wanting him to tell me I was mistaken.

There was a murmur amongst the group but no one answered. I turned again to Christabel who seemed to be collecting herself. When at last she did look at me, the expression on her face was one of resignation.

"He doesn't mean you," I said, willing her to tell me that indeed he didn't mean her. That in fact, he'd thought someone else had rescued me and that she was just covering up for them. How I managed to think all of that in the time it took for her to nod her head I don't know. But I did. And she did. She nodded.

Against my will, my attention was drawn to the child whose legs were draped over hers and whose upper body disappeared inside her loose fitting blouse.

"This is my sister," she said, caressing one of the little legs with what could only have been fondness. "Her name is Thomasina."

I touched the small, stockinged foot and Thomasina's toes curl reflexively round my finger.

"She is quite lively at times," Christabel said. "Other times, she sleeps. I'm always very careful that her diaper is clean and dry. And see?" She placed my hand upon the tiny chest. "She even has her own little heart."

I could feel it beating.

With my hand already on Thomasina's chest, it was easy to follow her body up to the place where it joined Christabel's. Thomasina had no arms. She had no head. Her body protruded from beneath Christabel's own sternum. I looked up at Christabel and our eyes met. Strangely enough, I was not repulsed. Only saddened. The vulnerable expression on her face told the tale of a lifetime of countless hurts and I could clearly see she was steeling herself for another. What could I possibly say to her? For the second time in as many days, my ready mouth failed me. Instead, I put my arms around her once more, including little Thomasina in my embrace. This time, Christabel was able to put both her arms around me, firm and strong.

At last, she held me away. Her eyes glittered strangely.

"I'm sorry you were hurt in there," she said. "A sweet girl like you should only have nice things happen to her. Are you going to be all right now?

I nodded.

Her smile was a little tremulous as she smoothed my hair.

"Then I think maybe it's time for you to go. Your mother must be very worried about you."

I didn't dare to say that my mother was nothing of the sort. I only nodded.

The bearded lady came up then and in her deep masculine voice said, "I can help you find your family, if you like."

She was dressed as a man and I realized she was the only one who could safely venture out into the light of day. Her disguise was so complete that no one would guess what lie hidden beneath her clothing.

I took her hand.

Outside there still seemed to be a deal of commotion going on over by the Crocodile Man's tent. A lot of angry villagers were roaming around, eyeing the other tents. The ringmaster himself was out there trying to shoo people away, repeating over and over that the show was over and that everyone should go home.

Chapter Five

On the way back to Cook's house, the children managed to needle me about my reaction inside the tent in that sneaky, venomous way that never seemed to draw the attention of the adult in charge. At first, I was able to ignore them, caught up in the enormity of my recent adventure. But they wouldn't allow me my reverie. However unwilling, my mind was drawn from the depths of reflection to the moment at hand and to the numerous little bites and stings they inflicted upon me. The sensation was similar to coming awake from a dream. I felt my eyes focus on the impish little faces. They'd become bold at my initial lack of response and so I think I caught them off guard when I said "You'd be scared too, if the Crocodile Man lived in your house."

"Hush now," Cook said, typically having heard only my response and completely ignorant of the comments that had goaded me.

I increased my following distance.

"You better be careful," I said to the children a few moments later. "There's a ghost in my house and he doesn't always stay there. He can hear you talking about him twenty leagues away and he'll come if he thinks you've called him."

To my satisfaction, the eyes of the younger ones shone round with fear.

"Don't talk about him then," one of them whispered.

"Maybe I will and maybe I won't." I said, having become the center of attention and gained a respectful silence all around. "But if you keep reminding me of the Crocodile Man, you're going to make me think of the ghost because they look just the same. And then I might accidentally say something."

Shh," said a few others.

"Don't worry," I said. "If I were to be very careful, I could tell you stories about all the things he's done quite safely. I'd just have to remember not to say the magic word."

They jumped at the bait like a cat at a dangled mouse.

"What magic word?"

"I can't say it," I told them. "If I say it, he'll come and since you don't know what the word is, maybe you'd better stop talking about him. You might say it without even knowing."

Obviously, I was not the first to have mentioned the ghost. It was quite the dark secret around the village so my show of bravado was enough to silence their comments and gain their respect. Indeed after supper, one of them approached me and asked shyly if I really had seen the ghost.

"I've done a lot more than see him," I answered with a knowing wink. That was all it took. Shortly thereafter, they managed to draw me outside the house, all of Cook's children and some of their friends as well.

"Tell us about the ghost," one of them demanded.

"This is hardly the place for a bedtime story," I chided with an air of superiority.

"She doesn't know anything," one of the older boys said. I recognized him as Yves, the hapless lout who'd been stuck in my finger trap one afternoon.

"I spend the night in that house all the time," I said without surrendering any of my haughtiness. "Even your parents aren't brave enough to do that."

He seemed to be casting about for an adequate retort but I didn't give him the chance.

"Come with me to that haystack over there," I said, gesturing to the shadowy mound I could see in a nearby field. "I'll tell you all about him if you're not too scared."

I headed toward the field, knowing that the darkness and the distance from the house would make the prospect frightening to one and all, knowing also that they wouldn't allow me to outdo them. Sure enough, they followed. I sat on the far side of the haystack where we'd be cut off from sight of the village. The spot was satisfactorily isolated to make any ghost story come alive. Right on cue, a chilly breeze kicked up, starting the goose bumps even before the story had begun. I sat down cross-legged with great nonchalance though I would have been hard put to go out there by myself. Slowly the others settled around me. They were subdued but there was an underlying current of expectancy.

"Before I tell you about the ghost," I said, "I have to tell you what to do if you ever see one, in case I accidentally say the magic word. My Maman taught me this and I'm sure it's saved my life. If a ghost ever looks at you straight in the eye, your hair will turn white and you'll die. They found my aunt that way one morning. You see Maman had forgotten to warn her before she went to bed that night. My aunt was lying there with her eyes wide open and her hair standing straight up. It had turned completely white. Her mouth was open too because she'd been screaming when she died. So you must never look a ghost in the eye. The best thing to do if you see a ghost coming is curl up in a tight ball and pretend you're asleep."

The moonlight broke away from the clouds, revealing the circle of horrified faces around me. I rubbed my hands together with glee.

"No matter what you do," I said, "You mustn't let a ghost know you're awake because then they'll try to test you. They'll touch you and poke you with their skeleton hands but you mustn't scream or all will be lost. Sometimes, when they haven't been dead long, the rotten flesh is trailing off the bones and they'll brush it over your face and comb back your hair and breathe on your neck with their stinking breath."

I was gratified to hear a few muffled shrieks.

"You must do better than that," I scolded in that general direction. "You must lie very still and not make a sound. You must keep your eyes shut. Sometimes even drawing in your breath too quickly will give you away. The one good thing is that the more times the ghost visits you, the better you get at playing dead. In our house, the ghost has become very bold but I never move a muscle. Not even when he's found a chink in my nightgown and sticks his bony finger inside. First he'll tickle you, ever so lightly, so that it makes all the hairs on your arms stand up. But then, just when you least expect it, he'll give you a nasty scratch with his sharp claw, just to test you. I think I've made the ghost very angry because he hasn't been able to make me open my eyes. So sometimes he even picks me up and carries me down to the cellar where its freezing cold but I don't dare shiver.

"One night he laid me down in the big wash basin and covered me from head to foot with frogs and snakes and worms and snails and left them crawling all over me until it was nearly morning and then he put me back in bed all covered with slime."

I knew without a doubt the maid would have spread the tale of the muddy sheets far and wide. Sure enough, my listeners were stealing surreptitious glances and nodding at one another.

Only Yves appeared unmoved. "How would you know the ghost looks like the Crocodile Man if you always stay rolled up tight as a hedgehog every time he comes?"

I hoped there was enough moonlight to reveal the disdainful smile with which I favored him, filling time as my mind raced to find an answer.

Suddenly inspired, I said, "He's around even in the daytime. My Maman talks to him all the time. He hides in the dark places because he can't be seen in the light. But sometimes – " I dropped my voice to a conspiratory whisper. "If you look into the big mirror in Maman's bedroom, you can catch him unawares. Inside the mirror, his power is reversed, you see. During the daytime, if you can look him in the eye while he hides in the mirror, he'll be destroyed."

There were all kinds of involuntary squeals from my restless audience but smirking Yves was determined to get the best of me. "Well, if it's as easy as that," he said, "why haven't you done it already?"

"You don't know anything," I said. "Do you think he just sits there staring out into the room waiting for someone to vanquish him? You have to be quiet and make him think the room is empty if you want to see him." *Hah. Let them try it.* "One time I hid in the closet and jumped in front of the mirror all at once. That's when I saw him. Just before he turned and leaped behind the dresser. Then at night when he was poking me, I felt all those bumps and things growing on his body and I smelled his rotting flesh."

"I smelled it too," one of Cook's brats said. Other voices timidly concurred. They were remembering the Crocodile Man.

"Anyway," I said, so certain I'd won that I didn't mind gloating, "that's the reason only Maman and I can ever spend the night in that house. That's the reason she makes all the servants leave at sunset. Who would take care of the house if all of *you* were dead?"

"Does he do the same thing to your mother as he does to you?" someone asked.

I stopped and thought. "I don't think so," I said. "Maman and I don't talk about him much. But I get the feeling it's different with them. She likes him. She goes looking for him." I stopped, painful memories flooding my mind of Maman holding conversations with the wall. *Why was I choking up and getting ready to cry?* I swallowed the lump in my throat, suddenly tired of the whole business. "I really don't know what goes on between the two of them." I turned my face aside and tried to flick away a tear without anyone noticing but I'd only whetted their appetite for the macabre.

Someone, as stupid as she was bold, asked, "Is that what your mother is doing when she has her arms around the mirror? Is she talking to him?"

Or kissing him?" Yves added.

Laughter, all be it nervous, exploded all around me and I could feel my face getting hot. Mercifully, the clouds had cut off the moonlight once more.

"You better shut up." I said, "or he'll come after *you*. He never lets anyone insult my mother and live. You remember that dead beggar they found in the creek. All I can say is that he was rude to my mother the day before when he came demanding food at our house. A dog that shows its teeth to Maman is as good as dead. They show up around the water too."

"What about the chickens?" a timid voice asked.

Someone cried out in terror. "There's something in that tree over there."

"Where?"

Everyone was trying to see at once.

"It's just the wind," said someone else.

"No, I see something white."

Suddenly there was a lonely howl. It was probably just one of those miserable village curs but it sent a panic through the entire group and instinctively, as a single unit, we went dashing towards the house as if the devil himself were on our tail.

Chapter Six

I don't believe that any storyteller anywhere could have wished for a better response than the one I got from the yarn I spun in the hayfield. Indeed, the ghost must have been very busy that night, for the following day I heard tell that many of the smaller children had been visited. Some of them were truly terrified. Older brothers and sisters gave me reproachful looks but were afraid to say anything to my face. My gratification was short-lived. That night, several adult visitors appeared at Cook's front door. I recognized them as the parents of some of the children who had listened to my story. A few of the older children were also present, including my good friend Yves with that "now you're going to get it" look on his face. You'd have thought it was a town meeting the way they all came inside, making a mess of the recently swept floor with their muddy clodhoppers. Some removed dirt encrusted hats to turn them nervously around in their hands. Others took a seat on the hearth or the floor. One of them, apparently the leader, took Cook to one side so that both their backs were to the assembly and proceeded to have a whispered discussion. When this breach of etiquette had finally concluded, they turned back toward the rest of us and Cook called my name much more loudly than was necessary.

"Yes, ma'am," I said, all innocence.

"These good people are here," she said, "because you've been giving their children nightmares with your wild stories. Now what's the meaning of this?"

"What's the meaning of what, Cook?"

The farmer who had initially conferenced with Cook said, "Lying's going to get you in trouble, Mademoiselle. You'd do well to remember that we are under no obligation to offer you shelter. If you continue telling these lies to frighten our children, your mother will have to make other arrangements in the future. Do you understand me?"

The fact is, I didn't care what they told my mother. There were a myriad of impertinent responses that occurred to me, the best and truest being that I'd be happy if I never had to stay in the village again. Maybe then, Maman would have to take me to Paris with her. But there was a very important factor to take into account. The children themselves were present. To go back on my story in any manner with them right there in front of me would have been the equivalent of suicide. I knew I was only barely tolerated and was painfully aware of the treatment outcasts received. I'd joined in plenty of times myself in hurling cow pies at the clubfoot and dumping newcomers headfirst through the hole in the outhouse seat. Not going along with it would have been the same as offering myself up for the same treatment next. With no idea how long before Maman returned from Paris, I took the only viable option I really had. With my chin raised and my tone defiant, I stuck to my story. "I wasn't lying," I said, "It was God's honest truth."

There were gasps all around the room.

"You be careful now, Mademoiselle," the man said, his eyes dangerous and a distinctive note of warning in his voice. "The Lord will punish you for blaspheming."

"Is the truth blasphemy then?" I asked, throwing covert glances around the room to determine the humor of my audience.

The men looked at each other gravely. I suppose they'd expected to bully me into submission. Perhaps my very refusal to be cowed gave an air of truth to the story.

They conferred briefly in whispers.

"We want to hear this story of yours again," the leader said. "We especially want to hear what you have to say about the dead beggar and the animals that have been dying all over."

"All over?" I asked.

"Our livestock," said another. "Our milk cows and our goats have been dying in the night. There's no explanation for it. They're perfectly well in the evening and in the morning they're bloated and dead."

"I don't know anything about your cows," I said.

"My boy Yves said this ghost of yours is responsible for the carcasses found all along the road leading to your house," the leader said.

I shrugged again but had to clasp my hands together to keep from trembling. A feeling of foreboding rose up inside me.

"Look," I said, trying to keep the tone of panic out of my voice, "I never saw the ghost kill anyone. All I know is what my mother told me and what I've seen."

"What exactly have you seen?"

"Shadows in the darkness. And in the mirror."

"What else?"

"Nothing else."

"What about that whole tale of being carried to the cellar at night?"

"What about it?" I shouted, "Ask Mme. Jenner. Ask the housemaids. They're the ones who had to clean me up."

I started to cry.

There was some more discussion. At last Yves' father came towards me and knelt on the ground. He took hold of my shoulders with his callused hands and looked at me with both fear and pity in his eyes. Somehow this frightened me more than his anger and I understood that he believed. God help me, he believed the whole story and I knew something terrible was going to come of it.

"Listen to me very carefully, child," he said. "There have been many unexplained incidents here in the village and we need to know if this thing that lives in your house has anything to do with them."

"I don't know," I whispered.

"Just tell us," he said, "everything you told the children last night."

I bit down hard upon my trembling lip but was unable to control the telltale whimpering that was coming up from deep within me. A quick glance confirmed my worst fears. The children had taken note of my reaction and were watching avidly, though none so much as Yves who looked as though he might wet his pants so eager was he to see me disgraced. One slip and they'd get me. If not today then tomorrow. Nothing I said to any adult would change that. So with much trembling and sobbing I condemned myself, repeating the essence of the half truths and lies I'd spun together so artfully and so carelessly the night before. The silence of my audience was grim. They were listening with an intensity that was frightening. Words continued to spill out of me as if some cowardly spirit had taken over my body. I wished that God would strike me dead, as the priest was always warning, for I thought it would have taken a miracle of that magnitude to halt my runaway mouth. But at long last, and with no divine intervention, the torrent came to an end. I'd said it all. I was empty. Fully expecting them to put on their hats and leave, I was astonished when no one made a move. The end of the world had come and gone and those fools hadn't even noticed. Yves' father appeared to be speaking, though at first I didn't realize it. He gave me a little shake and repeated his question.

"How much of this does your mother know?" he asked.

"I don't know."

"But you say she speaks to him."

"I think so," I said. "But no one can see him or hear him in the daytime, except maybe her. That's why people say she's crazy. But she's not."

"Hush now," he said. "No one's saying your mother is crazy. At first perhaps some foolish tongues were wagging but now we've seen the evidence for ourselves. The entire village is being terrorized. Animals are dying and maybe even people. You've told us a great deal but we'll need to know more if we're to fight this thing. Is there anything else you forgot to tell us?"

I shook my head. I truly had nothing more to say.

He stood. "All right men," he said. "I think we've heard everything we're going to, tonight."

There was a great shifting about as people got to their feet, brushed themselves off and gathered their things. Yves' father lagged behind until the last of them had left. He approached me one last time.

"Mademoiselle – " He seemed to be considering very carefully what he was going to say. "I know you've witnessed strange and frightening things but I must ask that you refrain from recounting your experiences to the children. Do you understand? If anything else happens, tell one of us. Tell me. But don't say any more about this to the children. It has frightened them terribly."

"I'm sorry," I said. No truer words had ever been spoken.

He stood looking at me and I thought to myself, tell him now. Tell him it was all a lie. There's still time.

But at that very moment, he turned to leave and I was too much a coward to call him back. As the door opened and closed, I saw outside that the crowd was still milling about. I had the distinct feeling the meeting wasn't over, only that it was going to be continued elsewhere.

Cook had also seen them. She bolted the door and then looked at me thoughtfully. "There's no doubt you've started something, Mlle. Charlotte," she said. "I only hope it isn't someone innocent who suffers for it in the end."

Chapter Seven

Cook's ominous words found an echo in my heart. I had the frightening feeling that I'd set in motion something that couldn't be stopped. The ethereal voice of the siren and the insubstantial flitting of shadowy figures hardly seemed a match for the physical strength and dumb volition of the garlic-eating mob. How could I have ever believed the house on the hill to be impenetrable?

That night I dreamed it was on fire. I stood outside and saw my mother through one of the windows. How could she still be inside, walking back and forth folding linens as if nothing were happening? I called to her. I stretched out my arms toward her and saw they were covered with blood.

"Lotte," cried a voice. Its timbre was sweet and familiar. I looked toward the roof where stood a figure I'd never seen before but that I knew instantly to be my angel. My heart swelled at the sight of him, beautiful like the painting of Jesus in our church. His eyes were filled with compassion and his arms were extended toward me. But flames surrounded him on every side.

"Come down," I cried.

"I can't," he said.

"Please."

"You've taken my wings,"

I'm unable to say how I knew what I was going to find but the dread I felt wasn't enough to prevent my gaze from shifting downward. There, at my feet, as I somehow knew there must be, were two quivering wings, freshly amputated.

I screamed and awoke, the sound of the flames and the moans of the dying fading as I stared at the moonlight that shone through the window. I was trembling and covered with sweat. The children curled up on either side of me stirred in their sleep. For a moment, I felt relief at having escaped the dream but this relief was short-lived. Events of the night before came flooding back into my consciousness. The villagers had believed what I'd told them. They'd taken themselves off to meet elsewhere, a bad sign. Yet even before that they'd started attributing things to the ghost that couldn't possibly have been his doing. *Dead livestock indeed.* I stayed awake with my eyes open and my heart pounding for a very long time. I didn't think I'd be able to get back to sleep and frankly I was afraid to try.

Instead, I prayed. "Please God, don't let anything bad happen. I was a bad girl and I know it. But I promise to be good from now on. I'll be nice to Maman and I'll do whatever my tutors tell me and if there's anything else you want me to do, I promise to do it only please God, don't let anything bad happen."

Sleep must have claimed me for I opened my eyes again and found sunshine streaming in through the windows.

For the next several weeks, there were few signs that my story had any lasting effect. It was quite obvious the younger children of the village had been told to stay away from me but many of the older ones still came around, including Yves. No doubt his father had forbidden him to mention "the ghost" but he gnawed around the edges of his prohibition whenever opportunity arose. I think he maintained that scoffing tone of his to cover up an avid credulity. He plied me with questions about vampires and changelings and the myriad supernatural beings that were supposed to gather at crossroads. He seemed obsessed with the measures one would use for counteracting these assorted demons. And so I told him the vampire could be vanquished with a stake through the heart or by burning the coffin that contained its native soil. I told him changelings too could be overcome by burning. I fed the flames of his voracity with anecdotes I'd read.

Then one morning, when I'd been in the village for nearly six weeks, Yves didn't show up. I was foolish enough to be relieved. It wasn't until that afternoon that I heard his father was looking for him. That same afternoon, Maman's carriage came rolling into town and the plight of the villagers stopped being my concern. Maman wasn't in her carriage, of course, she'd just sent the coachman along to collect me and to tell the servants to get back to work. I'd been uncommonly well-behaved during most of those six weeks, so it was with a pang that I perceived Cook's relief when she sent me on my way.

Maman seemed to have done some shopping while she was gone. Boxes were piled in the entryway and Maman herself came to greet me in a dress I'd never seen before. She looked very smart. But nothing else had changed. She gave me a peck, handed me a sweet and almost immediately began bustling about as if she were very busy and didn't have time to talk to me. I felt an undercurrent of remembered anger but recalled the promise I'd made to God and stifled it at once.

Besides, I told myself with an inner snarl, you don't deserve anything after what you did and here she is giving you kisses and gifts. What more do you want, you ungrateful little beast?

I climbed the stairs to my room. It wasn't my fault I had to walk past that corner in the hallway where I knew a door must be hidden. But I remained strong. I averted my eyes and hurried past, proud of myself for having accomplished that simple act.

Self congratulations turned out to be premature, however. That night, the siren sang and I was halfway out of bed before I remembered my new resolution. Furious with myself, I got back under the covers, the voice of my conscience scolding me as angrily as Cook ever had. The truth is, I'd underestimated the raw power of the siren's lure when I was making my little promises safely away from its influence. I tried to ignore it. I tried, silly goose that I was, to go back to sleep. But how could I sleep when invisible filaments with tiny hooks in my gut were exerting an almost tangible, physical pull? I writhed and became tangled in the twisted sheets. An actual moan escaped me and I knew my resolution was doomed.

It was then I decided to run away. If I couldn't go *to* the music, then maybe I could flee *from* it. I pulled the blanket from the bed, wrapped it around my shoulders and dashed out of the room. I swear to you I intended only to run out the front door of the house and perhaps even down the road a short distance. Just far enough away so I couldn't be tempted.

But I didn't make it past the hall. I stopped as abruptly as if I'd slammed into some unseen barrier. An unseen barrier, of course, situated just inches from the hidden doorway. The music was so loud that the siren might have been just the other side of the wall.

"Please, help me," I said to that voice.

It never faltered.

I don't know quite how it happened but I discovered that I'd pressed my body up against the wall as if trying to melt into it. A secret desire, unacknowledged for so long, came bursting forth in a whispered plea.

"Take me."

But nobody took me and nothing changed. When the music finally released me, it did so of its own accord and not because of any regard the siren may have had for my broken psyche. I stumbled back to my room, fell into bed and slipped into oblivion.

The next morning, my lessons began despite my lethargy upon waking. It was like I'd never been gone. Although it was true I'd made a heartfelt promise to be good, I think my exemplary behavior was due more to exhaustion and defeat. The chiding I received from M. Duprès for my rusty playing after six weeks without access to a keyboard was enough to elicit a caustic remark from a saint. I, however, lacked the energy to sustain a lively argument and so, let it pass.

When the morning's humiliations came to an end, I was allowed to return to my room. Heavy despondency weighed me down and I noticed for the first time the number of stairs I had to climb. Though it was more usual for me to run up them without a second thought, I found myself quite uncharacteristically pressing one hand against the wall for support. Even when I reached the second floor, my fingertips remained in contact with the carved molding that divided the top of the wall from the bottom. It was when I neared that fateful corner in the hallway that I felt a piece of wood moving beneath my hand. I pulled away, certain that my cursed touch had brought on destruction yet again.

And then I saw that I hadn't really broken anything. The carved rosette had merely turned up on a hidden axis, revealing a button. I turned it back to its original position, chagrined but excited, and hurried away.

Back in my room the knowledge of that button burned a hole in my brain. I couldn't help being intrigued by my accidental discovery. My mind grew heated and I examined every possibility that occurred to me, not the least of which was that I'd been had. So involved did I become in my speculations that I never noticed when the heavy cloud of morose humor lifted, though later that afternoon when I found myself once again standing by that fateful rosette, I realized my body was infused with vitality.

I contemplated the carving for some time without touching it. All at once, my traitorous hand darted out, turned the rosette and pushed the button before I had a chance to stop it. Immediately, a panel opened at my feet. It was a trapdoor, completely invisible when shut. Two of the sides matched exactly with the junctures in the hardwood floor. The third was hidden by the edging at the bottom of the wall. The fourth was covered by the runner. Without taking a step nearer, I looked down to discover the beginnings of a stairway steep enough to resemble a ladder. Unbidden, I relived the memory of Maman and the shadow man shrinking and disappearing before my very eyes. It was suddenly clear that what I'd actually witnessed were the two of them descending the hidden stairs.

I pushed the button and the trapdoor closed. I was so excited by this discovery that for a moment I actually became dizzy. I rested my head against the wall until it cleared and then went bounding back to my room. I was there only long enough to light a candle and then returned with it to the hallway. Had my hand passed through solid wood, had something else that defied explanation occurred, I'm sure I'd have given that wall as wide a berth as I gave the mirror. But instead what I'd found was something so obviously the product of human ingenuity that my previous resolution to leave the mysteries alone seemed to have been made under false pretenses. At least, that was what I told myself as I pushed the button once more and descended the hidden staircase.

Down below, I found a set-up of pulleys and counterweights. I examined them. The design was simple and I was able to close the trapdoor from below. In the darkness, the feeble glow of the candle took on greater importance. I looked around and found that I was in a passageway of wood planking and unfinished walls. When my eyes adjusted, I made out the shape of another ladder, not far from the first. Curious, I climbed it. There was a pinhole of light at the very top and I put my eye to it. A familiar scene at a very unfamiliar angle greeted me. It was the hallway again, as seen from near ceiling height. One of the maids walked by. I drew back but she didn't even noticed me. I realized that although I could see, I myself was invisible – like a ghost. I estimated my position to be directly behind the portion of the wall that sounded hollow. It wasn't a doorway at all. It was a hidey hole. No wonder I'd found no way to open it.

It came to me that not only was our ghost actually human, he was a man who spent his time sneaking around and spying on us from behind the walls of our house. Seen in this light, I felt justified in carrying out a thorough search.

I climbed down the ladder and began to follow the passageway back beyond the trapdoor. As the darkness retreated ahead of the candle glow, I made out other ladders, going both up and down, as well as other passageways that branched off every so often from the main one. I stood for a moment at one such intersection and something like a vision descended upon me. I saw the whole house more riddled with wormholes than a Swiss cheese and realized that anyone who could master this maze would be able to go virtually anywhere, watching and listening in complete anonymity. I knew that I would have to return here many times and explore each tunnel and ladder until I knew it all by heart. But I also decided that on this, my first adventure, I would do best to follow the main artery to its end. This I did but the passageway didn't really end. There was a spiral stairway leading down so that my passage actually extended to lower levels. There were landings at certain intervals and I thought each one probably led off toward another, different labyrinth.

The extent of this hidden world staggered me but I pressed on. At some point, the wood gave way to stone and the chill increased so that I imagined I must be under the ground. I even wondered at one point, if that staircase spiraled all the way to hell. It didn't of course. It came to an end where the ground was flat stone in what appeared to be catacombs. Right away I saw it was a maze I couldn't penetrate without warmer clothing, lots of candles and perhaps even food and water. Still, I couldn't help taking a peek down the nearest passage. It didn't seem as though it went very far so I followed it to where it ended in front of a stone wall.

Knowing the ways of our spy a little better by that time, I examined the stones and the junctures in between them. Sure enough, there was a hidden lever. I pulled it. The whole wall in front of me that had looked to be so solid and so heavy moved easily to the side. I stepped in and found myself in a furnished music room. The stone of which it was constructed was mostly hidden by either carpet or tapestry. There was a fireplace that took up an entire wall, like the kind they sometimes have in old castles. I supposed it would have taken a very large blaze to warm the chill of that room and indeed there were enough logs stacked up to start a bonfire.

I touched the wick of my candle to some of the others that were placed all around the room and tried to imagine the way it would look with all of them lit and the fire going as well. In my mind, I beheld what would most certainly have been a beautiful, otherworldly sight. There was a pipe organ set up against one wall, a piano more or less in the center of the room and other musical instruments arranged on shelves. Furniture placed here and there gave the room an odd homeliness and a big bookcase proved to hold perhaps fifty leather-bound volumes. I pulled one down and discovered musical manuscript written in red ink. I pulled down and leafed through others at random and discovered in one, the very polonaise Maman had been copying the day she left for Paris. In case I had any doubts, the very page I'd manhandled was there, slightly crinkled and with a soup stain on one corner.

Guilty and embarrassed, I closed the volume. Too late. The notes had already jumped to my head. I heard them as I knew they must have sounded, long past the page I'd actually seen. I wasn't remembering the ink strokes. I was remembering the sound of it. I must have heard it one night when I was asleep. This was the room where the music came from. This was the place where the siren sang. The reason the music always seemed to surround me was that the tunnels all radiated out from this room and then passed behind every wall in the house.

As I continued my investigations, I noticed one of the tapestries stirring. I pushed it to one side and discovered a hidden alcove that I saw at once to be a bedchamber. Despite its location in the catacombs and the chill of the air all around me, I thought it must be a very cozy place when the candles and fireplace were lit. Another memory tickled the edges of my conscious mind, the memory of a man in black with his arm around a lady in white and I understood that this was their place. With a touch of annoyance, or perhaps it would be better to call it jealousy, I made bold as to open all the armoires and drawers. They were full of clothing, both a man's and a woman's. I even recognized some of my mother's dresses.

I set down my candle on the dresser, illuminating the items upon its marble surface: a lady's combs, several flasks of perfume, a miniature in a small gilt frame, a hand mirror, a jewelry box.

I opened the jewelry box. It played a tinkling melody, also familiar. Inside was a veritable king's random in jewels. I couldn't help plunging my hands into the treasure and letting it spill through my fingers. Shyly at first, I fastened a pearl necklace around my neck and clipped on some earrings. I went to pick up the hand mirror and noticed that the name "Christine" was worked onto the back surface. I turned it over and took a look at myself, nearly bursting into "The Jewel Song" from *Faust.* I stopped myself because I remembered all too well the imprisonment and death of poor Marguerite who'd sung that song before me. Instead, I contented myself with turning my head this way and that and admiring my bejeweled reflection.

After some minutes, I thought to try on some of the other jewels in the box. I put the mirror down, accidentally bumping the miniature and knocking it to the floor. I picked it back up and held it closer to the candlelight. When I saw the image in the frame, though, I almost dropped it again.

It was a portrait of me. I could tell it had been done a few years ago because I still looked like a chubby little baby. Closer examination revealed it to be a reproduction of the big portrait Maman had commissioned and for which I remembered sitting endless hours. Most impatiently I might add.

How can I explain what I felt at that moment? I was profoundly touched that I'd somehow been included in the happiness that was a part of this beautiful room. Somebody down here loved me. Gently I replaced the portrait where I'd found it. Carefully, I removed the jewelry and put it back in the box. I ran my fingers over the objects on the dresser and outlined the letters that spelled "Christine." I wanted to stay in that room forever.

And then I heard a scream.

I spun around but no one was there. I ran out of the bedroom, extinguished the candles in the music room and left that sweet refuge, pushing back the lever to close the stone door behind me. I heard voices echoing up and down the passageways and I looked about for a place to hide. But there was no place. I thought to blow out the candle and allow the darkness to hide me but the inky blackness just beyond the feeble light seemed too frightening to face. I stood there trembling as the voices continued to desecrate the silence of that darkness. They were speaking rapidly, loudly and all at once.

It was then I realized I recognized them. It was just the servants making a great fuss over nothing, no doubt. That was a daily occurrence. They really were going on this time, though, and I wondered what had got them so excited. It was unnerving the way the sounds carried through the passageways. No one was in the catacombs with me but if I'd closed my eyes I'd have thought myself surrounded.

I climbed the spiral stairs up one level. The voices seemed to get louder. I put my eye to a spy hole and immediately recognized one of our cellars. For some puzzling reason, the smell of kerosene was very strong. I could see by looking through the hole at different angles that three people were standing there having a discussion. What I couldn't do was view all three of them at the same time. Something seemed to be hanging down from the ceiling and was blocking my view.

"This is not the work of any ghost," said Blaise the gardener.

It was hard to make out faces but I recognized his voice. I tried to see what they were all looking at but apparently it was beyond the range of my spy hole.

"Shh," said Lianne, the scullery maid. "You remember what Mlle. Charlotte said. If you talk about him, he'll come."

"Let's get out of here," said Heloise, that little snip Maman had taken on as her personal maid. The three hurried out, leaving a lamp burning on the floor in their haste.

Still mystified as to the specifics, I understood something serious had happened. Deep down I knew that whatever it was, it would ultimately turn out to be my fault. Drawing in a quick breath, I was only just able to stifle the whimper that tried to escape me when a shadowy figure detached itself from a dark corner and moved towards the center of the cellar. I held my breath as it climbed upon a pile of debris and began making sawing motions toward the top of the object hanging from the ceiling. It turned on the rope from which it was hanging and I saw what it was. I clapped my hands over my mouth and ducked down beneath the hole, drawing my knees to my chin and hugging myself with all my strength to keep from screaming. What I'd seen was a face. The face of someone who was hanging by the neck in our cellar.

Unable to stand any more, I crawled away from the spy hole and crept toward the spiral staircase as quietly as I could. Once I'd ascended a couple of levels, though, I pounded back up the remaining stairs as fast as I could, wanting only to be out of there and safe in my room.

I glanced back over my shoulder a few times as I ran but no one was following me. When at last I climbed back out of the trapdoor and into daylight, no one was there to see me rising up from the floor. I ran to my bed, completely unobserved, threw myself upon it and wept.

All my fears had been justified. The nightmare had begun.

Chapter Eight

I don't really know how long I stayed there indulging in my grief as if there were nothing more important I might be doing. At some point, though, I realized it was nighttime. I began to wonder why no one had brought my supper but inside I think I already knew. The servants had abandoned us. They'd all left after that body was discovered in our cellar and I was alone in the house with Maman. And with him. Was Maman even here? I got up and ran to her room only to find it vacant and dark. I didn't leave at once, however, because I heard what sounded like a crowd of people. I followed that sound to the open window, giving the mirror a wide berth, and looked out. Standing on our front steps was the whole village, or so it seemed. They were talking to Maman who'd apparently opened the door to them herself.

So she hadn't left me.

As I watched, she admitted several of the men into the house. All the guilt and all the fear that had been with me to a greater or lesser degree since that ill-fated narrative in the hayfield rose from my belly and my hands began to shake. My first instinct was to hide. But then I thought about Maman who spoke to angels but was at a loss for words with anyone else. Maman, who lived in a waking dream. Maman, who in her own confused way loved me. I remembered that portrait so lovingly placed on the dresser next to her other treasures in that secret room. She couldn't have put it there to impress me or the servants for no one even knew the place existed. No, she'd put it there because she wanted it there. She wanted me close to her even when she was with *him.* With that unbelievable realization came the knowledge that I couldn't let her face the crowd alone. I'd started this mess. I would end it. Somehow.

I went down to the sitting room where I knew they'd be meeting. In my mind I'd already decided to come clean. The taunting of the children during my next exile seemed a vague and distant threat just then. All I wanted was to set things right. All I wanted was for everyone to leave us alone and for life to go back to the way it had always been.

I saw, when I entered, a delegation of four men from the village and two gentlemen I'd never met. Only the gentlemen were seated. One of those standing was Yves' father. He turned at the sound of my footsteps. Over night, he seemed to have turned into a sick old man. He was stooped and tired. His eyes were red-rimmed and the flesh of his dirt-streaked face sagged. Even so, he seemed glad to see me. He came over and knelt down just as he had that evening at Cook's house. "Ah, Mlle. Charlotte," he said. "These are terrible times." He shook his head and wiped at his eyes. "We should have believed you. You told us everything and we did nothing. Forgive me for scolding you. If only I'd acted, my Yves would be alive now. I'm sorry, mademoiselle. I'm so sorry."

He broke off, released an actual sob and gripped my shoulders painfully.

An awful foreboding seized me. I tried to speak and nothing came out. I cleared my throat and tried again. "What happened to Yves?"

He looked at me in his misery. "They haven't told you?"

I shook my head.

"Dear God," he murmured, shutting his eyes as if to brace himself. He remained that way for a long moment. Then, as if he'd somehow gathered sufficient strength, he said in a rush, "Your ghost has murdered my boy."

"How?" I cried.

"They found him hanging in your cellar."

I came to on the floor. The focus of the group had shifted from my mother to me. One of the gentlemen was waving something pungent beneath my nose. Memory came flooding back. Yves' grieving father. The body dangling from a rope in our cellar. The dark figure peeling away from the shadows. I looked quickly around for Yves' father and found him behind me, supporting my head and shoulders. Our eyes met.

"Tell them everything, Mlle. Charlotte," he said. "It's the only thing we can do for Yves now."

I sat up carefully, still feeling dizzy. Strange the way your head can feel foggy and your mind so perfectly clear. I was aware enough to make sure Yves' father was out of my line of vision – where I wouldn't have to see his reaction – when I addressed the rest of the group. "It's all a lie," I said. "There is no ghost. I made the whole thing up."

Maman turned toward me. "Lotte, what have you done?"

My mind picked up her question and repeated it with increasing intensity. *What have you done? What have you done?* The aromatic vinegar kept me from losing consciousness a second time and I felt myself being lifted and carried over to the chaise lounge. I heard a voice say something about letting me have a few minutes to recover and then the rest of them seemed to gather again around Maman. Only Yves' father stayed near me though I still didn't have the courage to face him.

The same gentleman who'd been waving the vinegar under my nose turned to Maman. "Look at your child," he said. "Can't you see she's suffering. How can you allow this man to abuse your own little daughter."

"He would never hurt Lotte," Maman shouted. I was startled for Maman rarely raised her voice. She startled me further by wringing her hands and moaning the way the scullery maid did when in the grip of her courses.

"Ah, so you admit there is someone."

She turned away from him and started to cry.

"Is it possible," asked the gentleman in a quiet aside to the farmers, "that she isn't aware of the treatment this child has received at his hands?"

It was Yves' father beside me who responded. "Mlle. Charlotte said her mother often speaks to the ghost. Perhaps she was afraid to tell her."

"Is that true?" the gentleman asked, directing his steely gaze at me.

"I'm a liar," I said.

"But what about the muddy sheets?" asked one of the other men. "My wife changed them herself and bathed the girl as well."

"And she's sick," supplied another, "the first Sunday of every month."

"And the beggar," said another, "and all the dead animals."

"And François' wife, her twins were both stillborn."

"Our children are afraid to go to sleep at night."

"He visits them, I tell you. My little daughter has scratch marks all over her body."

"And Yves . . ."

"Enough," the gentleman shouted.

In the sudden quiet my mother's weeping seemed inordinately loud. It was more like howling than crying and the way she tore at her handkerchief with her teeth made her seem a mad woman.

"We're getting nowhere," the gentleman shouted. "If you can't control yourselves you'll have to leave."

"Get them out," Maman shrieked.

"If that is your wish," the gentleman said, "then they will certainly leave but you must promise to answer my questions after."

"Out, out," she screamed.

"Maybe all of us should leave," said Yves' father. "Maybe we should bring Madame la Comtess and Mlle. Charlotte as well. I think," he said, addressing the gentleman, "that neither of them will tell you anything as long as they're inside this house."

"And since when did you become inspector?" the gentleman asked, dilating his nostrils as if he smelled something bad. "No, I believe the Countess is correct and all of you should go."

He signaled for the other men to leave. Only Yves' father balked, remaining stubbornly beside me. The two gentlemen called him aside. All three conferred for some minutes. At last, Yves' father went out, his jaw stiff, his face angry. But he glanced at me one more time before closing the door and his eyes filled with compassion. Once he had gone, the gentleman in charge looked from me to Maman and back again. Maman had finished with her tantrum or fit or whatever that remarkable display had really been. She sat limply on another couch, her face slimy with wetness and her expression totally vacant. The gentleman turned to me.

"I think, Mademoiselle, that we have had a very bad start," he said. "I am Inspector Beauford from Rouen and this is my assistant, Officer Duval. What is your name?"

I told him.

"Charlotte," he said, "do you know why I'm here?"

I shrugged

"I'm here, Charlotte, because someone died here in your house. A friend of yours, I believe. His name was Yves."

I waited for him to tell me something I didn't know.

"The Mayor called me out here to see if I could find out more about his death. Now I think, Charlotte, that somebody killed him. And I know that the man who killed him was not a ghost. You know that too. Don't you Charlotte?"

I almost nodded.

"You made up that story about the ghost, didn't you?"

"I'm a liar and I'm going to hell," I said.

I'd expected surprise. He gave no sign of it. "Now why would you feel you had to lie, I wonder?" He didn't give me time to respond even if I'd wanted to. "I think you're a very smart girl, Charlotte. I think that some terrible things have happened to you but you knew better than to tell, am I right? You lived with it for a long time and then something happened, didn't it Charlotte? Something happened and you couldn't keep it inside you any longer. But even so, you had to be careful. You had to say it without saying it. You had to change the story. But now, Charlotte, things have got worse. Now we've gone past scratches and mud. Now we're talking about murder. If you don't help us find the murderer he could kill someone else. Maybe next time it could be your mother. Or you. Think about that."

"What was Yves doing in our cellar?" I asked.

Inspector Beauford paused for a moment, perhaps trying to decide how much to say to me. "We think he broke in with the intention of setting fire to it. There was a can of kerosene there that his father identified as belonging to him. All the items in the cellar had been doused. Three of your servants report having found him hanging by the neck from one of the beams at approximately 3:30 this afternoon but there is no body hanging there now and none of the people we've questioned has admitted to knowing where it is. I am told that this is not the first time such a thing has happened.

"He doesn't understand," Maman said.

Everyone turned in her direction. Her face was still slack, her voice monotone.

"All his life people have hurt him. That's all anyone has ever done. He learned to save himself by hurting them first."

Inspector Beauford glanced to see that his assistant was scribbling in a notepad, turned his full attention to Maman as if I were nothing more than a newspaper he'd been reading and asked, "Who is he?"

"Lotte's father," she said.

There were amazed glances exchanged but the inspector continued, "The Comte de Chagny?"

"Lotte's father."

Her pupils were big and dilated and I knew her mind was elsewhere. Somehow, I also knew she was speaking the truth. Fear gripped me, not for what I'd just learned but from what was being revealed to this outsider.

"Maman," I shouted, "What are you saying?"

She didn't seem to hear me. "He never wanted to hurt anyone, not even at the Opera. All he wanted was for everyone to leave him alone. But they never left him alone and he had to leave the bodies out where people could find them so they'd be afraid and stop looking."

"Maman," I screamed.

The inspector made a hand signal for me to be quiet but instead I got up and began tugging at her hand.

"Stop it," I said. "*You* are hurting him."

She turned her languid gaze upon me and I watched the transformation take place. Slowly her eyes focused and her slack jaw firmed. "My God, Lotte," she said in a strangled whisper, "What have I been saying?"

"All sorts of nonsense, Maman." I said loudly enough for the two men to hear. "You went into one of your trances again."

"Did I?" She passed her hand over her eyes. "I'm sorry."

"Madame, please," begged the inspector, looking at us both with confusion, "we're going to need to talk to your . . . er . . . husband. It's imperative we speak to him."

"My husband is in Monte Carlo," she said.

"The count?"

"Of course."

"What about Lotte's father?"

"He is away," she said impatiently. "Now gentlemen, if you please, I must have some rest. I just returned from Paris and am very tired."

"Madame," Beauford said, "we haven't yet concluded this inquiry."

"It's finished," she said. "It is *all* finished. Go away. You're tiring me."

The inspector seemed to weigh his options. At last he said, "All right, Madame. I shall return on the morrow with a warrant from the judge that will allow us to search this house from attic to cellar. In the meantime I'm placing you under protective custody. I shall post an officer at every door and if either of you tries to leave this house I will be forced to place you in prison. Do I make myself clear?"

"Good night, Inspector," Maman said.

"Good night, Madame." He gave each of us a curt bow. Duvall did as well and then Maman and I were alone in the sitting room. I heard Beauford's voice out in the hall shouting orders.

Maman looked bereft. After some time, she looked over at me. "Oh, Lotte," she said, "What shall we do?"

"I think we better warn him," I said.

She dismissed the suggestion with a wave of the hand. "They'll never catch him. But he'll have to go away. Oh, God." Her eyes brimmed yet again. "Who's going to take care of me now?" The tears spilled. Her face crumpled and a long whine escaped her.

"I'll take care of you, Maman." I jumped onto the couch and wrapped my arms around her. She was sobbing again and I petted her as the angel had once petted me. Maman's arms hung down at her sides and I wished she would put them around me. I was crying too. I recalled another time when I'd cried. I recalled a sweet voice, filled with concern and gentle hands that comforted. But that was over now. He could never comfort me again because I'd made it necessary for him to leave me.

I had a sudden vision of my entire life, spreading out before me a cold, endless void. I looked at poor Maman again. She was innocent and yet she was facing that same void because of me. Even so, it seemed she didn't hate me. I'm not sure I could have been so charitable had our roles been reversed. So what did it matter that she couldn't return my embrace? I didn't deserve to be comforted.

I kissed her and hugged her again and again. I vowed I'd do anything to make her happy. And I told myself I had no right to expect anything in return.

Chapter Ten

I awoke with a start to hear the siren once more. I wasn't in my room and felt strangely disoriented until the last of my dreams retreated and the corporeal world reestablished itself around me. I was lying under the covers of Maman's huge bed and remembered, all at once, tucking her in as if she were a little girl. I'd fully intended to return to my own room but found myself instead, drawn to the mirror. I'd knelt down in front of it and without further thought, poured out the whole story, sparing myself nothing. With brutal honesty, I admitted my betrayal. With open-faced frankness, I explained the logistics of our "protective custody." And with remorse, I begged the forgiveness of that entity who had terrorized my childhood.

There was no sign that anyone had heard me. I put my hand upon the mirror and when nothing happened, pressed myself against it as I'd often seen Maman do. Cupping my hands around my eyes to shield them from the candlelight, I looked into that mirror much as I might have looked through a window. And realized that was exactly what I was doing. The relative darkness of the bedroom allowed me to see past my own reflection and into the passageway beyond. It was like the ones I'd explored earlier that day.

As my eyes grew accustomed to the darkness on the other side, I became aware of a shadow on the right that was not quite beyond my line of vision. With a jolt, I leapt backward, sure it was the ghost but when nothing else happened I checked a second time. What I'd thought I'd seen was no longer there. This little experience, as illuminating as it was unnerving, gave me the impetus I needed to disobey my mother's decree about violating her privacy. I joined her in bed, snuggling up against her and telling myself it was for the sole purpose of being nearby in case she needed me.

Wide awake now and alone in the bed, I realized I'd not done a very good job of watching over her. The siren, cause of all of my woes, continued to sing. For some time I stayed where I was, wrestling with my fears, my desires and the dictates of my conscience. At last, I threw aside the covers, got out of bed and went back to my own room where I lit a candle and dressed in my warmest clothing. I went out to the trapdoor in the corner of the hallway and pushed the button. A fathomless darkness unfurled at my feet, the music washing over me in sudden, pristine splendor. Follow or die. It was as simple as that. So I followed the call into the void. I followed it past the vaguely branching corridors flashing by me like the countryside as seen from a train. I followed it into the bowels of the earth where its dominance grew and I seemed to be weightless. I followed it into a warm golden glow that, small in the distance, began to approach, looming closer and larger and then all around me, merging at last with the soul of the music. What resistance could there be in the face of such power? All I could do was to open my mind and allow it to penetrate deep and insistent. There was no passage of time. There was only the "now." There was no sense of self, only vibrant sensation – sensation that filled me with rapture.

There was a moment when the intensity was such I thought my poor mortal heart would burst. But then there was a fading, a palpable subsiding. The singing, I realized, had stopped, though I couldn't pinpoint when exactly this had occurred. I became aware of myself in much the same way as one who awakens from a very deep sleep. I took note of my physical state, of my dry unblinking eyes, my slack, drooling mouth and came dully to the conclusion that I'd gone into a trance as Maman always did. I rubbed my eyes into focus and saw her. She was standing in front of me by the curve of the piano, swaying a little from side to side. Clearly, she was still in that strange place from which I'd just emerged. The golden aura surrounding us had, at least for me, resolved into the light of a thousand candles and the blaze of a truly impressive fire.

I understood then that I'd followed the music to the secret chambers under the house. I also understood that at last I'd found my siren, my Maman, the angel's Christine. An unexpected wave of tenderness welled up inside me – a tenderness that was not, even at that almost religious moment, completely divorced from a pang of envy and the ache of a wound that was too deep to heal.

I wiped my mouth on my sleeve and was ready to take a step toward her when I realized she and I were not alone. There was someone sitting at the piano. The figure was in shadow but I sensed the penetrating eyes. I may have been eight years old but even then I was fully aware of the moment as a turning point in my life. I was also aware that I knew exactly what to do.

Without hesitation, I walked to where my father was seated, the details of his shadowed face gradually becoming evident. I'd not been wrong in comparing him to the Crocodile Man but his disfigurement was so much less that it seemed almost nothing. What I found most striking was the apprehensive expression in his eyes, the stiff, pulled-back posture of his body. He was afraid, just as Christabel had been afraid. With an odd sort of detachment, I realized I had the power to destroy him. It was this very realization that gave me the courage to be kind instead. I sat down on the piano bench. Only when I noted that he'd started breathing once more did I take the final step, wrapping my arms around him and laying my head against his shoulder. I heard him gasp but at the same time his own arms came up.

"Lotte," he murmured. "Oh my precious Lotte." He began to rock me and to cry.

For the next few moments, I struggled to contain the physical response engendered by such an extreme proximity to the stench. I realized the risk he was taking in opening himself to me so completely. I was aware that even the slightest hint of repugnance on my part could ruin forever the miracle of his trust. So I closed my eyes and willed my gagging throat to relax and my churning stomach to calm, grateful as my nose accustomed itself to a smell that gradually became unimportant.

Only then was I hit by the full impact of what was happening. This was my angel. He was here with me, holding me. Never had I been more certain of anything than I was at that moment of his love for me.

He scooped one arm under my legs and lifted me onto his lap with a flowing grace that seemed second nature to him. I put my arms around his neck and he repositioned his own around my waist, placing a kiss on top of my head. I reached up to wipe at the wetness on his cheeks.

"I'm sorry about everything," I whispered. My voice was hoarse and I couldn't meet his gaze.

"We all make mistakes," he said and brushed back a strand of hair from my face. "I've certainly made my share." Our eyes met briefly and he continued. "If I'd known how you'd be . . . how you'd react when you saw me, I would have come to you years ago."

I understood what he was saying but his belief that he should have revealed himself sooner gave me pause. I remembered all too well, and with no little embarrassment, my initial reaction to the Crocodile Man. I wasn't certain I'd have known what to do without having first met Christabel and Thomasina.

"All things considered," he said, "I think the worst mistake I ever made was with Christine."

He looked over at her then and saw she was wandering aimlessly about the room. With a sigh he set me on the piano bench, stood up and went to her. The embrace was spontaneous, the kiss tender, but she wasn't there to appreciate it. In the end, he took her hand and guided her as if she were blind to one of the upholstered chairs. He told her to sit and she sat. He told her to sleep and her body went limp. He came back and sat down beside me, a wistful expression on his face.

"I loved her," he said. "I needed to have her with me. In the beginning I couldn't imagine anyone loving me, least of all someone as beautiful as she. That was why I thought I had to ensnare her. It's still unclear to me how anyone could forgive such a violation. But Christine did more than that. She came back to me after I set her free, with full knowledge of what I'd done and accepted me for what I was.

"Only then did I understand the hypnosis had never been necessary. The damage was done, though. I've never met anyone more susceptible to suggestion. She began falling into trances by herself and staying that way for hours. She liked it, I think. The harshness of the real world always seemed to affect her more strongly than it did others and the trance allowed her some respite. When she's like that – " He nodded at her catatonic form. " – I think, she's in her own private heaven where evil is unable to touch her. Unfortunately, someone has to care for her body while her spirit is traveling."

He looked back at me almost resentfully. "So don't talk to me of mistakes. Yours are nothing compared to mine. At least you're not guilty of ruining the mind of the only person who ever mattered."

"I think she's happier this way," I said.

He gave me a skeptical look.

"I mean it," I said. "She always seems so nervous when she's *here*." I felt my face flushing and was compelled to add, "I haven't been very nice to her either. Maybe it would have been better if she'd stayed in her own world and I'd never been born."

"There you're wrong," he said. "You're the only thing that's forced her to keep some hold on reality. Without you, she'd have slipped away entirely by now."

I digested that. What he said made a strange kind of sense yet I couldn't comprehend how it absolved me. Any good that came of my behavior was completely unintentional. I looked into his eyes to see if his expression would belie his words but the gaze with which he met mine was tranquil and steady. In the end, I was the one who looked away – so he wouldn't see the embarrassing contortions my face was making in an effort to hold back the tears. His hand clasped my shoulder and it came to me that he didn't care about my petty sins – that he would still have loved me no matter what I'd done.

And then I lost control quite thoroughly.

He took me in his arms, offering the undeserved comfort for which I could never have asked. He stroked me and held me for a very long time.

"Beauty though you are," he whispered at last, "I can see myself in you. Why must there always be such pain?"

I wiped my face on my sleeve and looked up. "Am I like you, then?"

"In many ways."

"I'm like her too." I glanced in Maman's direction. "When I was listening to her singing just now, I went into a trance just like she always does. It was – " I struggled for words to describe it and failed.

"I noticed that too," he said. "You're going to have to be very careful all your life. Whatever you do, don't let anyone hypnotize you."

"Why can't I sing like her?"

This time he was the one to look away. "There is the unfairness of it all," he said. "Christine has a talent like nothing I've ever seen. I'd hoped, when you were born looking so much like her, that you'd inherited the gift."

A feeling of despair gripped my heart but I allowed myself one last moment of hope. "It's not just what you're born with, is it?" The desperation was so plain in my voice that even I could hear it. He turned back to look at me. "Doesn't work have something to do with it?" I pressed. "Doesn't practice make perfect? What if I were to practice very hard for years and years? Don't you think that one day – "

"No, my darling," he said. "Christine was born with a superior instrument. All the work in the world would only develop your own instrument to the fullest of its potential and still she, without trying – without even caring – would effortlessly and unthinkingly achieve a perfection that will remain forever beyond your grasp."

If I hadn't cried so recently, I'm sure I'd have done so then. But my tears were all gone, and this, the greatest disappointment of my life, elicited only despair.

"I know," he said as if reading my thoughts. "It's discouraging. Life bestows treasures on those who are least deserving. It gives a pig the face of an angel and an angel the face of a monster. Be glad, at least, that you've been spared that little joke."

The horror of this statement took a moment to penetrate.

"You mean I might have – "

"Don't even say it. When I learned that Christine was with child, it occupied my every waking thought. My every nightmare. I'd cursed my own mother for bringing me into the world and yet I feared my own selfishness would be responsible for the birth of yet another monster. But then you were born and I was as filled with joy as ever I've been."

"I was born because you were selfish?"

He smiled at my naïveté – despite himself, I think. "I remember when I was a boy," he said. "My mother truly couldn't stand the sight of me. I used to watch the other children with their mothers. Even the naughtiest of them got their share of hugs and kisses. I grew up, Lotte, never knowing what it was to be held in someone's arms. It wasn't until Christine came to me at last that I ever knew the trusting warmth of another in my bed. You cannot know what it is to have someone treat you so kindly after so many years of cruelty and loathing. She came to me willingly and I couldn't let her go. And after the first time, I refused to think any more about it. I lost myself in the sweetest of dreams and only awoke when she told me she was with child. I should never have allowed it to happen. The risk was too great. After you were born, I felt as though I'd been given a second chance. I made sure never to give in to my selfish desires again."

At the time, I didn't truly understand what he was saying but there was a sense of loss and longing even I couldn't miss.

He continued, then, more to himself than to me. "Even so, I'm happy. I'd built this house for her so she could want for nothing. At night I made alterations outside the knowledge of the workmen I'd hired so that there might be a few shadows in her world of light where I could hide and still be near her. And as if her love weren't enough, she tried to repay me by accomplishing something I'd thought to be impossible. She went to Paris and had some of my music published. Since that first time both royalties and commissions have been steady. The letters I receive now are so courteous as to quite overcome me. I even allow myself to forget sometimes that these unseen well-wishers would never be so kind if they were once so unfortunate as to meet the composer *face to face*."

He interrupted himself with that sinister chuckle that had once terrified me. Now, it inspired only pity.

"But that is neither here nor there," he continued. "My only other regret is having built this house so quickly. I didn't have the leisure of fourteen years to install all the necessary backdoors and escape routes, as I was able to do when I worked on the Palais Garnier. This place could be a trap if I tried to hide here indefinitely. Those fools would eventually blunder into my hiding place no matter how many precautions I took."

"So you're leaving?" I asked.

He sighed.

"Do you know where you're going?"

"Someplace more isolated than this," he said. "A place with good water and no farmers to decide that I'm responsible not only for my own failings but for stillbirths and plagues amongst their livestock as well. I'll take plenty of time to build my house right so I'll never be forced to leave it again. Perhaps we could make use of some of your own devices. I rather like your idea of employing machines instead of people. So many fewer idiots to endure that way."

He smiled at my discomposure.

"You know everything, don't you?" I said.

"Why of course, child," he answered almost jovially. "You know very well where these passages lead. And to be quite frank, there isn't anything that amuses me more than watching you at work in your laboratory." He spoke this with such fondness that I couldn't be angry, only extremely embarrassed as I remembered once again, certain things I'd done when I'd thought myself alone.

But then he sobered. "I shall miss you, Lotte."

"Can't I go with you?"

"Someone needs to look after Christine," he said.

"Couldn't we both go?"

I realized the answer even before he began to shake his head. He could never move freely and invisibly if burdened with Christine who was no longer fully in control of her actions. Her outburst during the police interrogation was proof of that. If he took us with him, it would only be a matter of time before we slowed him down and he was caught.

"I'm sorry," he said. "But be assured this is not the end. I shall send for you both when all is ready."

"How long will that be?"

"I can't know that."

"But you'll be alone."

He sighed. "There was a time when the world without exception seemed to have nothing better to do with itself than persecute me. I was truly alone then, hating everyone and hated by all. But for a little while now, I've had a safe haven. I've had this time of happiness. And I have you too, don't I Lotte?"

He paused to wipe away the tears that had begun to roll down my face.

"Just knowing you're here and that you care, knowing too that poor Christine loves me, in her way . . . That is enough. I have the two most precious treasures in the world. Nothing else matters."

"I love you, Papa," I said.

"I love you too, my little Lotte."

Epilogue

Inspector Beauford and company returned in the morning with the promised warrant. Strange though it may seem, I'd given no thought to the guards who were supposed to be stationed at every door until the moment Beauford arrived. If I'd thought of them at all, I surely would have wondered why they too didn't try to follow the voice of the siren down to the hidden chamber. As it turned out, though, someone had thought of them – someone who wanted more than anything else in the world, to have one last perfect night with Christine and with me. I remembered his hands, so long-fingered and graceful, hands that had so gently wiped the tears from a little girl's face. Those same hands had apparently served quite a different purpose earlier that evening. For the inspector, upon his arrival, found all his men dead at their posts. Each throat had been brutally crushed. Each neck broken.

As for the next time I saw my papa, well, that is a story for another night. Sleep well, my dears, and may you too dream of the Angel of Music.

Acknowledgments

I wish to thank Gaston Leroux for writing *Le Fantôme de l'Opéra* in the first place. Without his brilliant work, the world would be a poorer place, I think.

A special thank you to John Legg who did the 1996 line edit and offered suggestions for the improvement of "Phantoms of the Mind." That said, this story has been twice reworked since then so the fault for any errors that may have crept in rests entirely upon my own shoulders. Furthermore, it would be impossible to express enough gratitude to Cindy Marie Christine Fernandez, Author Representative at Xlibris, for all her help, kindness and patience throughout the entire publication process.

Thanks too, to Suzy McKee Charnas and Madeline Baker (a.k.a. Amanda Ashley) both for encouraging me in my own writing and for the creation of their own unique tributes to the tale (*Beauty and the Opera or the Phantom Beast*-SMC, *Embrace the Night*-MB and *Masquerade*-MB).

I will forever value the works of all those other authors who have taken the *Phantom* story and made it their own in the various literary, film, theatrical and television incarnations too numerous to list here in their entirety. Still, if not for Lon Chaney and Andrew Lloyd Webber, chances are I myself would never have heard of Leroux's *Phantom.*

I also think it important to thank those great lovers of the *Phantom* story without whom *The Phantom of the Opera* would not be the phenomenon it is. I stand by the belief that the fans are the ones behind the success of many *Phantom* versions by repeatedly supporting the efforts of – and providing free publicity for – those who have created *Phantom* works. Of these many, I have only the space here to name those individuals who helped make my own work better known by publishing it in their zines or on their websites. They are Bethany Cap, Britta Rutkowsky, Carin Klabbers, Christine Daaé-Clemens, Diane Flogerzi, Karin Willison, Kathleen Resch, Krista Sigler, Tom Atkins and also Nicole Hudson of Alan Wasser Associates who in 1998 published two of my reviews on the official Cameron Mackintosh/Really Useful Group *Phantom of the Opera* website. I thank you all for your kindness and for your faith in me. I thank PhantomFans.net, the IMDb, Le Phorum, The Lair, The LiveJournal Phantom Community and PhantomOfTheOpera.com for the exposure on your forums. I thank anyone who's ever linked to my site.

Finally, I'm grateful to my friend Sandra Andrés Belenguer for the promotional photos she sent, to my family for their moral support, to my brother for his advice on writing a treatment, to my sister for the PR and marketing advice as well as for the use of her apartment as a writing refuge, and to my husband for the leaps of faith he made and for not giving up on me.

Contributions to the Great Body of Phantom Lore

The following list is the merest taste of the vast number of works written with the "Phantom of the Opera" as a central theme. I've stuck mainly to print incarnations but without really touching upon children's versions or comic book versions. I've also had to leave out all the cinematic versions, television versions, ballet versions, radio versions, on-line versions and those versions published without an ISBN. Still, since the vast majority of theatrical *Phantoms* are most easily accessible via their print formats, I've included a list of scripts/librettos that I consider to be recognizable adaptations of the original story. For more comprehensive lists of *Phantom* works, please refer to Leonard Wolf's *The Essential Phantom of the Opera* and John Flynn's *Phantoms of the Opera: The Face Behind the Mask.* There's also a plethora of *Phantom*-related reference sites on the internet.

The Original:

Le Fantôme de l'Opéra by Gaston Leroux, the French-language story that started it all, published as a serial in the periodical *Le Gaulois* in 1909 and as a novel (Paris: Lafitte) in 1910.

Leroux's Phantom in English Translation:

Various print editions by translators Alexander Teixeira de Mattos (1911), Lowell Bair (1990) and Leonard Wolf (1996).

Retellings/Spoofs/Sequels:

D'Arcy, Brigitta. *(Le) Fantôme.* London: Minerva Press, 1999.

Ebert, Roger. *Behind the Phantom's Mask.* Kansas City: Andrews and McMeel, 1993.

Forsyth, Frederick. *Phantom of Manhattan, The.* New York: St. Martin's Press, 1999.

Kay, Susan. *Phantom.* New York: Delacorte Press, 1991.

Meadows, Becky. *Phantasy.* Lincoln, Nebraska: Writer's Club Press, 2002.

Meadows, Becky. *Progeny.* Lincoln, Nebraska: Writer's Club Press, 2001.

Meyer, Nicholas. *Canary Trainer, The.* New York: W.W. Norton & Co. Inc., 1993.

Pettengill, Nancy. *Journey of the Mask.* Lincoln, Nebraska: Writer's Club Press, 2000.

Pratchett, Terry. *Maskerade.* London: Victor Gollancz Ltd., 1995.

Sicialiano, Sam. *Angel of the Opera.* New York, Otto Penzler Books, 1994.

Vehlow, Gwenith M. *Phantom of Paris, The.* Frederick, Maryland: PublishAmerica, 2003.

Novellas

Ashley, Amanda. "Masquerade," *After Twilight.* New York: Dorchester Publishing Co., 2001.

Charnas, Suzy McKee. "Beauty and the Opera or the Phantom Beast," *Stagestruck Vampires and Other Phantasms.* San Francisco, California: Tachyon Publications, 2004.

Herter, Lori. "The Phantom of Chicago," *Shadows Short Story Collection.* New York: Silhouette, 1993.

Reference:

Fearon, Globe. *Phantom of the Opera Teacher's Resource Manual, The.* Published by Globe Fearon, 1999.

Flynn, John. *Phantoms of the Opera: The Face Behind the Mask.* New York: Image Publishing, 1993.

Hogle, Jerrold E. *Undergrounds of the Phantom of the Opera: Sublimation and the Gothic in Leroux's Novel and its Progeny, The.* New York: Palgrave MacMillan, 2002.

Husson-Casta, Isabelle. *(Le) Travail de l«Obscure clarté» dans LE FANTÔME DE L'OPÉRA de GASTON LEROUX.* Paris: Lettres Modernes Minard, 1997.

Perry. George. *Complete Phantom of the Opera, The.* New York: Henry Holt & Company, 1987.

Riley, Philip J. *Phantom of the Opera: The 1925 Shooting Script.* Galloway, New Jersey: Magicimage Filmbooks, 1996.

Scripts/Librettos

Phantom by Arthur Kopit with music by Maury Yeston. Produced by Theatre Under the Stars, Houston, Texas in January, 1991. Book published by Samuel French, Inc. in 1992.

Phantom with book by David H. Bell, music by Tom Sivak. Commissioned in June, 1991 and opened September 1991 at the Drury Lane Oakbrook Theater, Chicago.

Phantom of the Opera with book by Bruce Falstein and music by Lawrence Rosen and Paul Shierhorn. Commissioned by Abe Hirschfeld. Opened February 1990 at the Clarion Castle, Miami Beach, Florida.

(The) Phantom of the Opera by David Giles. Produced by the Wimbledon Actor's Company in cooperation with the Wimbledon Theatre, Southwest London, UK, 1975.

(The) Phantom of the Opera with book by Richard Stilgoe and Andrew Lloyd Webber, lyrics by Charles Hart and music by Andrew Lloyd

Webber. Act One staged at Sydmonton, July, 1985. Full version premiered at Her Majesty's Theatre in London, October, 1986. Libretto published in George Perry's *The Complete Phantom of the Opera.*

Phantom of the Opera with book by Michael Tilford and music and lyrics by Tom Alonso. Played at Toby's Dinner Theatre in 1992.

(The) Phantom of the Opera (a.k.a. *The American Phantom of the Opera: A Love Story*) with book and lyrics by Helen Grigal and music by Eugene Anderson. Produced by the Oregon Ridge Dinner Theater in cooperation with the Baltimore Actor's Theater, 1987 to 1992.

Phantom of the Opera: A Musical Play by Ken Hill. Original version with music by Ian Armit and Charles Gounod. Produced by the Duke's Playhouse Lancaster, July 26th, 1976.

Phantom of the Opera: A Musical Play by Ken Hill. Second version with incidental music by Alasdair MacNeill and with excerpts from Operas by Offenbach, Gounod, Verdi, Boito, Dvorák, Bizet, Weber, Donizetti and Mozart. Produced by the Newcastle Playhouse and the Theatre Royal, Stratford East in 1984. Book published by Samuel French, Inc.

Phantom of the Opera: A New Victorian Thriller by Gene Traylor. Book published by The Dramatic Publishing Company in 1979.

(The) Phantom of the Opera: An Exciting New Musical Adaptation with book and lyrics by Joseph Robinette and music by Robert Chauls. Book published by The Dramatic Publishing Company in 1992.

(The) Phantom of the Opera: Or the Passage of Christine with book and lyrics by Kathleen Masterson and music by David Bishop. Produced by the Capital Repertory Company, Albany New York, April 19 to May 18, 1986.

Phantom of the Opera: Original Family Musical with book by Rob Barron and music, lyrics and orchestration by David Spencer. Produced by Theatreworks/USA in 1998.

(The) Phantom of the Opera: The Musical adapted by Ivan Jacobs from the play by John Kenley and Robert Thomas Noll as well as from the novel by Gaston Leroux. Handled by the Joyce Agency Entertainment Services, Inc.

Phantom of the Opera: The Play by John Kenley and Robert Thomas Noll with music by David Gooding and Charles Gounod. Produced by Prescott F. Griffith in Association with John Kenley in the Carousel Dinner Theatre, Akron Ohio. Book published by Samuel French, Inc., 1988-1989.

(The) Phantom of the Opera on Ice with narration and lyrics by Roberto Danova, Tony Mercer, Kathy Dooley and Stephen Lee Garden. Music composed and arranged by Roberto Danova. Featuring the Russian Ice Stars. Toured England from Nov. 22, 1995 to June 29, 1996.

Phantom of the Op'ry: A Melodrama with Music with book by Tim Kelly, music by Gerald V. Castle and lyrics by Michael C. Vigilant. Premiered at the Baldwin Theater in Royal Oak, Michigan. Book published by Meriwether Publishing Ltd., 1991.

(The) Pinchpenny Phantom of the Opera: An Affordable Musical Comedy by Dave Reiser and Jack Sharkey. Book published by Samuel French, Inc. in 1988.

Printed in the United States
42246LVS00002B/259